PARTIES OF THE FIRST PART

Katharine Anne Prescott Millholland, a daughter of Chicago society, wants nothing to do with money or privilege. A smart and tough lawyer, she takes chances no one else does and goes her own way, no matter the danger.

Stephen Azorini has spent his life trying to shake off his family's mob connections. Now a respected doctor and founder of a multimillion-dollar pharmaceutical firm, he faces a takeover bid that could cost him everything to keep.

Edgar Eichel, the corporate raider, wants respectability more than anything else and will buy his way into it if he has to. He has a short fuse, a nasty temper, and never worries about consequences.

Joey Azorini, Stephen's older brother, makes money the old-fashioned way: illegally. He lies, steals, and would kill his own brother if he were in the right mood.

PRINCIPAL DEFENSE

Gini Hartzmark

IVY BOOKS • NEW YORK

Ivy Books
Published by Ballantine Books
Copyright © 1992 by Gini Hartzmark

ISBN 0-8041-1074-3

Manufactured in the United States of America

First Edition: September 1992

To Michael

I'd like to thank Charles V. Wetli, M.D. of the Medical Examiner's Office of Dade County and Joel Howell, M.D. for sharing their expertise with me. I am also grateful to Nancy Love, Susan Randol and most of all, my husband Michael for their input and encouragement.

CHAPTER

All the other lawyers in the room were men. Women may have made inroads in every other area of the law, but mergers and acquisitions is still the locker room of the profession. On the few occasions I allowed myself to think about it, I wondered what that said about me. But then, of course, one of the things I like best about mergers and acquisitions is that it doesn't give you much time to think.

It was right after Thanksgiving in the quiet weeks before Christmas when even the most relentless capitalists take some time off. I had just finished a big textile takeover, the Byzantine course of which had been burning up the business pages for months. My colleagues were taking advantage of the lull in the usual office frenzy to reacquaint themselves with their wives and children. I was reduced to digging my office out from under an avalanche of paper and generally trying to fill the hours with anything but thinking about Christmas, or Russell, or being alone.

That was how I came to find myself in the Friday morning securities meeting. Some whey-faced wonder was trying to bring us up to speed on regulatory changes. Instead of listening, I studied the portraits of past partners, all dead, that lined the dark mahogany walls and watched Howard Acker, sitting next to me, do a lovingly detailed sketch of a trout on his legal pad.

I was rescued from the doldrums of the meeting by a Nike-shod clerk who sidled shyly into the room and slipped me a note. In John Guttman's small and difficult handwriting it read: "Eichel has just sandbagged Azor. Come to my office. P.S. Bring the mayonnaise."

"Good news?" Acker inquired in a whisper. "You look like you just won the lottery."

"Better," I replied and headed out the door.

In the eccentric jargon of mergers and acquisitions, M&A for short, the note was a call to battle. It meant that corporate raider Edgar Eichel had just made a hostile bid for one of our biggest clients, Azor Pharmaceuticals.

I had been watching Azor's stock for weeks, listening to Wall Street rumors and talking to the arbs. I'd had a hunch that someone was putting Azor Pharmaceuticals into play. My boss, John Guttman, thought I was crazy and never tired of telling me so. He contended that too much of Azor's stock was held by the Azorini family, including the company's founder and president, Dr. Stephen Azorini. These shares held by insiders, pronounced Guttman, made Azor an unattractive takeover target, so unattractive in fact that if anyone were idiotic enough to make a pass at the company he would eat his socks. I assumed that he wanted the mayonnaise to make his argyles go down easier.

John Guttman was my mentor and tormentor. He had come to Callahan Ross as a partner from a rival firm and had brought with him an impressive stable of clients and a well-earned reputation as an asshole. An oft-repeated anecdote about Guttman concerns a junior partner whom Guttman once reprimanded for abrasiveness. "Coming from you," replied the brash young man, "that advice has to be taken seriously."

When I was fresh out of law school I finagled a job in Callahan's M&A department in part because of my family connections. But while the Millholland name may have helped me land the job, no one was willing to give the woman lawyer anything of interest to do. My in-tray was empty from lunchtime onward. In the end, Guttman took me under his wing. The problem was that four years later he still expected me to be fawningly grateful.

I got to his office only to find him on two phones at once. I plopped down in my usual seat and waited for him to finish. He had a corner office the size of a small ranch house, complete with conference table, couch, glass-fronted bookcases and a desk big enough to land a plane on. Unlike the rest of the firm, which was full of antique furniture, hunting prints, and the muted shades of old money, Guttman's office was incongruously modern. Everything was either black or white. His desk was bare except for the file he was working on and a Baccarat vase that held a yellow spray of perfectly sharpened pencils. Guttman never came to my office if he could help it. The clutter seemed to cause him almost physical pain.

"I was right," I said when he was finally off the phone.

"So you were right. Don't make a career of it."

He was an unattractive man in his late forties. His kinky black hair was on its way to gray, and he wore it brushed aggressively back from his forehead. His glasses with their thick black frames accentuated his heavy brows.

"I can't help it, John. The market speaks to me."

"So that's how the Millhollands got to be so rich."

"No. My great-grandfather sold opium to the Chinese."

"So Miss Clairvoyant, how much did Eichel offer per share for Azor Pharmaceutical stock?"

"I have no idea. The stock closed at thirty-seven dollars and some change yesterday."

"Forty-eight a share."

"Eichel means business."

"Eichel always means business. I just got off the phone with your friend Stephen Azorini. There's a meeting at Azor's office in twenty minutes. I want you to pull a copy of their corporate charter and meet me in the lobby in ten minutes."

"And go with you?" I asked, not sure I'd heard right.

"Of course," he replied, as if it were the most usual thing in the world. "I think Stephen needs to see as many friendly faces as possible today."

It was almost unheard of for a lowly associate like myself to go to a meeting with a client, especially one as important as Azor Pharmaceuticals. At a big law firm like Callahan Ross, they won't even let you go to court and file a motion by yourself until you're a partner.

"So get going already," Guttman snapped.

My initials were on my briefcase, embossed, appropriately enough, in gold. KAPM—Katharine Anne Prescott Millholland. My family's money is so old that no one is exactly sure who made it to begin with—though the line I fed Guttman about my great-grandfather was true. There was also a Prescott who started a paper company and a Millholland who, before the days of unions and environmentalists, had made a fortune strip-mining. From there the family went or married into shipping, real estate, and a long list of other enterprises so varied and lucrative that there is a small office on Monroe Street where three people work quietly all day long just managing the trusts and investments belonging to my parents, my sister, and me.

But, as my mother will point out to you after she's had five or six martinis, it's not just that we're rich, *we've* been rich for a long, long, time. For generations the Millhollands have gone to the right schools, worn the right clothes, belonged to the best clubs, and given to the correct charities. From the time I was born my family's expectations for my life have stretched out before me in a well-defined path: prep school, cotillion, Bryn Mawr if I was brainy, a year or two in Switzerland if I was not, followed by a couple of hundred parties until I found someone with a similar portfolio to marry, then children, a nanny, and a lifetime of parties, galas and clothes, clothes, clothes. As soon as I was old enough to figure it out (my junior year of high school) I ran like the Red Queen.

On my way I ran into Stephen Azorini. Like an orchid in ivy, he was simply the most exotic boy I had ever met. His father was an aging businessman known to have ties to organized crime, and Stephen's admission to the exclusive North Shore Country Day School had reputedly been purchased in the form of twelve new tennis courts and an audio-visual center. Even if Stephen hadn't been handsome, sophisticated, and a kick to be with, the scandal we caused when we started dating would have been worth it in and of itself.

We burned through our senior year, ducking out of cotillion parties to go to the racetrack, the fights, to blues clubs in neighborhoods I'd never known existed. We used his father's apartment in the city when he was away, cut school and took my parents' boat out when there were small-craft warnings. Stephen taught me about sex and drugs and rock 'n' roll. His foreignness, the sense that he came from a place that I'd never been to, only added to the attraction.

We lost track of each other in college. I went to Bryn Mawr and made a haven for myself among people who'd never heard of the Millhollands and couldn't have cared less. Stephen went to Harvard and fell in love with the cool objectivity of the lab. He transferred to M.I.T. his sophomore year and confounded everyone upon graduation by entering medical school.

I didn't give much thought to Stephen after that. I was consumed by the travails of law school, and by then I'd met Russell. When Stephen and 479 other invited guests crowded under the white canopy at St. John's Church he was just another face in the receiving line. But six weeks after the wedding, when Russell was diagnosed with brain cancer, it was Stephen, then an intern at the University of Chicago, who appeared at Russell's bedside to shield us from the medical bureaucracy and the daily barrage of bad news. Near the end, when the time wore away too fast for me to manage even the short drive from our apartment downtown, Stephen gave me the keys to his apartment near the hospital. He slept in the on-call room while I lay in his bed and wept for my dying husband.

In the cab on the way to the meeting Guttman observed the firm's strict prohibition against discussing cases outside the secure confines of the office. Callahan Ross spent thousands of dollars every year on shredding machines and anti-eavesdropping devices. No one wanted the firm's secrets peddled by some market-savvy cab driver with sharp hearing. So Guttman, naturally allergic to small talk, maintained a grim silence while his hands did an eloquently nervous dance over the top of his briefcase.

Guttman loathed Edgar Eichel. They'd first gone up against each other during a particularly bloody takeover of a drilling company. Our client was eventually rescued by a white knight, but not before Guttman had developed an abiding and obsessive hatred of Edgar Eichel. Guttman contended Eichel had used blackmail and intimidation to get shareholders to sell him their shares. I had heard similar stories but put the lion's share of them down to Guttman's legendary paranoia. Since then, Guttman's opinion of Eichel had simmered somewhere between revulsion and loathing. I could imagine how he felt about going up against him again.

While Guttman paid the driver I braced myself against the wind that blew in sharp and fast across the lake and checked for the watchers and photographers that are the pavement artists of the takeover trade. Eichel was certain to have someone keeping tabs on who came calling on Stephen Azorini, but the only person who caught my eye was a thin black man dressed in a greasy raincoat who sat, eyes closed and swaying, at the entrance to the train station.

Azor's corporate offices were in a newish office building on South Michigan Avenue across from the Art Institute. Stephen had taken the space at the same time he had moved into a bigger apartment. He had surprised me by taking considerable pains over the interior decoration of both. The offices were muted and modern, with a certain pared-down elegance well suited to a young, high-tech company.

We were immediately shown into a large, spare conference room. The table was milled from a single slab of rose-colored marble and ringed by those black leather chairs that someone won a design award for, but are an agony to sit on. There was no art on the walls, only the view from the window of Buckingham Fountain, drained and deserted for the winter, and the cold, gray lake beyond.

I recognized only a few faces—Danny Wohl, Azor's chief in-house counsel, and a woman from public relations whom I'd met once somewhere. Mostly there were just tense, corporate faces I'd never seen before. No one spoke. My guess was that they were all busy mentally updating their résumés.

In law school they teach you that a hostile takeover is the means of acquiring what cannot be otherwise gained by negotiation. The same, of course, can be said of rape. In my line of work I tried not to dwell too much on the similarities. But for Stephen Azorini, and even more so for his employees, Edgar Eichel's bid was no intellectual exercise.

Azor Pharmaceuticals was Stephen Azorini's brainchild, the product of his best instincts about science and about people. He'd gotten the idea in medical school of handpicking young scientists and offering them generous salaries and freedom from the teaching and grantsmanship that fettered them in academia. In the half dozen years that Azor had been in business, Stephen's premise had borne dazzling fruit. The company's long list of successes and Stephen's renegade style had put him at the head of one of the fastest growing biomedical companies in the world. The company had developed a drug used successfully to treat migraine headaches, machines that were used by blood banks to screen for the AIDS virus, and a powerful anticoagulant that reduced mortality for coronary bypass patients by 12 percent. In the pipeline was a powerful new drug to treat children suffering from fetal alcohol syndrome and a revolutionary antischizophrenia medication.

Now Edgar Eichel, who had never graduated from college and who had gotten his start manufacturing mufflers, had decided that he wanted to buy Azor Pharmaceuticals. Most likely he figured he could turn a profit selling it off division by division, or that the company's patents and physical assets—the computers, buildings, research equipment and manufacturing facilities themselves—were worth more than the price of the stock he would have to buy to acquire them. Good for Eichel, who lived in baronial splendor in Lake Forest, but potentially disastrous for the more than 400 Azor employees caught up in the corporate shuffle.

Stephen came in quietly. My roommate, Claudia, always said that he was so handsome it made your fillings hurt, and she was right. He had the chiseled features of an Italian matinee idol, smokey blue eyes and black hair worn just a little bit longer than corporate propriety allowed. At 6′5″ he was also hard to overlook. He walked into the room and simply absorbed all the attention. I had known him for more than a dozen years, and it still always took me a minute to get beyond the impact of his looks.

He sat down at the head of the table while his assistant, Richard Humanski, began passing out some papers. Richard was the kind of fresh-faced, high-I.Q. kid the University of Chicago seems to mint. If he wasn't always standing next to Stephen, he might even have been considered good-looking.

The top sheet was a copy of a letter from Edgar Eichel that began, "Dear Dr. Azorini." Outside, it had started to rain, and fat, cold drops smeared the windows.

"As you can see, we've received greetings from Mr. Eichel," Stephen began, pronouncing the name, "I-kill."

"He tells us that he has secretly acquired four point nine percent of the outstanding shares of Azor Pharmaceuticals and intends to purchase any or all shares for forty-eight dollars per share or a thirty percent premium over the last traded price. The offering period is the legal minimum—twenty business days, which means that our shareholders will have less than four weeks to consider whether we are doing our jobs or whether they should just take the money and give Mr. Eichel a crack at it. Mr. Eichel says that he looks forward to negotiating an amicable merger." Stephen paused for a moment.

"Well, we all know that Mr. Eichel's idea of an amicable merger is a little bit like a strange man walking up to a woman on the street, tearing off all her clothes, and proposing marriage." There were titters around the room.

"I just want you to know that there is no way that Edgar Eichel—or anyone else for that matter—is going to gain control of this company. Azor Pharmaceuticals is a special company, a unique company. We do not make ball bearings, or toilet paper, or mufflers. We develop and sell drugs and medical products that improve people's lives. We sink millions of dollars into research that would otherwise go unfunded. Scientists burn their bridges when they come to work for us. If Azor goes out of business, many, many people will be hurt. If we beat off Edgar Eichel, the only person who will suffer is Edgar Eichel."

This was moving, inspirational stuff, but the oft-quoted odds of deterring a well-financed and determined takeover bid are one in five. It would take much more than a heady mixture of wishful thinking and bravado to fend off Edgar Eichel.

"From now on, dealing with the takeover is the first

order of corporate business. This group will meet every morning at eight o'clock to briefly preview the day's actions and again at six o'clock to review the day's events. I cannot emphasize enough the danger of gossip or idle chatter outside the walls of this room. Eichel has been planning this for months. His only handicaps are his need to move quickly and his lack of direct information about our company and our intentions.

"I have been on the phone already this morning and First New York has agreed to act as our investment banker. Brian Gould and his team are on their way from New York, and we will be meeting with them later in the day to plan our course of action more specifically. So far, I have notified the exchanges, and trading in Azor stock has been suspended for twenty-four hours. I am also calling a meeting of the board of directors for noon Sunday. Several board members are out of the country, and I'm afraid this is the earliest we will be able to convene."

Stephen seemed confident that the board would back him in his decision to unilaterally fight Eichel. I hoped he knew something I didn't. When Azor went public two years earlier, the founders drastically diluted their stock holdings and had been forced to take on four new directors, three of whom represented the interests of Azor's new, institutional shareholders. The fourth new director was an old family friend, Tucker Sweet, who was charged with representing the public shareholders. The original three directors were all scientists with close personal ties to Stephen.

Three of the new directors were bankers interested in maximizing short-term returns for their investors. I couldn't see any of them turning down an offer as juicy as Eichel's. Stephen would cast the seventh vote, but it would only take one turncoat scientist or Tucker Sweet siding with the bankers, and Stephen would be sitting across the table from Eichel negotiating the terms of surrender.

When the meeting was over, Stephen worked the door like a host at the end of a party, shaking hands, patting shoulders. As I trailed Guttman out the door Stephen pulled me aside, and I fussed with my briefcase until everyone else had gone. Guttman, impatient, came looking for me, but when he saw me with Stephen he slipped me a leering wink and disappeared from view.

"How are you holding up?" I asked Stephen when everybody had gone. Even in heels I had to look up to him. It made me feel like a little girl, and I didn't like it much.

"I'm pretty pissed off, but otherwise I'm okay. The problem is I know it's going to get a lot worse before it gets better." He paused. "I can't believe you were right about someone putting the stock into play."

"I'm sorry I was."

"No, I'm glad you told me. I did a lot of the things you suggested last week. I signed on Gould, someone's been updating the shareholder lists. . . . I wasn't caught off guard."

Stephen's assistant, Richard Humanski, stuck his head in the door.

"I'm sorry to bother you, Stephen, but Eli Wexler is on the phone for you."

"Tell him I'll be right with him." Wexler was one of Azor's biggest shareholders.

"Kate, I've got to go."

I nodded my good-bye to his retreating back.

During the short course of my career I have been a witness to much corporate carnage. I have seen several men stand where Stephen stood. I knew much better than he did the incredible forces that stood ready to flay him. I wanted to reach for him, but I could not.

I had known Stephen for a lot of years. We had been many things to each other. We were connected yet governed by a mysterious restraint. From the beginning there had always been the sense that each of us had many doors that would always remain closed to the other.

For both Stephen and me there would always be bridges the other would never cross. I had given my full share of affection to Russell and had it snatched away. My well was dry. Stephen saved his love for Azor Pharmaceuticals.

But during the silent cab ride back to the office, I thought of the losses in my life. I wished desperately that Edgar Eichel could be turned away.

CHAPTER

The rest of Friday was crazed, but by Saturday we'd hit stride and the office hummed with the electricity unique to the start of a big case. In two weeks everyone would be functioning on too much coffee and not enough sleep. Lawyers would bitch and scream and hang up the phone on one another. Secretaries would quit. Mail clerks would go around mumbling that no amount of overtime was worth being abused by a bunch of suits. But at the beginning there was an unmistakable rush. We were poised to make one huge, complicated roll of the dice—collectively holding our breath, shaking them up, getting ready to let them roll.

The office had buzzed until well past midnight the night before. Already there was an impressive agenda of first steps to be taken against Eichel. The M&A department was split up into teams to launch the first wave of defense. One group was preparing a barrage of lawsuits to be filed in each state in which Azor Pharmaceuticals or any of Eichel's holding companies were incorporated. There were lawyers working on potential conflict of interest issues to be raised with the Food and Drug Administration. Another group was preparing defenses against the legal challenges Eichel was sure to file in an attempt to unravel the maze of the anti-takeover defenses we had woven into the Azor bylaws. There were lawyers in the file room and in the library, hunting down precedents and dreaming up stalling tactics. There were dozens of secretaries, paralegals, photocopying clerks (Guttman actually managed to call them xerographers with a straight face) and word processing personnel racking up double overtime and generating the avalanche of paper that constituted the ammunition of corporate conflict.

Driving us all was the fear that the twenty days specified in Eichel's offer was just too little time to avert the steam roller of Eichel's takeover machine. Eichel, we knew, had a team, too, and our faceless counterparts had already been working on this for months, guaranteeing that he had the necessary legal and financial resources. Worse, there was an undercurrent of uneasiness that Stephen was being overconfident in his belief that Azor's board of directors would back him and that Azor's defenses, no matter how brilliantly conceived, would be shut down by the time the board had finished meeting Sunday afternoon.

I was busy on the first draft of Azor's formal answer to Eichel's offer. It was mostly legal boilerplate, but there were a few critical sections that needed to be carefully worded. My desk was thick with papers, my shoes were off, and I had popped the Elvis Costello classic, "My Aim Is True," into my Walkman. I had the volume cranked way up. Cheryl, my secretary, had to come in and tap me on the shoulder to tell me my mother was on the phone.

"Didn't you tell her I wasn't taking any calls?" I groaned.

"She said it was an emergency."

I rolled my eyes. Cheryl was a smart kid from Bridgeport who went to Loyola law school at night.

''Don't start making faces at me,'' she warned. ''She's *your* mother.''

''I know,'' I replied. ''And it's not your fault she's a witch.''

As Cheryl closed the outer door to my office behind her, I braced myself for conversation with my mother, the famous socialite beauty, Astrid Millholland. I picked up the phone.

''Hello, Mother.''

''Kate. I'm so glad I could reach you before Timothy starts on my hair. The caterers will be here any minute and, of course, Mrs. Mason is having hysterics at the thought of them in her kitchen, and Neuchatel can't deliver the chocolates, and if I don't rest for an hour this afternoon there is no way I'll survive tonight.''

I had completely forgotten. My parents were having a big party that night.

''Mother. You told Cheryl it was an emergency.''

''It is, dear. Anna is on her way down to your office with that little black and gold Adolfo. I've had it taken in twice, and it still doesn't hang right. I thought you could wear it tonight.''

I weigh eight pounds more than my mother. Given the number of ways she manages to find of reminding me, you'd think it was eighty.

''I'm not even sure I'm going to be able to come. I'm working on a big case.''

''I know. Azor Pharmaceuticals. But when I spoke to Stephen Azorini this morning, he assured me that he would be there. You can't expect him to come alone. What would people think?''

The last year or so Stephen and I had come to rely on each other a lot socially. There were a certain num-

ber of "important" parties I couldn't get out of, and
Stephen genuinely enjoyed being seen in that crowd. I,
on the other hand, liked the scientists and inventors that
Stephen was called upon to entertain. Both of us were
thus spared the hassles of having to come up with a
presentable date.

"Mother, Stephen of all people will understand if I
have to work. I have things that have to be finished
today."

"They can't make you work on a Saturday," she announced in an injured voice. "I'm going to call Skip
Tillman."

Skip Tillman was Callahan Ross's managing partner.
His wife, Betsy, and my mother played bridge together.

"You can't," I burst out, sounding and feeling exactly like a third grader. "I'll try my best to be there."

"That's better," she purred. "Anna is going to stop
by before she picks up the chocolates. I had her bring
her little sewing box. Try the dress on. If it's too tight
she'll let it out for you."

"I don't have time to try on dresses today, Mother.
I'll just wear the blue dress I wore to Lizzie Simpson's
wedding."

"You absolutely can't wear that dress one more time.
It will only take a minute. Anna works very fast. You
can give shorthand or dictate or whatever it is you do
while she does the fitting. And be sure you curl your
hair and wear it down. You look so frumpy in that
French twist—like you just came from the office. You
could be a beautiful young woman if you just paid a
little more attention to your appearance."

When Tucker Sweet stopped into my office later that
day, he found me standing on my desk reading a revised
draft of the answer, while my mother's tight-lipped

Filipino maid, Anna, pinned the hem of a rather daring black and gold Adolfo evening gown.

"Hullo, Anna," he announced cheerily as he plunked down in my chair. "This looks like something that was your mother's idea, Kate."

"Please, Tucker, don't get me started." Tucker was an old friend of the family's and an exception to my almost universal dislike of everyone in "society."

Tucker had not inherited his great wealth, he had married it. The son of an Iowa dentist, he had wooed and won the horse-faced little sister of his Princeton roommate. And while the money and the pedigree belonged to his wife, Eunice, it was Tucker's wolfish grin and natural charm that put the couple securely at the top of the "A" list.

Still, behind the Brooks Brothers' facade, Tucker was a genuine sweetheart. He had earned my affection by always taking an interest. He had treated me as a grown-up, even during those awkward years when nobody else did.

"So what brings you to the working world, on a Saturday no less?" I asked.

"I just dropped in for a preview of what you'll be wearing tonight. You should plan on looking your best. Your mother's invited Edgar Eichel, and rumor has it he's planning to attend."

"I can't believe it. My mother would never invite the Eichels."

"She's trying to get a couple of million out of him for the Art Institute."

In the philanthropic pecking order, the Art Institute board was the pinnacle. But admission to that cliquish inner circle was fiercely guarded and not easily bought, certainly not by a pushy newcomer like Eichel, no matter how many dollars he had managed to put between himself and the muffler business.

"Since when is he interested in art?"

"Since his wife decided she wants to be on the Art Institute's board."

"That won't happen in my lifetime, no matter how much money he gives."

"Of course, but they'll be sure not to let him know until the check clears the bank. Serves his nouveau-riche little self right."

"Turn, please," Anna said, her mouth full of pins.

I obediently rotated forty-five degrees.

"Well, he's going to be there tonight. Are you and Stephen going?"

"I guess so. I haven't heard from Stephen one way or the other, but Mother says she talked to him this morning and he was planning on it. I guess I'll go with him if Guttman gives me the night off."

"I'm sure he will. He was just telling me how great it was that you were going to be available to hold Stephen's hand and keep him posted on Stephen's emotional temperature."

"He didn't really say that. I'm beginning to find the role of tame girlfriend extremely tiresome."

"Yep." Tucker nodded. "Guttman's convinced you're going to cheerlead Stephen through this, keep him from getting angry or depressed or doing anything stupid."

"For this I went to law school. So you just dropped in to see my dress and check on Stephen's emotional temperature?"

"I predict it will go up considerably when he sees you in that dress. It's really quite fetching on you. But seriously, I dropped in to have a chat with your friend, John Guttman, about the Azor board meeting."

The day that Tucker Sweet walked down the aisle with Eunice Worthington, he withdrew as an active participant in the nine-to-five grind. But he still kept his hand in by serving on several corporate and charitable boards. He'd been an Azor director for two years. It had been my idea for Stephen to ask him to serve. Stephen had been trying to raise money for the new hematology research division, and he was hitting up a lot of Tucker's well-heeled friends.

"What about the board meeting?" I inquired.

"I just assumed they'd want to convene as soon as possible. Today, as a matter of fact. But two of the directors are abroad. I guess there's some sort of international confab of chemists going on in Scandinavia of all places—whoever heard of going to Norway in the winter for god's sake?—and the soonest they can get back is Sunday afternoon."

"That's just a twenty-four-hour delay."

"I know, but elk season opens Sunday. I'm heading east to the Adirondacks to get a little hunting in."

Heaven help Stephen, I thought to myself, if the responsibilities of serving on Azor's board ranked right up there with murdering elk.

You cannot see my parents' house from the street. It sits well back from the road at the far edge of Lake Forest behind a tall stone gate at the end of a little lane marked "private." A manicured wood fringes the lawn, which, in summertime, is kept improbably short, like an enormous putting green. Now there was a dusting of snow that made it look as if the big Georgian house were set on a skirt of silver.

For the party, every light in the house was on. Cars lined the circular drive and were parked on the frozen west lawn as well. Valets in red jackets and green bow ties shivered under the portico. They sprinted between the cars, holding doors and easing Bentleys and BMWs into parking spaces. There was a special spot for parking limousines behind the house so that the drivers could come in and have a cold supper in the servants' wing.

Stephen and I had smoked some Thai stick as we drove up from the city. I wondered whether that fit Guttman's admonition, delivered in Dutch-uncle tones earlier that afternoon, to keep Stephen happy. As we pulled up to the door I sprayed my hair with a small atomizer of Joy that I kept in the glove compartment of Stephen's BMW for just such occasions. Stephen handed the car keys to the valet, who suppressed a knowing smile at the smell of the dope, and I entered my parents' house just like any other guest.

It had not been a good place to grow up. It was too big and too cold—a furniture museum for parents too absorbed in their own pleasures to give much thought to a child. But that night, filled with people and conversation, it was very beautiful. At the foot of the big, curved staircase was a fourteen-foot Christmas tree decorated with hand-blown ornaments and strung with pearls. The chandeliers sparkled, and the warm light reflected up from the polished floors. There was the deep glow of mahogany, the lushness of cabbage rose chintz and rose satin.

My parents stood in front of the tree greeting the arriving guests. My father's patrician face was already flushed with gin as he genially flirted with a covey of my mother's friends. They were all so impossibly thin and beautifully presented as to have a generic quality about them.

My mother, closing in on sixty, was the most beautiful woman in the room. Her trademark mane of chestnut hair was swept back from her high, ivory

forehead, setting off her perfect skin and perfect bones.
She wore a simple floor-length sheath of fuchsia silk
and a diamond necklace that was probably equal in
value to the gross national product of several small
African nations.

Strangely enough, my mother and I look a lot alike—
same hair, same basic features, same basic build—but
somehow when you put it all together my mother has
the face that still turns heads, while I have the face of
a basically presentable corporate attorney. Beauty
skipped me and passed to my little sister Beth instead,
who derived perverse pleasure from torturing my mother
by wearing nothing but sweat pants and refusing to wash
her hair.

"You fill that dress out nicely," she whispered as she
pecked the air next to my cheek, "but I wish you would
have let Timothy do your hair."

I was starving from the dope. Stephen and I plucked
two flutes of champagne from a waiter's proffered tray
and mingled our way deeper into the house, pausing
for forgettable conversations and wonderful hors
d'oeuvres. There were pea pods stuffed with pink
salmon mousse, warm twists of puff pastry flavored
with pesto, slices of goose liver paté on thin rounds of
toasted brioche topped with a thick slice of truffle. We
had more champagne. Party conversations washed over
us like surf.

I led Stephen on a detour through the greenhouse
and the back sun parlor through the mudroom into the
kitchen. It was an enormous room, as big as a restaurant kitchen, with a table at one end where the regular
house staff of eight took their meals. The female caterers giggled and flirted around Stephen, who looked
as if tuxedos had been invented especially for him.
They offered him samples of the dinner about to be

served, which he amiably tasted and pronounced excellent. I helped myself to a thick slice of roast beef on a Royal Copenhagen plate and sneaked it into the scullery.

"You're going to make that dog sick," Mrs. Mason warned from the darkness of the servants' television room. Mother had given her the night off, but she could never bring herself to leave while there were invaders in her kitchen. Instead, she sat in the dark, muttering Cassandra-like warnings about the state of the floor and the crockery once the caterers had finished.

"He'll be alright," I replied. "There's no one left to spoil him besides me."

"Hmmph," grumbled the ample black woman, "you'll be long gone when that dog sicks-up on the floor."

Rocket rattled his kennel at the sound of my footsteps. He was an old black Labrador with a fat body and arthritis in his hips. He had originally belonged to my older brother Teddy, who had hanged himself one night in the garage. He had wanted to be sure that my parents would find him when they came home from their party.

"Hiya, fella," I greeted him as I opened his cage. He heaved himself to his feet and barked and wagged his entire backside in excitement. "I brought you something." I rubbed his ears and scratched his stomach. Then, once he had managed to get his paws all over my dress, I put the plate on the floor of the kennel.

"Hi, Rocket," Stephen said coming up behind me. "How's he doing?"

"He's really getting old. My mother wants to have him put to sleep, but Dad won't stand for it. Teddy loved that dog."

* * *

Stephen and I spent the next three hours talking to anyone who was likely to own shares of Azor Pharmaceuticals. Stephen didn't lobby—it would have been bad manners to talk business at a party. But whenever anyone mentioned the takeover he would joke that he had arranged it all himself to keep me busy and out of trouble. He left them laughing and with the subtly laid impression of a man confidently handling a bothersome problem.

From time to time I caught Stephen watching Edgar Eichel across the room, though he was careful not to get so close as to make conversation a necessity. I caught a glimpse of him in the music room—a balding little man with a cigar and a paisley cummerbund. He looked like he'd been abused for being a nerd in high school and spent the rest of his life trying to get even. His wife was a typical social X ray: very, very thin, blond hair, a strapless Oscar de la Renta gown and too much jewelry.

As they served dessert (poached pears in crème anglaise or chocolate raspberry gateaux), Stephen and I went upstairs to the children's wing.

The girls were in the little upstairs sitting room, engaged in what appeared to be a sci-fi horror movie festival on video cassette. My little sister Beth and her best friend, Gretchen Azorini, were sitting on the floor among diet Coke cans and videotape boxes. On the screen a slimy reptilian monster exploded out of a man's chest—*Aliens*.

Gretchen was one of those closed doors between Stephen and me. Three years ago I had been in Kansas City for months working on a case involving the takeover of a meat packing company. When I returned, Stephen mentioned that his niece would be coming to live with him in a week, and asked if I would be able to help expedite her admission to Chelsea Hall. Up until that point I hadn't known he even had a brother.

Gretchen was the daughter of Stephen's half brother, Joey, who was in the international import-export business and traveled much of the time. Her mother had been killed in an accident, and the family had decided that the best thing would be for Stephen to act as guardian. Gretchen was thirteen years old at the time and an insulin-dependent diabetic. Stephen, a physician, was, at least on paper, a big improvement over an absentee, globe-trotting father.

I knew there was more to the story than that. There would have to be. Stephen frankly cherished his stripped-down executive's life-style. Before Gretchen became his ward he hadn't found time to take care of even a houseplant.

So we pulled some strings. Tucker Sweet, who was on the board of Chelsea Hall School, was called upon to meet the girl and pronounced her an asset to any institution. Stephen's family wrote an appropriately generous check to the Chelsea Hall Scholarship Fund, and Gretchen Azorini, refugee from who knows what, joined the ranks of green-kilted predebutantes at the Chelsea Hall School for Girls.

Chelsea Hall is not a boarding school, but there is a house on campus that is used as a dorm. Girls live there while their wealthy parents travel, divorce or detox, and are watched over by Mrs. Milnickel, the retired Latin teacher. Gretchen lived there during the week and spent weekends with Stephen or with my little sister, Beth.

Beth also went to Chelsea Hall. She and Gretchen were both in the same class—the only two "dormys."

Beth lived at school in the winter when my parents were in Palm Beach and in the spring when they were in Europe and most of the other times because she was just sick of them.

The girls were quite a pair: silent, friendless, suspicious of the adult world, and cut off from other teenagers by their perverse disdain. They were, I thought for not the first time, a creepy pair.

Gretchen was a plain girl with doughy features and pasty skin splattered with freckles. Her carrot red hair was long and curly, beautiful in and of itself, but somehow it only seemed to draw your eye to the ordinariness of the face it framed. I had never heard Gretchen speak above a whisper and never utter one word more than was necessary.

On the other hand, my sister Beth was a beauty. Perfect bones, beautiful skin, a thick mane of chestnut hair. Looking at her offered a glimpse of what my mother must have been. But Beth did everything she could to stamp out the resemblance. She wore no makeup, refused to wash her hair, dressed only in black, and composed her face into a mask of perpetual sullenness.

Mother was forty-two when Beth was born. She has never been shy about telling the story of how she misconstrued the symptoms of Beth's conception as the onset of menopause. By the time she guessed the real reason, it was well past the point she could have safely ended the pregnancy.

When I was sixteen I was as angry as Beth. I was infuriated by the indifference of my parents and shamed by the opulence around me. But while I embarked on a campaign of rebellion that took many forms, Beth seemed to have turned her anger against herself. She embraced a hundred little self-destructive behaviors designed to drive my mother up the wall. The problem was that they could easily drive Beth into a psychiatric hospital if they went too far. My mother had little patience for unpleasantness. I harbored the secret fear that my mother could make the decision to hospitalize Beth with the same compunction as she could make up her mind to redecorate the dining room.

"We just thought we'd leave all the boring stiffs downstairs and find out where the real good time was," Stephen said. The two girls just looked at him morosely.

Stephen plopped down on the couch near Gretchen and feigned an interest in the movie.

"Hey, what are you guys watching?" he asked.

"*Aliens*," Gretchen replied in her usual whisper. "Last night we did slasher movies."

"Did you get dinner?" Stephen asked his niece.

"Four ounces of roast beef, an artichoke, and some of the stuffed potatoes from the caterer."

"I ate her dessert," Beth announced.

"My blood sugar was one twenty," Gretchen continued.

"I fed my roast beef to Rocket," Beth said.

"Oh, no," I exclaimed, "he really is going to be sick. I just gave him a big piece, too."

"Mom and Dad had a big fight about him this morning. You know that Mom wants to have him put to sleep. She just keeps on going on and on about what a pain it is to have to take care of him and how it's so unfair that Raoul always has to drive him to the vet."

Raoul was the gardener.

"Daddy was talking about how Rocket was Teddy's dog and how he wouldn't allow him to be put down for the gardener's convenience. They were really going at it. Finally I told her they might as well have me put to sleep while they were at it; you know, cut loose from all their unpleasant responsibilities all at once.''

''I bet Mother loved that.''

''The witch grounded me for two weeks for having a poor attitude.''

''Well, what did you expect?'' I asked.

''I expected her to have me put to sleep.''

It was past midnight and the party was still going strong when Stephen and I decided to leave. The other guests could spend their Sunday sleeping late, but I had a full day at the office, and Stephen had to get ready to face his board. Mother had converted the little study off the foyer into a coatroom for the party. We stood there waiting for the maid to find my black wool coat among the racks and racks of minks.

By the time Stephen realized that Edgar Eichel was standing right behind him it was too late to do anything but say hello. Eichel barely came up to Stephen's shoulder, but he had the pugnaciousness in his bearing that little men sometimes have and a fighter's set to his jaw.

''Good evening, Edgar,'' Stephen said. His voice was frosty, his tone dismissive.

''Surprised to see you out on the town this evening, Stephen,'' Eichel replied in a too loud voice. He had obviously had more than a few glasses of champagne. ''I'd think you'd be at the office, drafting your letter of resignation.''

''Edgar,'' bleated his wife, Nadine, in warning. She was a recent acquisition, quite a bit younger than her husband.

''I think you're being a trifle premature. You might want to go home and count the diplomas hanging on your walls and reconsider whether you have what it takes to run a pharmaceutical company.''

Eichel was notoriously sensitive about having never gone to college.

"I can do anything you can do, you little dago asswipe," he growled.

"Oh? Can you do this?" asked Stephen, and to my astonishment popped him neatly in the jaw. He threw the punch so fast I barely saw it. Eichel's knees folded under him, and he collapsed onto the marble floor.

CHAPTER

3

Sunday morning I dragged myself into the office with the smell of Stephen's dope still clinging to my hair and the putrid taste of a hangover in my mouth. Guttman was already waiting for me. It seemed that watching Stephen deck Edgar Eichel wasn't exactly what he meant by monitoring the client's emotional temperature. I hoped he'd never find out about the bottle of Scotch we killed driving back from Lake Forest while Stephen ranted that he shouldn't have hit Eichel, he should have killed him.

The problem, I considered ruefully and not for the first time, was that while Scotch, even good Scotch, tasted wonderful going down, the next day it left a taste in your mouth like you'd eaten excrement. Some day-afters are just like that.

Guttman didn't improve the situation. He read me the riot act. When he finished, Skip Tillman, the firm's managing partner, in an unprecedented Sunday appearance, stopped in for a hushed and somber discussion of "the unfortunate events of last night." A reporter from the *Wall Street Journal* had gotten hold of the story and had called Tillman at home that morning for comment. They hadn't yet managed to connect my name with the story, but it was just a matter of time. Worse, the reporter had let it slip that Eichel was planning to press criminal charges.

Tillman not very tactfully reminded me about the firm's policy regarding talking to the press—if you did, the partners would have your tongue cut out and nailed to your office door. I was also under no circumstances to talk to the police without having a criminal attorney, presumably of the firm's choosing, present. He left my office with a disappointed shrug of his shoulders, making me feel vaguely guilty as well as incredibly hung over.

It was my mother's turn next. She called to tell me at great length and in no uncertain terms how disappointed in me she was. She was finding the humiliation of having a fist fight in her front hall unbearable, and her phone was "ringing off the hook" with reporters asking for a first-hand account of the goings on. She had, she informed me, been forced to take to her bed. The fact that Gretchen Azorini was still under her roof was adding further insult to injury. It was too embarrassing. Blessedly, Gretchen and Beth were going back to the dorm at dinner time.

Once I finally managed to disentangle myself from my mother, I got a call from a rather obsequious Lake Forest police detective who wanted to speak to me regarding the events at my parents' party. I took his number and told him I'd call him right back. I passed the bad news along to Tillman who said he'd see what he could do about finding a criminal lawyer on a Sunday afternoon when the Chicago Bears were playing at home.

To make matters worse, the New York airports were closed down because of weather, so two of Azor's directors were fogged in. Guttman was, in consequence, a complete basket case. He spent the afternoon galloping around the office like the hyperactive three-year-old he most certainly must have been, bellowing out weather updates like some demented Paul Revere.

Skip Tillman finally managed to reach Elkin Caulfield, the renowned criminal lawyer, in his sky box at Soldier Field. He agreed to stop off at Callahan after the game, and a police interview was hastily arranged. Late that afternoon, when the detective from Lake Forest came to obtain my statement, he seemed blessedly unaware that Elkin's presence was a little like Dr. Michael DeBake, the famous heart surgeon, dropping in to check your pulse.

I had already made up my mind. There were only two witnesses to what had happened between Stephen Azorini and Edgar Eichel, other than the two combatants. The coat-check girl had been busy retrieving our coats, and there had been no one else in the foyer at the time. There were only the two of us: Nadine Eichel and me.

"Miss Millholland," the detective finally managed to ask after a lengthy round of introductions, "could you please tell us what occurred between Mr. Azorini and Mr. Eichel last night at your parents' house?"

"You know, I'm not really sure. Whatever it was must have happened really fast. Stephen and I were waiting for our coats when the Eichels came up behind us. They must have been planning on leaving, too. The two men said hello, and Eichel said he was surprised, under the circumstances, to see Stephen out at a party."

"Under what circumstances?"

"Edgar Eichel is trying to buy Stephen Azorini's company, Azor Pharmaceuticals. So Stephen said something like 'don't count your chickens yet, it's early in the game.' Then Eichel answered him, I don't remember what exactly, I wasn't paying too close atten tion. I was watching the woman in the coatroom; she seemed to be taking so long finding our coats. Then all of a sudden Edgar Eichel was on the floor, and his wife was chirping, 'oh Eddy, oh Eddy,' and Stephen was helping Eichel to his feet and asking him if he was alright.''

"So you did not see Dr. Azorini hit Mr. Eichel."

"Hit him? Why, no. I assumed that Eichel fell. Someone must have spilled a drink because there were those little lozenge-shaped ice cubes on the floor. I just assumed that he slipped. Why would Stephen want to hit him?''

"Edgar Eichel is not without motivation in this," interjected Skip Tillman, who was nattily attired in green corduroys festooned with mallard ducks, and Top-Siders. (I hoped that being on the Lake Forest Police Department hardened you to the more gruesome aspects of preppy menswear—sort of the way Chicago cops were inured to corpses.)

"He's spending hundreds of thousands of dollars to publicize his attempted buyout of Azor Pharmaceuticals. If he can generate free press, especially in the form of a story like this, which makes Dr. Azorini look foolish or hotheaded, well, so much the better for him.''

"Was he hurt at all?" I asked. "I know that Dr. Azorini was very concerned and tried to check him over, but Eichel wouldn't let him. He seemed quite angry, but I just put that down to his being drunk.''

"No, just a bruise over his jaw.''

"Well, that must have been from hitting the floor. I honestly can't say for sure because I wasn't paying attention at the time, but I've known Stephen since we were teenagers. He doesn't have a temper; I've never heard of him hitting anyone. He and Eichel were just talking to each other in a normal tone of voice, just making conversation, waiting for the coats.''

"And Dr. Azorini didn't threaten Mr. Eichel?"

"No."

"Mr. Eichel did not call Dr. Azorini any derogatory names?"

"Names? No. These men are not steelworkers, Officer, they didn't call each other names. They were just making small talk."

"Well, Miss Millholland. I guess that does it. I'll have your statement typed up and sent to you for your signature."

"Why don't I just stop at the police station next time I'm out visiting my parents?"

"That'd be just fine."

"So—can he press charges?" Guttman asked after the detective had left.

"He can file a complaint," Elkin Caulfield answered. "Whether the D.A.'s office would pursue the matter and whether, if it did, a jury would convict is another matter."

"Tillman's going to have a word with the D.A. tomorrow," Guttman replied. "But if Eichel presses charges it's a public relations nightmare on top of everything else. I can see the headline in tomorrow's *Journal*. 'Azor's CEO throws sucker punch at society gala.' Won't the big stockholders love reading that."

They both glared at me as if it were my fault.

The Azor Pharmaceuticals Board of Directors finally met at 5:00 P.M. Richard Humanski, Stephen's assistant, had supervised the hanging of a special baffling device in the Azor conference room that very afternoon. Venetian blinds had been installed to prevent surveillance photography and to make the use of long-range microphones more difficult.

The board met in secret. No aides, assistants, or secretaries. Only a court stenographer, at Guttman's insistence, to make a transcript of the proceedings to protect the directors from a potential lawsuit. The plan was for Stephen to address the board, followed by a presentation by Brian Gould of First New York. Stephen had sworn he wasn't going to let anyone out of that room alive until he received permission to fight Edgar Eichel to the death.

Guttman and I waited out the meeting like expectant fathers in a Frank Capra movie, killing time over take-out food in Guttman's office. He talked with great vehemence but only partial attention about the viciousness of Edgar Eichel. The financial community was rich with Eichel lore, not very much of it positive. Fueled initially by junk bonds and perpetually surrounded by a coterie of hungry young men with modest backgrounds and immodest ambition—they were often unsmilingly referred to as "the sharks"—Eichel had always been the focus of rumors of sleazy dealings. He had been fined several times by the SEC for playing fast and loose with reporting and filing regulations. He had been censured as well for improperly soliciting shares in several of his early takeovers.

Much of the malice against Eichel was of the under-the-breath "he's not our sort" variety, aimed at his garish life-style, his chest thumping in the press, and the infamous "muffler blowouts" that were the cornerstone of his incentive program for the managers in his muffler chain. The parties, three days long, were said to feature oceans of booze and female companionship, courtesy of Eichel. They were the object of much snickering (and envy) from the button-down types whom Eichel now rubbed shoulders with.

But those stories were not the focus of Guttman's diatribe. Instead, Guttman rehashed the Beckman Corporation story. Guttman had helped defend Beckman, a medium-size manufacturing company, against one of Edgar Eichel's first corporate takeover attempts. The company was old and respected, and like Azor, it had a substantial block of stock in the hands of the founding family. Like Azor, I think there was a personal connection with Guttman as well—an old client or a family friend.

Eichel bought up a big block of the company's stock. He had made his purchases quickly, parking the stock in the names of third parties right up until he made his position public. Then he called a meeting with management and offered them a deal. They could either buy back his shares at a hefty premium or he would tear the company apart with a bloody takeover attempt.

Guttman counseled fiercely against caving in to greenmail. But the board, pressured by management, agreed to Eichel's terms and leveraged themselves to the max to write the check to Eichel, the budding corporate terrorist. The rest is a sad but familiar story. Interest rates skyrocketed. The company, burdened by debt, floundered, saw its equity slide to zero, and is now in the process of being liquidated. The lawyers and investment bankers had taken their hefty fees and moved on to the next deal; the professional managers who'd pushed to accept Eichel's terms moved on to other jobs. The directors shook their gray heads sadly and agreed over lunch at their clubs that it was truly a shame what had happened to the company. But the family that had founded the company, whose fortune had been in its stock, was bled to death by Edgar Eichel.

Guttman paced and muttered. I gripped the arms of my chair and was reminded, not for the first time, of what Balzac once wrote: "Behind every great fortune there is a great crime." I wondered whether, four generations from now, snobbish and inbred Eichels would snigger about another generation of strivers.

At 6:45 the phone rang, and we both jumped. Guttman nodded and whispered. Then his ugly face split into a big grin.

"The board voted to back Stephen," he announced as he hung up the receiver. "Halfway through Gould's presentation Tucker called a vote. Four to three."

"Close," I remarked.

"A majority is a majority," Guttman said.

"I hope he can hold it when it starts getting bloody," I replied.

By 9:00 P.M. I'd had enough. I'd had four hours of sleep the night before and knew enough to pace myself for a big case. I called Stephen before I left. I wanted to congratulate him. I also wanted to let him know that I'd perjured myself on his behalf. When I tried the office, Richard said that he'd gone home right after the board meeting. When I rang his home number, his answering machine picked up. I left a message: "Good job with the board, and I hope your knuckles hurt like crazy." I turned off my office light, picked up my Burberry, and headed for home.

Living in Hyde Park was one of my continuing acts of rebellion against my parents. I had lived there over their strenuous objections during law school, and had moved back after Russell died. Claudia, my roommate, was doing a surgical residency at U. of C. She'd bought a rambling railroad apartment on Hyde Park Boulevard near Fifty-fifth Street, and she was tired of living alone.

Later, when Gretchen came to live with him, Stephen gave up his trendy loft apartment in Printer's Row and bought a co-op three blocks away.

I liked Hyde Park. It is the kind of neighborhood you get when you drop a world-class university into the middle of the ghetto. I liked the eccentric mix of mansions and public housing, physicists and pimps—the fact that you could never be sure whether the man in the greasy raincoat whose shoes were tied with fishing line was a bum or a Nobel prize winner. Besides, you couldn't beat being ten minutes from the office and a block from the lake.

Claudia was home when I got there. I found her in the living room, sitting cross-legged on the couch in a set of bloodstained scrubs, rolling a joint. She was tiny and looked about twelve years old, but there was a core of toughness to her. When she told people she was a surgeon, they were only surprised for an instant. She had round, wire-rimmed glasses and wore her dark brown hair in a single, thick braid so long that she could sit on it. Her mother was a sculptor and her father was a professor of Russian literature at NYU. She came from a long line of socialist Jewish intellectuals and felt that I took my family much, much too seriously.

"I can't remember the last time we were both home at the same time," I said, plunking down in a big chintz-covered armchair. All of our furniture had come from one or the other of our parents' houses and the mixture was every bit as odd as you would expect. I poured us both a glass of wine while Claudia wet a joint carefully in her mouth and handed it to me.

"It's been a long time. I just got off my rotation. I was going to go to sleep in the on-call room since I've got rounds at five-thirty tomorrow morning, but after eighteen hours in the OR, I'm too wired to go to sleep, so I thought I'd come home.''

"That's a long day for a Sunday," I commented, lighting my joint. There was a time, in college, when Claudia and I would have shared one joint, jealously conserving the smoke. Now we each smoked our own, a sign of our revised yuppy sensibilities.

"There was a big accident on the Dan Ryan last night. Some guy driving a semi-truck fell asleep at the wheel and hit a church bus head on. I'm surprised you didn't hear about it."

"I've been at the office since Friday morning. Someone's made a hostile bid for Azor Pharmaceuticals."

"Oh, no. Stephen's company?"

I told her about the takeover, ending up with what happened between Stephen and Eichel. Whether from fatigue or the dope, we laughed until our sides ached. Eventually I said: "I'm glad you managed to find humor in it. It's so easy, sitting in an office downtown, to come to believe that a hostile corporate takeover is the world's biggest tragedy."

"No," Claudia said, suddenly turning serious and pointing to the bloodstains on the green fabric of her scrubs, "this is what tragedy looks like."

It was still dark when I woke up Monday morning. I pulled on my sweats and took a dawn run along the lake down to McCormack Place and back. I made some coffee and checked the fridge: one bottle of club soda, two cans of diet Coke, and a container of coffee yogurt dated July 29. I closed the refrigerator door. I took a long, hot shower, put on my robe, wrapped my hair in a towel, and called Stephen Azorini. There was no answer at home, but Richard Humanski, Stephen's assistant, picked up Stephen's private line at the office.

Richard was a baby-faced kid from Rockville, Illinois, who'd gone to the University of Chicago on scholarship when he was sixteen years old. Since then he'd worked at Goldman Sachs for two years, gotten his MBA from Harvard, worked for Stephen for three years, and managed, at the ripe old age of twenty-four, to still look like he was in the throes of puberty. Cute, in a beach boy sort of way. It was said that there was lively wagering among the Azor secretaries as to whether Richard had to shave.

He was smart, hardworking, and fiercely loyal. Everyone agreed that Stephen was grooming him for some terrific position, but Stephen relied on him so completely I often wondered if, when the time came, Stephen would be able to let Richard move on.

"Hi, Richard. The boss in?"

"No, Kate. He's got a breakfast meeting at the Union League Club."

"I just wanted to congratulate him on the board's vote. I tried to reach him at home last night, but there was no answer."

"He was probably in the shower," Richard replied. "Hey, I heard Eichel got what he deserved at your parents' house Saturday night."

"The official version is that he slipped on an ice cube. If he'd gotten what he deserved, someone would have slipped arsenic into his drink. Was Stephen pumped after the board's vote?" I asked, changing the subject.

"Yeah. He was pretty fired up. When you think about it, it was pretty amazing. I think the whole meeting was over in an hour. Stephen said that Tucker Sweet just stood up and basically said, 'Are we going to stand up to this creep Eichel, or are we going to lie down and take this shit?' and then called a vote."

"What a relief," I replied. "Who voted against?"

"It's supposed to be a secret," Richard answered. "But since we can be fairly certain that Stephen, Tucker, Carl Swensen and Peter Chou voted with Stephen, it's pretty easy to figure out who the no's were."

Swensen and Chou were two scientists who'd had seats on the board since the company was founded. Peter Chou had been Stephen's roommate at M.I.T. The institutional directors had, as a unit, voted against Stephen. Tucker had been the swing man.

Too close for comfort.

"Amazing," I said. "I talked to Tucker Saturday afternoon, and he was really noncommittal."

"Maybe he decided that anyone who'd punch Edgar Eichel in the nose might be able to keep him from taking over Azor Pharmaceuticals."

"Maybe. Or maybe he just couldn't wait to shoot a few elk."

When I got to the office, I found my star clearly on the rise. Eichel had decided on advice of counsel not to press charges, and the *Journal* made only a one-line reference on the last page to the "alleged incident." Guttman was jubilant at Stephen's victory with the board, and not only used much of my wording of Azor's answer in the final draft, but also sent me to meet with the economic consultants to help coordinate the litigation side of our counteroffensive. By the time the clerks brought dinner, news of my newly exalted status had become common knowledge, and I got a lot of ribbing from my colleagues, not all of it good-natured.

Monday blurred into Tuesday; Tuesday slid into Wednesday. I was swallowed up in my work, caught up in the rhythm of the takeover. I slept for a few hours every night on the too short couch in my office. I went to Stephen's office every morning for the daily strategy meetings. If the client would have been anyone but Azor Pharmaceuticals, my contentment would have been complete.

Wednesday, six days after Eichel had launched his raid, I spent the day brainstorming with the litigators about the possibility of filing suit in the New York courts against Edgar Eichel, alleging that he had violated certain securities laws and thus damaged Azor Pharmaceuticals by attempting to manipulate their stock and approaching shareholders improperly with a proposal to break up the company. It was unclear whether there was a strong enough basis for the suit, but if we could make at least a prima facie case, it would do several things for us. First, it would set Azor on a totally new course. The company would be on the offensive and counterattacking. Second, we could seek discovery of Eichel's records and files. Third, we might be able to drag out the offering period and gain additional time to strengthen our defenses. We were ready for deadly combat.

At 8:00 P.M. I was sitting on the floor of my office with papers spread out around me, eating Kung Pao chicken from a greasy cardboard container and trying to fight back waves of fatigue. When the phone rang, I had to pick my way across my littered carpet to get to my desk.

It was Stephen Azorini calling from his car phone. He was on his way back from a meeting with Azor's bankers. He sounded tired and depressed. Did I want a ride home?

I considered for a moment. With us a ride home was sometimes just that, but it was often an invitation to Stephen's bed as well.

I told him I'd be downstairs in ten minutes. Stephen was waiting for me when I got there. A light snow was falling. LaSalle Street, so busy during the day, was deserted except for the occasional taxi, but lights burned in almost all the office windows: other drones, just like me, toiling for their corporate masters.

Stephen drove easily but fast, swinging onto Lake Shore Drive near Azor's offices at Balbo. He had taken off his tie, and there were dark smudges of fatigue under his eyes. On him, however, exhaustion managed somehow to look good.

"I heard you covered my ass Sunday with the police," he said.

"It wasn't too tough. I mean, the Lake Forest police aren't exactly the gestapo—they're so damn polite."

"Thanks anyway."

"No problem. So how did it go with the bankers?"

Stephen tilted one hand over the gear shift, meaning "so-so."

"With the outstanding bonds and what it costs to service the debt we took on to build the new hematology research facility, if we're going to beat Eichel, we've got to do it quickly. We just don't have the money for a long, complicated fight. What First New York is charging should be a criminal offense, and you guys aren't exactly cheap either. Besides, I don't want to find myself in the position where I have to loot the company myself in order to keep Eichel from looting it."

We rode for a while in silence, past Oakwood and the gaping windows of empty public housing projects. A red Porsche, one side scraped and crumpled, shot past us.

There were two squad cars drawn up in front of Stephen's building and Randall, the doorman, looked worried as he stooped to let me out of the car. I waited demurely under the awning while he whispered with Stephen, who then unfolded himself slowly out of the driver's seat and walked toward me, squaring his shoulders.

"It looks like I may be needing a lawyer," Stephen announced ruefully. "Randall says there are two policemen waiting to speak to me. They wouldn't say what they wanted, and they wouldn't go away, so Randall told them to wait upstairs."

"Not in the apartment!" I exclaimed, thinking about last night's Thai stick and wondering whether there was any more stashed in the apartment.

"No, just in the landing." Stephen's building had only one apartment per floor, and at each private elevator stop there was a foyer. Stephen's was decorated with two wing chairs, a gateleg table, and a watercolor of Venice at night.

"Eichel must have changed his mind about pressing charges," I said. "Be friendly. Tell them you want to cooperate fully, but don't say anything else until I can get Elkin Caulfield to come down."

"Are they going to arrest me?"

"There's a good chance."

"Christ," Stephen muttered as the elevator whisked us to the penthouse, "I need this like a hole in the head."

As Randall promised, there were two Chicago cops making themselves at home on the landing: a long, thin, dour-looking man with dark hair slicked back, and a muscular black woman with a neat afro and eyes that didn't miss a thing.

"Dr. Stephen Azorini?" asked the female officer. "I'm Sergeant Conway and this is Officer Barnes. May we come in and have a word with you?"

"Certainly," he answered, unlocking the door and switching on the light. The officers were taken aback by the apartment. The building had been built at the turn of the century, around the time of the Columbian Exhibition, and it had been built on a grand scale. There were fifteen-foot ceilings and intricately carved moldings. The doorways were arched.

"Please come in," Stephen said, always the good host. "Tell me what I can do for you."

Officer Barnes took a small spiral notebook from his back pocket before taking a seat on the couch across from Stephen.

"Dr. Azorini. Can you tell me whether you are still the owner of a current model, dark blue Jeep Cherokee, Illinois license number SWT one six?" asked Sergeant Conway.

"Why, yes," Stephen replied, obviously surprised.

"And do you know where that vehicle is located at the present time?"

"I . . . well . . . it should be at my niece's school in Lake Forest. I hold title to the car, but it's driven by my niece Gretchen. It was her birthday present."

"So you couldn't tell me what the car would be doing in Mannetuoc, Wisconsin."

"Mannetuoc, Wisconsin?" asked Stephen, incredulous.

"Dr. Azorini, could you tell us what your niece looks like?" asked the male officer.

"About five foot six, long red hair. Why do you want to know? What's happened?"

"Dr. Azorini. I don't want to unnecessarily alarm you, but this afternoon the body of a teenage girl of about average height and with long red hair was found dead on an unused private road outside of Mannetuoc, Wisconsin. The Jeep Cherokee, license SWT one six, was found abandoned in a K mart parking lot a few miles away. The sheriff's department in Wisconsin traced the registration and asked the Chicago PD if we could help locate the owner and see if that might help us identify the dead girl.''

"The car might have been stolen," I protested.

"That's certainly a possibility," Officer Barnes replied reassuringly. "Is there some way you might be able to contact your niece to see if she knows where the car is?"

"I'll call," Stephen said. He went to use the phone in his study. Officer Barnes strolled around the living room, commenting that she'd never known there were apartments like this in Hyde Park. She went to the window to check out the views of the park and the lake. The other officer asked if he might have a glass of water. I fetched one. We made stilted small talk.

According to Richard Humanski, Stephen hadn't looked the least bit rattled when he first received news of Eichel's hostile bid for Azor Pharmaceuticals, but coming out of his study, he looked shaken to his bones.

"She's not in the dorm," he reported flatly, "and her car's not there either."

CHAPTER

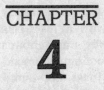

The police helicopter touched down at the lowest time of day—sometime after midnight and a long time before dawn. It was very dark. The makeshift landing field flickered beneath us, faintly ringed by blue lights. Everywhere else, it seemed, people were asleep.

I was feeling tired and defeated, pummeled by the events of the past few days. I could only imagine what Stephen must be feeling under the din of the rotating blades, staring out into the hostile night. My mind kept shuffling and reshuffling the variables, trying to work out plausible scenarios for this all being some horrible mistake.

The blades of the helicopter whined above us as we hurried, crouched over, through the bitter night, to a waiting highway patrol car. We were at least 300 miles north of Chicago, and it was much colder than it had been in the city. The air had a sharp flavor peculiar to the cold and to the country. The sky above the trees seemed filled with ink. The only light came from a low cinder block building about 500 yards away. Lights burned in a few of its windows and spilled neon onto the asphalt of the vacant parking lot.

The highway patrolman's name was Gunderson. He

had the smooth face of a child under the shadow of his hat, which was broad-brimmed and peaked like a Mountie's. He drove us the thirty or so miles to the hospital. He kept the siren on the entire time, though we passed no one on the road. The lines of Stephen's face were hard in the dimly flashing light. I wanted to slip my hand into his—to make some sort of contact— but I was gripped by a mysterious restraint. Instead, I pulled my coat more tightly around myself and fought back cold waves of fear. Let it not be her, I prayed.

The hospital was tiny, two story, and built of yellow brick like the uglier variety of public school. We pulled into a space marked AMBULANCES ONLY and followed Officer Gunderson into the brightly lit, deserted emergency room. The walls were painted brilliant yellow, and the whole place smelled of disinfectant. The highway patrolman left us on a row of orange vinyl chairs to stare at the Coke machine, while he tried to find someone in authority. It struck me that I had not been in a hospital since the night Russell died.

By the time Officer Gunderson returned, Stephen was pacing the floor, shaking his head in frustration and disbelief. The highway patrolman reappeared with a rumpled doctor in tow. The doctor had a sleepy face in need of a shave and a head of wispy, white hair that seemed to possess a life of its own. As they got closer I could read the name embroidered in red over the breast pocket of his once white lab coat—Proctor Van Dusen, M.D.

"I'm Dr. Van Dusen," he said, extending his hand to Stephen and bowing his head toward me.

"I'm Dr. Azorini, and this is Kate Millholland."

"Are you a physician?" Dr. Van Dusen asked.

"Yes."

"I'm told you've come to have a look at our Jane Doe."

"I understand my niece's car was found in the vicinity of the body. We haven't been able to reach my niece, who's at boarding school, so the police have asked me to come and have a look."

"Naturally. Even a negative identification is a great help in these cases," Dr. Van Dusen replied. "Why don't you follow me."

Stephen took my hand almost absentmindedly, and we followed the doctor down a long corridor, through two sets of automatic double doors, with Officer Gunderson bringing up the rear of the grim little procession. The smells, the swoosh as we waited for the doors to swing open brought Russell back to me. Not the laughing athlete who bounded ten minutes late into criminal law class with dirty knees and a soccer ball under one arm, but Russell, wasted, with tubes down his throat and his hair falling out in clumps from the sickening and useless chemotherapy.

The body was in an unused operating room, large but crammed with equipment, tools of the unspeakable things they do to you while you are under. On a gurney in the center of the room was a human form, tiny in death, under a sheet of surgical green. I stood back with the policeman while Stephen and Dr. Van Dusen went and lifted the sheet. I did not want to look but couldn't look away. My legs shook and my breath came in shallow, strangled gasps. I saw the tangle of red hair and looked away as hot tears began rolling down my face.

Only later did I remember Stephen's voice as he made the identification, the numb walk back down the corridor, Officer Gunderson's ministration with coffee from the vending machine.

* * *

The sheriff's office was even more forlorn than the hospital, but by no means deserted. It was clear that, the hour not withstanding, Stephen's identification of his niece was a big deal. The sheriff himself, in the person of one Donald J. Whittle, had been rousted out of bed for the occasion. He was flanked by two deputies, and while he made a great show of civility and condolence, it was clear that this was not going to be an entirely friendly encounter.

We sat in a room with cinder block walls that contained a battered wooden table, four folding chairs, and a tape recorder. As he spoke, Sheriff Whittle consulted a file that he held upright, like a choirboy, to prevent surreptitious glimpses on our part.

At first there had been some discussion about whether I should be privy to the sheriff's discussion with Stephen. But while I had been figuring how quickly I could get Elkin Caulfield up there, Stephen had introduced me as his attorney and insisted that I be present. My sense was that the relatively recent innovation of women attorneys had not yet penetrated this Wisconsin backwoods. My suit would cost him a whole month's salary. I felt as out of place as a fish on a bicycle.

"I know this must be very painful for you, Dr. Azorini," intoned the sheriff, "but in cases such as these you have to understand that we have a job to do."

Stephen nodded.

"You identified the deceased as Gretchen Maria Azorini, aged sixteen."

"That is correct."

"What was your relationship to the deceased?"

"She was my niece, my brother's daughter. In addition, she was my ward."

"Your what?"

"Dr. Azorini was his niece's legal guardian," I interjected.

"And why was that?" asked Whittle, not happy at having been interrupted. "Is your brother deceased?"

"No. But his business forces him to travel abroad a great deal. That is why Gretchen made her home with me."

"Your niece lived with you at your address? What would that be now?"

"Five eight four zero South Shore Drive. Chicago, Illinois. That was her legal address. However, during the week she lived in the dormitory of her school in Lake Forest."

"What school would that be?"

"The Chelsea Hall School for Girls."

"Is that a parochial school?" Whittle asked.

"No, just private," Stephen replied. His voice was flat, his answers automatic.

"When was the last time you saw your niece?" inquired Whittle, continuing to consult the file.

"Last Saturday night."

"And where was that?"

"At the home of Astrid and Edward Millholland."

"Any relation to Ms. Millholland here?"

"My parents," I replied.

"And what were the circumstances?"

"We were attending a party. My niece was spending the weekend with Ms. Millholland's sister, who is in her class at school. We just stopped up to say hi. The girls were watching videotapes."

"Was there any argument?"

"Pardon?" Stephen asked, as if he honestly hadn't heard.

"Was there any argument between you and your niece?"

Stephen pounded the table with the flat of his hand so hard that the room seemed to shake. He drew himself up to his full height and leaned over the table toward the sheriff. I reached up and grabbed his arm in a futile gesture of restraint.

"Listen, Sheriff. I understand that you have a job to do, but that doesn't give you permission to act like an insensitive idiot. I came home from the office to find two police officers waiting for me. They bring me up to this godforsaken spot in the middle of the night to identify the body of my sixteen-year-old niece, who I had assumed up until about thirty minutes ago was safely in bed in the dormitory of her school. And now, instead of being told what happened to her, I get to sit here and listen to you pretend to be every badass cop you ever watched on TV."

"You done now?" asked Sheriff Whittle. "Then why don't you just sit back down."

Stephen sat down slowly.

"I think it's quite obvious the strain that Dr. Azorini is under," I interjected. "I know that he is willing to cooperate with you in any way he can, but I think that he might be better able to answer your questions if you answered some of his."

"The body of your niece was discovered yesterday morning in the woods about twenty miles from here. Poachers found her. The body had been out in the open for some time. There was no identification on or near the body. We brought her in as a Jane Doe."

"Now, Dr. Azorini . . . Are you a medical doctor by any chance?"

"Yes, I am."

"Well, then, you'll understand that in most cases when you find the body of a young girl in an exposed area, the first reaction is to suspect rape/murder." Stephen sunk into his chair, his face completely white.

"I'd like to request an autopsy," Stephen said after a long silence.

"It's been done already," replied the sheriff.

"By whom?" asked Stephen.

"The pathologist over at the hospital. Now, I know what you're thinking, Dr. Azorini. You're thinking that we're a bunch of rubes up here, don't know anything about pathology or forensic medicine. But we got lucky in the pathology department. There's a young guy at the hospital, well trained, did a month at the Dade County Medical Examiner's office a while back. His wife's a large-animal vet so he's got no choice but to live in this godforsaken place, as you put it. Anyway, he's the one who performed the autopsy."

"And what did he determine as the cause of death?"

"He didn't. Not yet. He says he needs to wait for the reports to come back from toxicology. He's issued a pending death certificate so the body could be buried as soon as we'd made an identification."

"But how did she die?" asked Stephen.

"We don't know, yet. You might be able to help us figure that out by answering some questions."

"Certainly," replied Stephen.

"Had your niece ever run away from home?"

"No."

"Ever been in trouble with the law? Truancy?"

"No."

"Did she have a regular boyfriend?"

"No."

"Did she date a lot of different boys?"

"To my knowledge she didn't date at all."

"And she was sixteen years old?" queried Whittle, trying to mask his disbelief.

"Gretchen was a very quiet girl. Shy. She went to a girls' school. I don't think she'd gotten interested in boys yet."

"I see. We found her car parked in the K mart lot over in Ridleyville. Any idea what might have brought her up to these parts?"

"No. I thought she was at school. I can't imagine what would have brought her up here voluntarily."

"So you think she must have been forced?"

"Isn't that what you think?" Stephen asked. "You said it yourself, the circumstances make you suspect that she was . . ." He struggled to find the particular words that would be easiest to say, "assaulted and then killed."

"That is what it looks like," Whittle replied.

It was obvious, I thought, that he saw himself as very tough. I thought he was a macho jerk.

"But there are a lot of ways that a young girl can end up like your niece," Whittle said. "Some rape/murders are what we call stranger abductions. I guess it's not inconceivable that your niece was abducted somewhere in Chicago and forced to drive up here. It's also possible that she was killed elsewhere and her body was dumped up here. But then again there's also a chance that whoever is responsible is someone whom your niece knew."

"Could I ask you, Dr. Azorini," Whittle continued, "for how long had your niece been using drugs?"

"Drugs?" Stephen asked incredulously.

"Yes. The pathologist said that he found scar tissue formed under the skin, the kind you get from shooting up."

"She was a diabetic," replied Stephen wearily. "She injected herself with insulin several times a day. She was incredibly careful about her health. She would never take illegal drugs.''

''Then maybe you can explain why the pathologist says she must have been using cocaine.''

The trip back seemed shorter but more terrible than the journey there. My brain teemed with unspeakable scenarios culled from the carnage of the nightly news—horrible crimes that I had always assumed that people like Gretchen (and me) were protected from by the thick walls of class and privilege.

The entire way back Stephen's face was frozen into a basilisk, horrible in its absence of emotion. He did not speak, and I was silent as well. After all, what was there to say? Only questions for which there were no answers. Only fears that were better left unexpressed.

The helicopter brought us back to Meig's field, where the two Chicago cops had helpfully suggested that I leave Stephen's car the night before. The night had bled away to morning, and the sky stretched low and dirty over the city. Lake Shore Drive was clotted with the beginnings of rush hour going north, but our progress southbound was solitary.

The boat show was in progress at McCormack Place, the big convention center on the lake, and the indoor regatta of colored sails glimpsed through plate glass was incongruous and beautiful.

Stephen's apartment felt like a foreign place, transformed by grief into a series of rooms alien and unfamiliar. Only an empty glass, the contents consumed by one of the police officers who had come to ask Stephen about his niece's car, gave the events of the last night a concrete reality.

''I've got to take a shower before I go to the office,'' Stephen announced.

"Maybe you should try to get an hour's sleep first," I suggested.

"I can't. I have people coming in from New York at nine."

"They'll understand," I said.

"Yeah. But do you think Eichel will?" Stephen replied.

I left Stephen in the shower and went into the bedroom to make a phone call. Unsure whether Stephen might want to call other family members when he finished, I made my way down the hall to use the second line in Gretchen's room.

It was a pretty room but without much personality, as if Gretchen had done all her real living in her room at school. There was a four-poster single bed with a pink-and-white Laura Ashley spread and drapes to match. A desk, a dresser, a skirted vanity with its own mirror, and a rose-colored loveseat almost invisible under an avalanche of teddy bears of every size and description. The phone was on the nightstand, but it took me a while to compose myself to use it, sitting on a dead girl's bed looking at a teddy bear collection that would never get any bigger.

Her dresser was crowded with photographs, pictures of Gretchen before puberty standing beside a very, very pretty woman in a gaudy dress and too high heels who, I assumed from the resemblance, had been her mother. There was another of the two of them joined by a handsome man with a dark jowl who I thought might be Stephen's brother, Joey. There was also a big statue of the Virgin Mary on the dresser and one of a sad-eyed Christ in white robes, his arms open. Slid under the edge of the mirror there was a snapshot of Beth and Gretchen taken at an amusement park. Both girls wore shorts. They were standing in front of the log race ride, wet and laughing.

I needed to call Beth. I didn't want her to hear about her best friend's death from a stranger. I owed her that much. But when I finally picked up the phone, it was Guttman's number that I dialed.

He was already at the office, and in the silence with which he greeted the news of Gretchen's death, I could practically hear the gears in his brain turn as he worked through the implications of the tragedy.

"So where are you now?" he snapped.

"At Stephen's."

"How is he taking it?"

"How do you think?"

"Christ, this could kill us," said Guttman. "We've got fourteen days. Every fucking minute is important. Plus she was a big shareholder. We'll have to get an opinion from trusts and estates right away. I can't believe this is happening. When's the funeral going to be?"

"I don't know."

"Well, see what you can do about speeding things up. Let's not let this thing drag out. The kid's dead for God's sake, nothing's going to change that."

"I'll see what I can do," I answered, trying to smother my disgust.

"And get in here as soon as you can. Christ, this is a fucking disaster."

I stared at the teddy bears and the picture of my sister smiling out at me with her arm around her best friend's waist, and slowly laid the phone in its cradle.

My mother was annoyed to hear from me. She was on her way out the door to a meeting of the board of the Art Institute. I could just see her standing there at her writing desk in the morning room, wearing one of the Chanel suits she favored when she wanted to look businesslike.

"Mother," I said. "Something terrible has happened. Gretchen Azorini is dead. She died yesterday."

"Was she in a car accident?"

"No. They're not sure yet how it happened. They're waiting for some tests to come back from the autopsy."

"Does Beth know? This is really going to set her off."

"I don't think so. I wanted to let you know first so you could get a head start."

"A head start?"

"To pick her up."

"Pick her up where?"

"From school."

"From school? I told you, I'm on my way to a board meeting."

"Mother, her best friend's just died. I think she'll probably need to come home. I mean, I just can't see her trundling off to geometry."

There was a little pause while Mother tried to formulate a reason why doing what was most convenient for her was really what was best for Beth.

"I'll have to check with Dr. Weingart, but I would think Beth would need to be near her friends rather than home by herself." Harold Weingart was Beth's psychiatrist. Everyone who was annoyed by their teenager sent them to Dr. Weingart.

"Mother," I began, riding the wave of anger and no sleep that was rising up inside me, "the whole idea is that she wouldn't be home alone. She would be home with her mother who would be there to offer her love and support, but now that I think about it, I think she is better off at school. Of course, she'd be even better off with different parents, but you're probably too old for remedial mother school."

"Katharine Anne Millholland," began my mother in a tone I knew all too well, but by then I had had enough of it. I hung up the phone and hated myself for acting like a twelve-year-old.

I went into the bathroom, washed my face, and went back to the phone and called the number of Chelsea Hall School for Girls. I asked to speak to Mrs. Bigham, the headmistress. I told her as simply as I could about Gretchen's death and promised her that Stephen would call her as soon as it was convenient.

"This is such shocking news," she said. "I can't quite absorb it. This is going to be very hard on the girls. What an awful tragedy."

"I was wondering if I might be able to speak to my sister. I'd like to tell her what happened myself."

"Oh, by all means. Of course, this is going to be quite a blow to Beth. She and Gretchen were the absolute best of friends."

"Yes, I know."

"I'll have to find out what class she's in and have someone go and bring her to the phone. Do you mind waiting on the phone or shall I call you back?"

"I'll wait," I said.

It seemed like an age before there was a click, and then Beth's puzzled voice was on the line. "Kate? Is that you?"

"Beth. Hi. Listen. I have some bad news. Gretchen Azorini died yesterday."

"What?"

"She died yesterday. There are a lot of questions, since you were her best friend . . ." I began, but the question remained unspoken as I heard the crack of the receiver hitting something, probably the table, and the deeper, muffled thud Beth made as she fainted onto the headmistress's rug.

CHAPTER
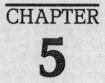
5

I made coffee and brought a cup to Stephen in his study, black with two sugars. He had changed into a black suit and a plain white shirt. His neck seemed to have shrunk away from his collar, and his cheeks were clawed with fatigue. He was speaking softly on the phone, in Italian, something I'd never heard him do before. I set the cup on the desk in front of him and nursed mine in the window seat in the arched bay that overlooked 57th Street where it curved into Lake Shore Drive. Commuters pulled out into rush hour traffic, school buses stopped in front of the Museum of Science and Industry—the beginning of another day.

"That was my father," Stephen said after he had hung up the phone.

"How did he take the news?"

"He's a tough old man."

"I called the school while you were in the shower. I told them about Gretchen, and I spoke to Beth. She was too upset to talk about what Gretchen was doing in Wisconsin. I'll call her in a couple of hours."

Stephen came over and joined me on the window seat. He looked at me for a minute, his leonine head cocked to one side.

"Kate, I want you to understand something," he said. "I know that Gretchen is dead. Nothing you or I can do can bring her back. But I can do something about Edgar Eichel and . . . I know this sounds cold, but I also think that you of all people will understand. I need to keep this thing with Gretchen on hold for a little while, keep focused on Eichel."

"I do understand," I answered. "It's horrible, but I do understand."

I dropped Stephen at his office and then took his car back to Callahan. Claire, the receptionist, told me that Guttman wanted to see me the "absolute minute I got in" and handed me a stack of phone messages. Skip Tillman, my mother, Richard Humanski, and about ten other people, several I'd never even heard of, all wanted to talk to me right away. I stuffed the messages in my pocket and dodged down the service stairs to my office.

"Get me a pot of coffee, a bag of M&M's, and don't tell anyone I'm here," I ordered Cheryl, my secretary. "And get me a mail clerk right away."

"And good morning to you, too," Cheryl replied, obviously taken aback. I generally managed to avoid Guttman-like behavior.

I went into my office and glanced at the mirror that hung behind the door. I looked as shitty as I felt. I checked my watch. It wasn't even 9:00. Leon, one of the mail clerks, tapped discreetly at my door.

"I need you to go to Field's for me. On the Wabash side of the store there's a door marked CORPORATE LEVEL. Here's my card. Ask for Linda Uhler, tell her I need either a dark suit or a jacket and skirt with a blouse and accessories to match."

Leon was unfazed by my request. Unexpected trips

were nothing new in M&A and the mail clerks often went out on underwear and toothbrush runs.

When Cheryl came back with the coffee and M&M's I told her what had happened to Gretchen Azorini.

"How awful," she said with a shudder. "I have a little sister her age."

"So do I."

"That's right. Weren't she and Gretchen friends?"

"Best friends. When I called my little sister at school this morning to break the news to her, she fainted."

"I'm so sorry."

"Anyway, I've been with Stephen all night. We flew up to Wisconsin to identify the body. I've had nothing to eat, no sleep, and if I don't get into clean clothes soon, I'm going to have a breakdown."

"Do you want me to send down for some real breakfast?" Cheryl asked, eyeing the bag of candy on my desk.

"No, when I feel this bad, coffee and M&M's are my drugs of choice. Just promise me you'll keep Guttman off my back until Leon comes back with some clothes for me."

"He's been screaming blue murder for you since he got in this morning."

"Well, let him scream some more."

"I'll just tell him you're not in yet."

"Thanks," I said. "And could you see if you can reach my mother on the phone?"

"Sure thing."

I only resorted to M&M's and coffee for breakfast on the very worst of days, and this certainly classified as one of them. Cheryl buzzed back to report that my mother was not at home, but when I asked she didn't know whether she'd gone to the board meeting or to pick up Beth. I peeled off my pantyhose—which after twenty-four hours felt as if they had become permanently attached to my legs—and put on a fresh pair from the supply in my bottom drawer.

When Leon appeared with the shopping bag from Marshall Field's, I emptied it onto my desk. There was a black-and-white houndstooth skirt a couple of inches shorter than I usually wore, a white silk blouse, and a black wool jacket with a bright red silk poppy pinned to the lapel. I took off my crumpled suit, rolled it up, stuffed it in the shopping bag, and changed into the new outfit. I removed the red poppy, threw it into the bag, and decided I was as ready as I ever would be to face Guttman and the day.

As I waited in Guttman's doorway for him to get off the phone, I reflected that while Guttman's ability to see the death of a sixteen-year-old girl purely in terms of business was grotesque, I, too, was worried about its implications for Azor Pharmaceuticals. Stephen had placed a substantial block of Azor shares in trust for Gretchen until her twenty-first birthday. The disposition of those shares could be pivotal. Worse, the business decisions that Stephen would make in the next few weeks would affect the lives of thousands of people. Would he really be able to focus as sharply on the takeover now that Gretchen had been killed, or would the tragedy turn out to be just the little edge that Eichel needed?

"So what the hell happened?" Guttman demanded without ceremony when he had finished with his call.

"I'm not sure. When Stephen went home last night there were two cops waiting for him. They said they had found Gretchen's car and the body of a young girl with red hair. Stephen said that there must be some mistake, Gretchen and her car were at Chelsea Hall, but when he called the dorm, she wasn't there. So Stephen and I flew up to some godforsaken place about three hundred miles north of here called Mannetuoc to take a look at the body.''

"He called you to come with him?"

"No. I was with him when he came home," I replied with an edge to my voice that warned against further questions.

"And was it her?" Guttman asked.

"Yes, it was her."

"So what happened to her?"

"At this point, nobody knows. She was found near a seldom-used dirt road by two poachers. The sheriff seems to think she was raped and then murdered, but beyond that he's not saying. They found her car in a parking lot somewhere up there. She could have driven up to Wisconsin for some reason, to meet somebody, and then been killed. She could have been killed somewhere else and her body dumped there. Christ, she could have been driving down the street in Chicago, and somebody with a gun could have hopped in at a red light. . . . Though the sheriff seems to think that drugs are involved, because they found some cocaine in her body.''

"Great," Guttman replied as if the whole thing were my fault. "Fucking great. We've got to keep this away from the press."

I was saved from further diatribes by Jeff Bassman. He was a partner in the trusts and estates department, and John hoped he'd be able to tell us what would happen to Gretchen's shares now that she was no longer going to reach her twenty-first birthday.

"It's possible that the terms of the trust set out what will become of the shares should she die before her twenty-first birthday," ventured Bassman. "It just depends on how cautious a bastard the lawyer who drafted the document was. Did we do it?''

"No," Guttman said.

"When was the trust set up?''

"Less than a year ago," Guttman replied.

"Can we get our hands on a copy?''

Guttman punched a button on his desk, and his secretary appeared at a trot, steno pad in hand.

"Call Vince DeGenova," he commanded. "Ask him to fax us a copy of the trust documents for Gretchen Azorini. Tell him we need them right away.''

"Yes, sir.''

"While we're waiting," Guttman continued, "we need to get probate started, provided it's in our best interest to do so.''

"A copy of the death certificate—''

"They're only issuing a pending certificate," I interjected.

"Oh, Christ, a pending certificate," lamented Bassman. "Well, then, you're in one hell of a mess when it comes to probate. The only thing a pending certificate allows you to do is bury the body. Everything else is locked up. No insurance pay outs, no probate, nothing. What are they waiting for?''

"Toxicology reports," I replied.

"How long do they think that'll take?" Guttman demanded.

"I don't know," I replied, making a note. "I'll get an answer for you today.''

Guttman scowled at me and looked as if he was about to launch into another tirade, this one for Bassman's benefit, when his secretary appeared with the slippery fax sheets of the trust agreement.

"Give those to Mr. Bassman," Guttman ordered.

Bassman quickly flipped through the trust agreement.

Then he looked up from his reading and tapped the sheaf of papers together on the edge of Guttman's desk.

"Don't make me put this in writing—I'd like to spend some more time on this—but my quick and dirty first guess is that in the event of Gretchen Azorini's death prior to her twenty-first birthday, the shares in the trust would go to her next of kin."

"Meaning her guardian?" I asked, knowing what the answer would be.

"Her father," Bassman replied. "Despite any custodial arrangements, the law goes by blood relation. It looks like the shares would go to the father, once the estate was probated."

"That's just fucking great," groaned Guttman.

Back in my office I consulted my list of things to do and spent the next half hour adding to it. Then I got on the phone.

My first call was to the Mannetuoc sheriff's department, where I worked hard to ingratiate myself with Sheriff Whittle's secretary, Martha. From Martha I got the name and phone number of the pathologist who had performed the autopsy. I also learned that the one and only detective employed by the Mannetuoc Sheriff's Department, Tom Morrisy, was officially in charge of the investigation. She professed herself "pleased as punch" to connect me with him.

Morrisy was a monosyllabic individual who, in response to all of my inquiries, replied that he'd have to check with Sheriff Whittle before parting with any information.

I didn't bother to ask him to connect me with Sheriff Whittle, as I had real doubts about the detective's ability to operate a phone unassisted. Instead, I thanked him, hung up, and called Martha again directly. The sheriff, she reported, was out, but she promised to have him call me as soon as he got in.

Next I rang the number Martha had given me for the pathologist who had done the autopsy: One Dr. Brian Yarbrough, who'd married the large animal vet and thereby doomed himself to a lifetime of exile in the country.

"Dr. Yarbrough," he announced after the first ring. I loved a man who answered his own phone, a trait especially rare in a doctor.

"Dr. Yarbrough, my name is Kate Millholland. I am an attorney in Chicago. I represent Dr. Stephen Azorini. He is the uncle and legal guardian of your Jane Doe."

"Yes, I heard that they'd made an identification last night. I was sorry they didn't page me. I'd have liked to have met the next of kin."

"From what the sheriff told me, you've issued a pending death certificate until you get the results back from the toxicology lab."

"That's true. I'm sorry about it. I know that it's very upsetting to the family."

"The Azorinis are as eager as you are to find out what caused Gretchen's death. Her uncle is a physician and, as such, is probably much less uncomfortable with the idea of postmortem investigation. You have to understand how sudden and inexplicable her death is. I think they're very eager to learn what actually happened to Gretchen. And I guess that's why I'm calling. I was wondering whether you might be able to fax me a copy of the autopsy report."

"I have to check it out with Whittle."

I groaned involuntarily.

"You have to understand, Miss Millholland. This isn't Chicago."

"Believe me, I know. I flew up last night with Dr. Azorini to identify the body."

"He brought his lawyer up with him?" he asked incredulously.

"It wasn't like that. He and I have been friends since we were teenagers. I was with him when the police came and told him that they might have found his niece. I just did what any friend would do under the circumstances, I went along for the ride."

"Had she been missing long?" he asked.

"She hadn't been missing at all. Dr. Azorini thought she was at school. That's why this is so disturbing, why the family has so many questions."

"Miss Millholland, you have to understand, we don't get many homicides up here, and the ones we do get are pretty straightforward. Two drunks with shotguns. Domestic disputes. This is the most exciting thing that's happened in Whittle's jurisdiction in ten years. He's overseeing the investigation personally."

"So the assumption is homicide?" I asked.

"That's Whittle's assumption. He's welcome to it until the autopsy's complete."

"What do you mean?"

"Don't get me wrong. I'm not ruling out homicide. There are a lot of things that point in that direction. For one thing, the condition of the body. First thing they teach you in forensics is when the body of a young female is found in a rural area you immediately do a rape kit."

"A rape kit?" I asked, not sure I understood the jargon.

"It's a series of procedures that you do when you suspect the decedent may have been raped. We do swabs of the mouth, anus, and vagina. We comb out the pubic hair. We take samples, do a blood type on any semen we find.''

"So did you do a rape kit first thing?'' I asked.

"Well, actually, the first thing I did was call a friend of mine who's a forensic pathologist in the Cook County Medical Examiner's Office to verify what I should do. Then I did the rape kit.''

"And what did you find?''

"Like I said. At first look, there are a number of things that point to a rape/murder. First of all, there's the fact the body was found outdoors.''

"Was she clothed?'' I asked.

"Yes. But that in and of itself isn't terribly meaningful. There were plenty of other factors that would make even a relatively inexperienced police officer suspect homicide and possible rape. First of all, her body was found outdoors. Second, the officers on the scene noticed that her eyes were swollen and bloodshot from broken blood vessels. There were scratches on her neck. Again, the vast majority of women who are murdered after they are raped are strangled.''

"So was she strangled?'' I asked.

"You're not going to catch me that easily. All I said was that the officers noted petechiae—''

"Noticed what?'' I interrupted.

"Petechiae. It's just the technical term for the characteristic bloodshot eyes and broken blood vessels. There were the marks on her neck. When we did the rape kit, we found that she had indeed had intercourse. Because of the lapse of time between death and discovery, it's hard to pinpoint exactly when.''

"How long do you think that lapse was?'' I asked. "When do you think she died?''

"I'm putting the time of death somewhere between ten A.M. and noon on Monday.''

"Monday?" I asked incredulously. "I'm sorry. I was interrupting. You said that she'd had intercourse. . . ."

"Yes, we did the blood type on the semen in the hospital lab. It was A negative. Swabs of the anus and mouth were negative. We combed her pubic hair and found hairs that were most likely not hers."

"So what are the test results you're waiting for before you'll issue a final death certificate?" I asked. "Whittle said toxicology."

"Whittle would kill me if he knew I've been having this conversation with you."

"Listen, Dr. Yarbrough. You have to believe that my client and I are even more interested in discovering what happened to Gretchen Azorini than you are. Can you imagine what is going through her family's mind right now? No truth can be worse than what they're imagining. The more information I can give them about what you suspect, how long it will take before you have something concrete, the more they deal with facts instead of inventing gruesome scenarios, the easier it will be for them."

"I sent urine and tissue samples to a crime lab in Chicago to do a drug screen—cocaine in particular."

"Why?" I asked.

"Let's just say that there were physical indications that she might have died of a cocaine overdose."

"What indications?" I asked.

"I'm sorry. I've been too forthcoming as it is. I'm going to have to clear any further information with Sheriff Whittle. I'm sorry."

"No. Don't be sorry," I replied. "I just have one more question. How long do you think it will be before you have the results of the toxicology tests?"

"I don't know for sure. Usually they take about two

weeks. I sent a note along with the specimens that they're for a case that's generating a lot of interest. They'll probably try to speed it along.''

"Thank you, Dr. Yarbrough, you've been incredibly helpful. Is there anything that I can do to help you, any information I might be able to give you?''

"Yes. I know that Whittle will get it for me eventually, but can you get me the name and number of the dead girl's physician and dentist if she had them?''

"I'd be glad to,'' I replied. "I'll call you back with them in ten minutes.''

It took a little longer than ten minutes to track down Stephen's assistant for phone numbers of Gretchen's doctor and dentist, but when I called him back, Dr. Yarbrough seemed grateful. I left him with my fax number on the off chance that Sheriff Whittle would see it in his heart to send us a copy of the autopsy report. If not, I'd have to think of another way to get my hands on a copy.

My next call was to Mrs. Bigham, the headmistress of the Chelsea Hall School for Girls. I wanted to know where the school thought Gretchen Azorini had been when she was in reality lying dead in the Wisconsin woods.

Mrs. Bigham seemed genuinely grieved by Gretchen's death. In addition, she was incredibly deferential. My parents had donated a minor fortune to Chelsea Hall in the years since Beth hit puberty. Beth's scholastic work had been so poor, her behavior so bizarre, that it took major-league bribery to keep her as a student in good standing.

"I know that this is very difficult,'' I began, "but there are a great many questions surrounding Gretchen

Azorini's death. I was hoping you might be able to answer some questions about Gretchen's last days.''

"Certainly. We are eager to have this mystery cleared up. I'm afraid the girls are working themselves into hysterics. It's been very difficult not having all the details to give to them.''

"I was just speaking to the physician who did the autopsy, and he tells me that they put the time of Gretchen's death to be Monday morning between ten and noon. I was wondering why Gretchen wasn't reported missing from school?''

"I don't understand," Mrs. Bigham replied in a mystified tone of voice.

"Gretchen died on Monday morning,'' I replied. "Her death wasn't discovered until Tuesday afternoon. I was just wondering why Dr. Azorini wasn't notified that she wasn't in school.''

"I don't understand," Mrs. Bigham replied. "You mean she didn't die in the hospital? Dr. Azorini called the school on Monday morning to say that Gretchen had come down with the flu over the weekend and had been admitted to the hospital. That sort of thing had happened before, nothing to worry about.''

"Did you speak to him yourself?'' I asked, totally confused.

"No, I believe he spoke to my secretary.''

"Could I speak with her?'' I asked.

"Why, certainly. But I don't understand what you're getting at. Did Gretchen not die in the hospital? We just assumed it must have been complications from her diabetes.''

"It looks like it was a bit more complex than that,'' I replied. "Why don't you let me have a word with your secretary.''

* * *

I sat at my desk and contemplated what Mrs. Bigham's secretary had told me. On Monday morning at around 10:00, a man who identified himself as Dr. Azorini had called the school. He just wanted the school to know that Gretchen had come down with the flu on Sunday night and had been admitted to the hospital. They expected that she'd be there for a day or so, no more. Had she recognized his voice? I asked. No, she'd only worked at the school for six months and had never had occasion to speak to Dr. Azorini, though she did say to him that he sounded like he had a cold, and he'd replied that he hoped he wasn't coming down with the flu himself. She'd marked Gretchen absent, written a note to Mrs. Bigham about it, and hadn't given it a second thought.

I didn't know what to think.

Cheryl had to knock twice to get my attention.

"I know you don't want to be disturbed, but it's Richard Humanski on the phone. He says it's an emergency."

"Thanks, Cheryl," I said and picked up the phone.

"Richard, what's up?" I asked.

"Gee, I'm sorry to bother you, Kate," (Richard did actually say things like "gee"), "but Stephen has just blown a gasket, and I don't know what to do."

"What do you mean, 'blown a gasket'?"

"He was in his office talking to his father on the phone when he buzzed me and asked me to get an atlas from the library. So I ran down the hall and grabbed it and brought it to him. Five minutes later I heard him screaming in Italian and banging around his office. You know how reserved he usually is, never raises his voice. I went in to see if he was alright. He screamed at me to leave him alone. His face was purple. Now he's in there slamming drawers and swearing—at least it sounds like swearing to me, I don't actually speak Italian. I've never seen him like this. Plus, there's a meeting set up with the guys from the Calder Insurance pension fund, they're big institutional investors. I'm afraid to let them see Stephen like this. . . . I didn't know who else to call.''

''You were right to call me,'' I answered. ''First thing you do is get on the phone and call the people at Calder and postpone the meeting. God knows if you explain about Gretchen's death they'll understand. And I'll be right over.''

''Please. Don't tell him that I called you,'' Richard pleaded.

''Don't worry. It just sounds like he's had about as much thrown at him in the last twenty-four hours as anyone has a right to have to deal with.''

CHAPTER

6

In the end, Stephen went home quietly. Perhaps he realized that there was little he could accomplish in the state he was in, or maybe Richard and I were able to convince him that it was dangerous for him to be seen by anyone involved in the takeover when he was less than completely in control of himself. A takeover is like any battle; the opposition can smell weakness, and after Gretchen's death everyone would be watching Stephen carefully.

We stopped at the little market in Regents Park on the way to Stephen's apartment. I picked up a roast chicken, a loaf of French bread, a cold bottle of ubiquitous chardonnay, and a hastily assembled salad from the takeout bar. Stephen wasn't going to eat any of it, anyway. He was in a state of shock. There is only so much one person, even someone as tough as Stephen, can absorb in the way of grief. I knew the signs—parts of him were just shutting down.

We had to wade through flowers to get to the front door of Stephen's apartment—baskets of fruit, too. The doorman had run out of space in the little foyer by the elevator and had started to stack flower arrangements inside the front door. The entrance hall was knee deep in lilies. They seemed to be mostly from business associates of Stephen's, a ghoulish testament to corporate efficiency. So far Stephen's family seemed strangely removed from the tragedy.

I unpacked the food and rummaged in the kitchen for things to serve it on. I poured out two glasses of wine and set Stephen's plate in front of him. The apartment seemed huge and empty around us, the kitchen noises—the clink of the glass on the table top as Stephen set it down, the rattle of my fork against my plate—seemed terribly loud. That's what you need a family for after someone dies, I thought, not as a buffer against the grieving, but to just fill up the silence.

"Did you find out about the autopsy today?" asked Stephen.

"I spoke to the pathologist who did the autopsy," I replied, looking down at my plate. I pushed it away, faintly revolted.

"What did he say?"

"He basically said that he doesn't want to say. He seems to be both competent and cautious, especially for someone practicing in his neck of the woods. The first thing he did when they brought in the body was to call a forensic pathologist he knows and ask him what he should do. He says he's not ruling out homicide, but he didn't seem nearly as certain as Sheriff Whittle. One thing he did say was that he thinks that Gretchen died on Monday morning, not Sunday night."

"On Monday?" demanded Stephen sharply.

"In the late morning. I called Mrs. Bigham to find out why the school didn't call to say Gretchen was absent from school. She said you called the school to say that Gretchen had come down with the flu over the weekend and had been admitted to the hospital for a few days."

"What!"

"The call came to her secretary. Did you call the school about anything on Monday?"

"No. Never!" Stephen replied, visibly upset.

"Then I wonder who called," I mused.

There was a pounding at the door.

"It's probably a messenger," said Stephen, leaving his untouched plate to go to the door. "I asked Richard to send me the projected sales figures for the Hospital Supplies Division."

I remembered thinking that it was odd that the doorman hadn't rung first to say that the messenger was on his way up. Security in Stephen's building was usually tight, but by then Stephen had opened the door, and I heard arguing in the front hall.

I had never met Gretchen's father, Joey Azorini. He was Stephen's older brother by eight years, and Stephen had never spoken of him, but the person in the living room couldn't have been anyone else. He was older, thinner, shorter, and dressed like a gigolo who'd won the lottery, but the family resemblance was unmistakable. They had the same curly, dark hair, the same aquiline features. But Joey's eyes lacked the sharpness of Stephen's quick intelligence, and his lips were wide and cruel.

He was so strung out with rage that he was having a hard time keeping on the ground. Hopping mad, I thought, so that's what they mean. There was a man with him, younger than Stephen and me, and enormous. In the course of my privileged and sheltered life, I had never come across a hired thug, but I had no doubt that I was looking at one now. His neck was as big as my thigh, and the muscles of his chest strained against the shiny fabric of his polyester shirt. His face was deeply pitted with acne scars, and his hair was bleached blond like a surfer's. He was watching his boss, Joey Azorini, scream obscenities at Stephen, like a leashed dog willing a squirrel to come closer.

"You fuck!" Joey was shouting as he pushed Stephen in the chest with the flat of his hand, thrusting him out of his way. "You fucking shithead. I should kill you right now. I should run a piano wire through your brain. I should cut you into little pieces and feed your balls to the fish, I should—"

"It's good to see you, too," Stephen said, taking a step backward with the verbal blows. "Would you and your piece of meat like to come in and sit down, or do you prefer to stand and call me names in the hall?"

"I ain't just going to call you names, fuckface. I'm going to rip your fucking head off."

"I see you haven't managed to expand your vocabulary since the last time I saw you," Stephen said in the matter-of-fact tone that seemed most likely to incite his brother.

"I'm going to kill you!" spat Joey.

"It's a good thing you brought Vito here with you, Joey, or I'd have killed you with my bare hands the minute I saw your ugly face at my door," Stephen said in his level, boardroom voice.

He turned and walked into the living room. Joey, after a moment's hesitation, followed him. I marveled at Stephen's calm. I found Joey's rage thoroughly frightening. I don't think I would have turned my back on him. Vito, the bodyguard, tagged along, looking visibly disappointed. Stephen sat on one cream-colored couch. Joey sat facing him on another. The thug took up his place, standing, arms crossed, behind Joey.

"Would you like a drink?" Stephen asked Joey.

"Who's the broad?"

"I'm sorry, this is Kate Millholland, my attorney. Kate, this is my brother, Joey Azorini."

"You fuckin' her?" Joey leaned forward and asked in a stage whisper.

"What happened in Wisconsin, Joey?" Stephen asked, ignoring his question. "You might as well tell me, because I'm going to find out anyway."

"What is it with you, anyway?" Joey asked angrily, springing to his feet. "I don't get it. Christ. I was in Colombia on a business trip."

"Don't start with me, Joey. That bullshit isn't going to work. I'm going to find out. Pop's going to find out. Why don't you just tell me, save us all a lot of trouble."

"What the fuck is going on?" Joey inquired plaintively, quizzing the walls. "I get home today from a little business trip, and I'm in bed with some babe who's showin' me she's real glad that I'm back, and two of Pop's guys bust into my apartment and drag me out in my underwear. They throw me in the back of some limo, and there's that little faggot DeGenova sitting there, and he starts giving me the third degree. 'Where was I? Who was I with?'

" 'Why should I tell you?' I ask. 'Because otherwise you'll be eating your balls for brunch,' they say. Then they turn on the muscle and dump me at Pop's house. For Christ sake, Stephen," he continued, his voice dissolving into a whine, "I was on a buying trip to Colombia. I didn't get back till today. You and Pop are being so unfair. I didn't do anything wrong."

"You have a lot of nerve," Stephen replied, his voice rising and clotted with rage. "You have a lot of nerve coming here . . . here to my house. Your daughter is dead, Joey. She was a sweet girl with her whole life ahead of her, and she was murdered and left in a ditch.

And you sit there telling me how unfairly *you've* been treated.''

"You were supposed to take care of her," Joey replied with the voice of a hurt child. "She was my flesh and blood, and all I get is shit from you and Pop treating me like dirt.''

"You're barking up the wrong tree, Joey," Stephen said shaking his head in warning. "I didn't say anything to Pop. He just knows you about as well as I do. 'My own flesh and blood.' You make me sick. Why is it that everybody who loves you ends up dead, Joey?''

When they fight in the movies it goes so slowly, you see every punch. The protagonists feint and jab, scowling at each other for the camera.

The real thing is much faster and infinitely more frightening. I'd never seen anyone try to kill someone with his bare hands before. I'd never witnessed that kind of naked, animal hatred. Joey didn't so much hit Stephen, as throw himself at him—his fists leading the way. And while Joey was driven by rage, even in the flurry of motion I could see Stephen thinking, analyzing the situation, defining the problem, and working out the solutions.

Stephen kicked Joey's legs out from under him and rolled on top of him as they both hit the floor, knocking over a drop-leaf table and sending the silver-framed photographs that lay on top of it to the ground like a house of cards. The bodyguard hung back, assessing, not wanting to spoil the fun if his boss was managing for himself.

Stephen tried to get away from Joey, but he took a solid punch in the face as he wrestled away. He grabbed his brother by the hair and smashed his head against the floor with a sickening thud. He hit him in the mouth. Then Vito grabbed Stephen from behind and pinned his arms back to give Joey a clear shot at him. Joey scrambled to his feet unsteadily and gave a twisted smile. Squinting through his rapidly swelling eye, he hit Stephen so hard in the face that he hurt his hand. Blood from Stephen's mouth splashed all over Joey's shirt.

I realized that I was standing frozen, like some helpless bimbo, with the back of my hand pressed to my mouth. I threw myself onto Vito's back, going for his eyes. He grunted from pain and surprise, letting go of Stephen. He whirled around, leading with his fist. The impact propelled me against the back of the couch and knocked the wind out of me. I got to my knees to try to stand, and he gave me a quick kick to the face. This is awful, I thought to myself, and checked for loose teeth while Vito went back to give Joey a hand with Stephen.

Joey's bodyguard pinned Stephen from behind, holding him while Joey landed blow after blow. I scanned the room for something that could be used as a weapon. Stephen kicked backward at his captor's knees and simultaneously landed an elbow in his stomach.

The soapstone carving was about the size of a flattened baseball. It was in my hand, and I was already in motion when I saw the gun in Joey's hand. I cracked Joey across the back of the head as hard as I had ever hit a tennis ball. He hit the rug, and I dove for the gun.

I picked it up fast and leveled it against the bodyguard, taking two or three steps back to get Joey in range, too. I hadn't fired a pistol since I was a thirteen-year-old at summer camp. But I'd hunted my whole life and knew enough to take the safety off and to hold the gun with two hands. I stood braced, feet apart, against the recoil in case I had to fire.

"Keep your hands where I can see them," I said in a voice that sounded nothing like my own. All the oxygen seemed to have suddenly gone out of the room. I gulped compulsively for air.

Stephen straightened himself up shakily. Vito bared his teeth, and Joey sat up, his eyes glazed and unfocused.

"Stephen," I said. "Call the police."

"No. These two are harmless. Joey just gets like this when he's having a tantrum, and Vito over here just does as he's told."

Stephen patted the bodyguard down and pulled a gun from a holster at the small of his back and a five-inch length of pipe from his pocket.

"Just get him out of here," Stephen ordered Vito, indicating Joey with a nod of his head.

Vito helped Joey to his feet. Joey was bleeding from his nose and assorted cuts on his face. Stephen threw him a handkerchief.

"Here, use this. This isn't the kind of building where you can bleed on the carpet. I don't want to see your ugly face here ever again. If you come back, I'll tell Pop. You are the lowest form of life there is, Joey. Go crawl back into the gutter where you belong."

"Give me my gun back," Joey demanded, his speech slurred. He stumbled over a basket of fruit.

"The only way I'll give it to you is one bullet at a time," Stephen replied with real menace. "Now get the hell out of here."

Joey had a hard time coordinating his legs. Vito, who had developed an ugly red flush to his acne-pitted skin, had to half carry him to the door. While they waited for the elevator, Joey turned to Stephen, half whining and half sobbing: "I was in Colombia, Stephen. Honest I was. It's wrong of you to be mad at me." His tears were mixed with blood.

It wasn't until Stephen had shut the door and was

leaning with his back against it that I lowered the gun. I was shaking—not just my hands, but my legs, my knees, my whole body was trembling as if from some terrible internal freezing. I was sweating, too, like tears all over my body, and gulping for breath. Stephen smiled at me, and I realized that blood was raining down over his face from a deep gash above one eye, white edged and ugly. His lip was mashed and bleeding in half a dozen places.

"You are one amazing woman, Katharine Anne Millholland," he said into my hair. I stayed there in his arms for a moment, feeling small and safe. Slowly, I realized that his shirt was wet not just with my tears, but with his blood. I pulled away to assess the damage.

"You need a doctor," I announced.

"I am a doctor," he replied.

"Seriously, Stephen, unless you'd like to stitch up your own face, you're going to the emergency room."

"I will tell you exactly where I am going," he replied. "I am going to get myself a drink, and if you're nice to me I'm going to get you one, too. There's no way I'm going to the emergency room. I am too tired, and I'm not going to risk the papers getting a hold of this, not after punching Eichel."

After some fairly tense negotiations, Stephen did agree to let me call my roommate, Claudia. I reached her in the emergency room, and she agreed to come over when her relief came in about an hour.

Stephen emerged from the kitchen with a bottle of Scotch and two glasses. The living room was a mess. There were smears of blood on the cream silk of the couches, and furniture was turned over. There were two handguns on the coffee table.

"You should see yourself," said Stephen.

"Why?" I asked, patting my hair.

"You look like you could use a stitch or two. How does your eye feel?"

I got up and went into the powder room and looked at myself in the mirror. My cheek was scraped where Vito had kicked me, and there was the beginning of an impressive bruise. My lip was bleeding, and my right eye was on its way to closing. My white silk blouse, new that morning, was torn and flecked with blood. My hair was wild.

I washed my face carefully and patted it dry. I started to take my hair down but stopped halfway. I was seized by a violent case of the shakes. I stood for a while, clutching both sides of the sink. I did not cry, but my chest heaved convulsively—from grief, from lack of sleep, from being scared, but mostly with the sweet relief of being alive and relatively unhurt.

Finally, I managed to steady myself with a few deep breaths. I drank the rest of my Scotch in one swallow, gasping as it burned its way down, and brushed my hair. I went back into the living room where Stephen refilled my glass and handed me a package of frozen peas. I looked at him like he had just arrived from Mars.

"No, thank you," I said. "I'm not hungry."

"It's for your eye. You're going to have a shiner."

"I thought you were supposed to put a steak on a black eye."

"Don't you know that red meat is bad for you?" he replied, and we both laughed much longer and harder than his thin joke warranted.

Stephen switched on a lamp behind me and examined my face.

"What a mess," he said.

Stephen didn't look much better. He had neatly taped a piece of gauze over the deep gash above his right eye, but his face looked like it had had a close encounter with a trash compacter.

"Listen," Stephen said, taking my face in his hands, "thank you. Joey might have killed me."

"I can't believe you wouldn't call the police."

"This is family. In my family, you don't call the police."

"So," I said, wincing as I put the bag of frozen peas over my eye, "will you at least explain what that was all about?"

Stephen poured us each a fresh tumbler of Scotch and fetched fresh ice cubes from the kitchen. As he walked back he seemed to weigh them in his hand before dropping them one by one into the glasses.

"Joey is my half brother, older by almost nine years. Joey's mother was an Italian girl from the old neighborhood, much younger than my father and, by all accounts, very beautiful. She killed herself when Joey was still a baby. I don't know why, though I can guess that my father gave her several thousand reasons. My father never speaks of her.

"He married my mother when Joey was six. She died of cancer four years later. After that, my father must have decided that marriage was unlucky for him. From then on, if there have been any women in his life, he's kept them elsewhere. My aunts raised us in the big house off Cicero.

"It was a lot like you and Beth, there was such a big difference in Joey and my ages. We never had much to do with each other. I was always the little punk.

"But from my earliest recollection, Joey was in trouble: girl trouble, gambling trouble, scrapes with the police that needed Pop's attention. He made the old man crazy. I can see now how growing up in that kind of environment was poisonous for a person like Joey. He didn't stand a chance. He was bent from the start.

"The other problem, of course, is that Joey isn't very bright. Pop never cared whether he broke the law, that he ran wild. He cared that he always fucked up, got caught. Joey has no judgment, and as a result he's been a continual embarrassment to my father.

"Then, when Joey was seventeen, he stole a car—which was ridiculous to begin with because he already had a car, a new one. It was a present from Pop, probably for staying out of trouble for a couple of weeks. But, as a dare and to impress a girl, he stole a car. Not just any car, mind you, but Father Calducci's new Cadillac. He hot wired the car and convinced this girl to sneak out of her parents' house with him and go for a joy ride.

"To make a long story short, they ended up drunk, driving on the Dan Ryan at about a hundred miles an hour. Joey slammed the car into a concrete bridge support. He was thrown from the car and walked away with a mild concussion and a sprained wrist. The girl was in a coma for four weeks before she died. She was fourteen years old and from a good family. Her parents didn't even know she was out until the cops called them from the emergency room.

"The whole thing cost Pop a fortune. He managed to have it covered up, but just barely, and not before a lot of people knew about it. After that Pop figured Chicago probably wasn't the best place for Joey to be, so he was sent to work for some friends in New Jersey who owned a construction company. He must have worked some low-level job, because I always remember his whining to Pop about how he was bigger than whatever it was that he was doing, and Pop always slapping him down.

"I didn't hear much about him for a long time. But when I was at M.I.T., Pop and Joey had a big fight. It seemed that Joey had decided to go into business for himself. He'd met this bunch of very go-ahead black guys, and he was dealing drugs—cocaine and heroin.

"Now, my father is of the old school, and the old school stays away from drugs. The profits are big and so are the losses. Pop made his money in the traditional ways: gambling, loan sharking, extortion. . . . And even then he was working to get away from all of that, using the money he'd made to build a legitimate business empire.

"Pop was furious. In the first place, drugs were forbidden, or maybe he just didn't think Joey was smart enough to play that game for long without getting caught and tying the Azorini name to drugs and crime."

"So why was everything so different for you?" I asked. "Why didn't you steal cars and get into trouble?"

"I think that by the time I was born, Pop had made a strong commitment to legitimate business. He'd gotten away from the old businesses, the old guys. He made a conscious effort to raise me differently. Besides, I'm a lot smarter than Joey. As I recall, you and I broke any number of laws. We just never got caught."

"And Joey?"

"Joey, it turns out, has found his niche in life. It seems that it pays to be a complete sociopath if you're going to deal drugs. Joey's done very well. By the time I started medical school, he'd moved his operation back to Chicago. The old families were moving into drugs themselves, and Joey was becoming a big shot right under Pop's nose.

"While Joey was a big success in the drug business, his personal life has always been a complete disaster.

Right after he moved back to Chicago, he married this girl. She was barely sixteen and German. She'd run away from home to come to America to become a movie star. Her name was Anja, and when Joey met her, she was making porno movies. Joey convinced her that he was Rockefeller, the Pope, and Elvis all in one.

"They had a baby girl, Gretchen, but Ward and June Cleaver they were not. For one thing, Anja had a drug problem; for another, she still wanted to be a movie star. She spent all of her time buying clothes, snorting coke, and fixing her hair. Joey bought into a nightclub on Rush Street so that Anja would meet show business people, but it ended up that he started running around with a lot of young, would-be actresses who were not his wife. Joey and Anja fought all the time.

"I have no idea how Gretchen managed to survive her childhood except that Pop always managed to see that there was some kind of housekeeper, someone to make sure that she got to school and had clean clothes.

"Then, when Gretchen was nine, she was diagnosed as having diabetes. Now, we tend to think of diabetes as no big deal. Partially that's due to technology. We're able to manage the disease better so that diabetics lead very close to normal lives. Still, juvenile onset diabetes, especially Type II, which is what Gretchen has, I mean had, is very serious. Her body produced no insulin at all. It is tricky balancing food intake to insulin dosage, constantly monitoring blood sugar levels. It's a huge burden to have a chronically ill, insulin-dependent child. Even the most organized, supportive families find it difficult.

"Joey and Anja didn't have a clue how to deal with Gretchen's illness—all they managed to do was fight about it. Anja would get coked to the eyes and forget to give Gretchen her insulin. Joey would be out of the country on a buying trip, and he'd come back to find Gretchen in the hospital. They would fight like cats and dogs; Joey would beat up Anja, who would drag herself, bleeding, to Pop's house and scream: 'See what he did to me!'

"This went on for years. Gretchen got better at managing on her own. Christ, she was an independent kid. I guess you'd have to grow up quickly with parents like that. Still, there were emergencies. A cold, diarrhea, the flu, anything that changes the rate at which the body metabolizes glucose and uses insulin is potentially life-threatening to someone with Gretchen's type of diabetes. Three or four times a year there'd be some sort of crisis. Gretchen would end up in the hospital, and Joey would beat the shit out of Anja.

"At one point Pop even tried to have a nurse come and live at their house, but you can imagine that very few nurses would be willing to live in that kind of environment, no matter what the salary was. They finally found one, but it turned out that she was a drug addict herself. Joey came home one day to find the two of them, Anja and the nurse, strung out together on the couch watching soap operas.

"Anja was really starting to lose it. Joey was running around with all sorts of young girls. Gretchen was getting to be a teenager and fighting with her mom, calling her a junky, telling her that she hated her.

"One day, one of the neighbors called Joey at the nightclub and told him that there was a terrible ruckus going on at his house, and that if he didn't do something about it, the neighbor was going to call the cops. So Joey came home to find the house all torn up, Anja screaming and throwing around everything that wasn't nailed down, and Gretchen locked in the bathroom with a huge hunk of her hair pulled out and a split lip—compliments of her mother.

"So, Joey, rocket scientist that he is, did the only logical thing and started beating up Anja. Only this time he went a little bit too far. He fractured her skull—cerebral hemorrhage. Anja ends up D.O.A.

"Pop covered it up. They coached Gretchen on what to tell the police. Cash all around.

"Gretchen lasted less than six weeks with Joey after her mother died. She went to Pop and told him she didn't want to live with her father anymore—she wanted to live with me. She barely knew me, but she knew I was a doctor and I wasn't part of the environment.

"It didn't take me more than twenty minutes to decide. I sat and talked to her in my father's house. She was so thin and scared and miserable. I felt like we were both refugees from the same war, only I'd been helicoptered out while she'd spent months in an open boat."

Stephen's face was wet with tears, and the gash above his right eye was bleeding again. The gauze had soaked through, and blood trickled along the side of his face. "She wanted to walk away from her life so far. I couldn't manage that, but I did get an agreement that Joey would make her my legal ward and only see her four times a year, supervised by another family member. Guttman and DeGenova arranged it. They're the only ones outside of the family who know even a part of the real circumstances. The day it was signed, Gretchen came to live with me."

"You've told me why Gretchen was your ward, but not why Joey came here tonight to try to kill you," I said.

"For the past year I've suspected Joey of seeing Gretchen. I don't know whether he's just getting older, regretting that he gave up custody, or whether there's some ulterior motive. I knew that Gretchen was getting some pretty expensive presents, and I knew they were from Joey. It wasn't technically in violation of our agreement, but it made me nervous. But Gretchen seemed happy, and I let it slide.''

Stephen shook his head sadly.

"I guess I only have myself to blame. I should have put a stop to it at the beginning.''

"I don't get it,'' I said.

"Gretchen was in Wisconsin to meet Joey. I'm sure of it.''

"How do you know?''

"Joey always has some sort of crackpot scheme going: riverboat gambling in Iowa, dog hotels . . . a couple of years ago it was a hunting lodge in northern Wisconsin, a sort of gentlemen's club meant to attract the big spenders from Chicago. He figured he'd sell memberships, lure them with a little gambling, some pretty girls. He got as far as he usually does. He bought a huge parcel of land. He built a cabin for himself. Then he realized he'd bought five thousand acres that contained no drinkable water and half of the world's mosquitos. The land is near a little town called Lee-High. That's about sixty miles the other side of Ridleyville, where they found her car. That's why I didn't figure it out at first. I had to see it on the map. I checked with Officer Gunderson. The land that the poachers were hunting on belongs to Joey.''

"So you think she went up there to meet Joey. But he says he was in Colombia. You can't believe he raped and strangled his own daughter?''

"I don't know what to believe. You have to admit a lot of things point to Joey at least knowing that she was going up there. . . .''

We sat quietly in the darkened living room, too tired to put the furniture back upright. When Stephen spoke again it was barely a whisper.

"Jesus, Kate. I've never felt like this before, like a wrecking ball has gone through my life. I wanted to help a sick and scared kid, and she ends up raped and murdered. I wanted to build a business, something of my own that is powerful and good, and this creep Eichel is going to take it away. I feel like one of those people in California whose houses get sucked into a mud slide—one minute everything's fine, in control. Then it's gone—obliterated."

The silence begged for me to fill it, but the only things that came to mind were the same worthless platitudes I heard in the wake of Russell's passing. Some of them were true—you're young, you have your health, times eases even the greatest suffering. But they were still shallow, worthless nonsense, just noise in the face of pain.

"Stephen," I said finally, "I want you to know that the whole awful time before Russell died, nothing helped me more than your being there for me. If there's anything I can do to help you with this, with Gretchen, with Eichel, I promise I'll do it. Just ask."

He looked at me, his handsome face battered, his eyes full of tears, and gathered me up in his arms. Sitting there in the big, empty apartment, with the pistols and the broken glass, I had no way of knowing to what dangerous brink that promise would bring me.

CHAPTER

7

I woke up, stiff and aching, to the sound of Guttman's voice amplified through my answering machine. He sounded pissed. I scrabbled for the receiver and discovered that I hurt everywhere.

"Hi," I answered, holding the phone up to the side of my face that wasn't swollen.

"What the hell are you still doing at home?" Guttman demanded.

"What time is it?" I asked.

"It's almost two in the goddamn afternoon. I can't believe you're doing this to me. Are you sick?"

"Something like that," I replied.

"I don't have any time for female complaints," he remarked unpleasantly. "I need you to get downtown right away. Do you have a pencil?"

"Yes," I answered, pulling one and a notepad out of a drawer.

"Three twenty-two West Washington. Suite two oh six six."

"Do I have time to take a shower?" I asked.

"You don't even have time to take a leak," snarled Guttman as he slammed down the phone.

* * *

The address was of a newly renovated office building on the western fringes of the loop. I found it wedged between a store that sold wigs and a Crispy Corn popcorn shop.

My face throbbed with every step. I had five stitches at the corner of my right eye and eleven more in my scalp behind my right ear—Claudia's handiwork. The sidewalk traffic was thin on a Saturday morning in that part of town, but in every person I passed I saw a stutter in their step. Even the people who didn't stop to rubberneck at the sight of my battered face probably would have liked to. I really was a sight.

I took the elevator to suite 2066, which turned out to be the law offices of Morganelli, DeGenova and Rocco. I had never heard of the firm. The reception room was decorated like a Victorian funeral parlor. Dark drapes, big black furniture, and ferns.

I told the receptionist, whose jet black hair seemed to defy the laws of gravity, that I was here to join Mr. Guttman.

"Yeah, sure," she replied. "I'll show you."

As she teetered ahead of me in her high heels, I kept on expecting to hear her crack her gum.

It turned out to be a family reunion with lawyers. Joey Azorini, sullen behind his taped and swollen nose, sat on one side of the table. Stephen Azorini, stitched up and serious, sat directly across from him. Joey was flanked by two men in pinstripes. Vito, his bodyguard, stood just inside the door, ugly and inscrutable. Guttman sat next to Stephen.

At the head of the table an old man sat alone. He had once been a big man, as big as Stephen. But time and who knows what sorrows had sunken his chest and stooped his shoulders. His hair was white and receding, slicked back from a high forehead and a beak of a nose.

It was a profile that could have graced a Roman coin. He had Stephen's eyes, blue and cold, incongruous in his old man's head. His hands were huge and gnarled, and they lay on the table in front of him like small animals at rest.

I saw a flicker cross Guttman's face as he registered the condition of my face and that of the two Azorini brothers, but he didn't mention it. Instead he interrupted the ongoing conversation and introduced me to Stephen's father, Anthony Azorini, the law firm's three name partners—Messrs. Morganelli, DeGenova and Rocco—and Joey Azorini.

"We've met," I commented tersely.

I couldn't even begin to guess what I had walked into. Guttman motioned me into the empty chair next to him. Mr. Morganelli, seated next to Joey, began speaking to him softly in Italian. He looked as if he were urging him to do something, trying to convince him.

Guttman slid a single piece of paper in front of me. It was a letter to Dr. Stephen Azorini, chief executive officer of Azor Pharmaceuticals. It stated the author's intention to tender the 304,477 shares of Azor Pharmaceutical common stock in his possession as well as the 50,000 shares in the estate of Gretchen Azorini. At the bottom of the letter was Joey Azorini's signature.

Anthony Azorini rapped one of his great knuckled fists against the conference table.

"In English," he demanded. Morganelli did as he was told.

"Death, especially the sudden, tragic death of someone as young as Gretchen Azorini, is a terrible, terrible thing," he intoned in the manner of a saddened parish priest who is surprised by nothing anymore. "Emotions get vented, things get said, actions are taken, some of which may later be regretted. These things are normal, natural, a part of life.

"But when important decisions," he continued, his voice rising, "business decisions are made at such a difficult time, grave errors can be made. Errors that have long-term consequences. I have seen families torn apart. Brother from brother." He shook his head sadly, bowed low as if by the weight of it.

"Business is business," Joey replied, his chin stuck out like a little boy who's finally worked up the courage to defy his father. "I have made a business decision. I feel no loyalty to my half brother. He obviously feels no loyalty to me. No loyal brother, no real brother would make the accusations he makes! Nothing I can do today can tear this family apart. That happened a long time ago."

"It makes no difference to me what you do," replied Stephen flatly.

"Stephen, don't say things that you will regret," warned Guttman, half under his breath.

"You know that if you treat me like a brother I will treat you like a brother. Everyone knows that Joey Azorini is loyal—loyal to his friends, loyal to his family. Who did you come to, Stevie, when Pop turned you down, when the banks wouldn't give you a dime? You came to your brother, and what did your brother do? Did I question you? Did I ask you whether you could pay me back? Did I ask you what you wanted it for? No. I trusted you! You are my brother!"

"I paid back the loan," replied Stephen wearily. "I gave you the shares, and they are worth many millions now."

"And now I'm cashing in my millions," spat Joey. "You pathetic little shit. When you needed me I treated you like a man, like a brother. When my only child is found dead, you treat me like an animal.''

"That's how decent people treat killers," replied Stephen. "I expect to be treated like a brother because I have always acted like one. You haven't behaved honorably for ten minutes in your entire life!"

"Boys!" Anthony Azorini growled, his eyes flashing. "Joey, you claim that you have chosen to sell your shares of Azor stock and those that you think you will inherit from Gretchen's estate to this enemy of your brother, Edgar Eichel, in order to make a profit. Fine. I will buy them from you at the price he is offering, forty-eight dollars per share. Right now, you will sign an agreement, and I will write you a check."

The old man patted his pockets and then reached into his jacket and pulled out a checkbook. You could see Vito tense into readiness as Anthony Azorini's hand disappeared from view inside the lapel of his suit for a moment.

Nice family, I thought to myself.

"How much does that come to, Vince?" asked Anthony Azorini as he wrote the check. Vince DeGenova took out a pocket calculator and punched in the numbers, 354,477 times $48. That was a lot of money, even for a Millholland.

"Seventeen million, fourteen thousand, eight hundred ninety-six dollars," DeGenova reported.

"Fine," grunted Azorini, Sr. "Here's your money, Joey. Vince will make up an agreement for you to sign, handing over the shares to me."

Stephen studied the table in front of him. Joey pushed the check away from him.

"No!" he exclaimed. "I don't want your money, Pop."

"What's wrong with my money?" Anthony Azorini

asked reasonably. I can afford it.'' He paused for effect.
''Or are you afraid of what I'll do with the shares? Are
you afraid that I won't tender them to Eichel? Or worse,
that I'll make a present of them back to your brother?''

''I wouldn't have done it if he'd only said he was
sorry!'' Joey burst out like a pathetic child.

''Oh,'' replied Anthony Azorini, like a man who was
carefully picking his way through a mental mine field.
''I see. Then it is not a business decision. Then what
you want is not money, but an apology.''

''Stephen made me lose face in the family, Pop,''
Joey pleaded. ''He hurt my honor in front of you.''

All eyes turned to Stephen.

''I did not say one thing that is not true,'' he replied,
looking only at his father.

''You must apologize,'' Anthony Azorini commanded.

''No,'' replied Stephen.

''But you don't know for a fact that your brother was
involved in Gretchen's death,'' Guttman interjected as
if thinking out loud. Stephen shot him a look that said,
Whose side are you on? Is this what I'm paying you
for?

''Your lawyer gives you good advice, Stephen,'' said
Anthony Azorini, picking up the thread. ''You are a
man of science, a man of reason. You suspect that your
brother is somehow to blame. You would like to believe
it. But what if it isn't true? Then you are indeed guilty
of a terrible injustice against your brother.''

''If you prove to me that I am wrong, I won't hesitate
to apologize,'' retorted Stephen in a tone that suggested
he didn't expect to ever have to make good on the promise.

''But what proof would be acceptable?'' Guttman
queried. I saw where he was going with it, and I
couldn't help but admire the way that the two of them

had laid the trap and were carefully walking Stephen into it.

"I'm sure that Joey could produce any number of witnesses who saw him miles away from Gretchen. But you wouldn't believe them."

"For a price anyone will lie," Stephen replied.

"Oh, I don't think so," Guttman responded in his most reassuring country doctor voice. "I bet you Joey couldn't buy Kate here, couldn't get her to lie for him for any price."

"So what's your point?" asked Stephen, obviously getting tired of this exercise.

"Well. The point is that if Kate examined the circumstances of your niece's death objectively, the way a special prosecutor might, you would believe her findings, wouldn't you?"

"Of course I would believe her," Stephen answered cautiously.

"And if she could prove to you that Joey wasn't involved in his daughter's death, that would satisfy you?"

"She'd never be able to prove it. The son of a bitch is responsible. . . ."

"But if she could prove it to you, you would believe her," Guttman insisted.

"Yes." His answer was reluctant.

"Then we'll have the lawyers draw up the papers," announced Anthony Azorini with the relish of a man who enjoys closing a deal. There were a lot of puzzled looks around the table. I had the distinct impression that I had been railroaded, but it was such a smooth job I wasn't exactly sure what I had been railroaded into.

"Kate Millholland will agree to oversee an investigation into the circumstances of Gretchen Azorini's death," said Guttman, while DeGenova took notes. "An impartial investigation whose object is to uncover the facts surrounding the death of Gretchen Azorini. Should her investigation prove that Joey Azorini was involved in his daughter's death in any way, she will present such evidence to Stephen Azorini, and he will act on it as he sees fit. However, should her investigation reveal that Joey Azorini was blameless, then Stephen will apologize to his brother.''

"And Joey will remove his shares and Gretchen's from the offering pool."

"Provided that such proof is procured before the offering pool closes."

"It closes in ten days," I whispered urgently.

"Vince. Draw up the papers," boomed Anthony Azorini.

"Hey!" interjected Joey. "How do I know she's not crooked?"

"From your point of view it doesn't matter," Guttman replied. "If you were not involved in your daughter's death, and Miss Millholland says that you were, then you are in exactly the same position that you are in now. If she says that you were not involved when you were, then you will at least receive the apology that you crave. Groundlessly, of course."

Joey squinted like a man trying to see in the dark.

"Vince will write up the agreement," commanded Anthony Azorini.

"Provided that Miss Millholland agrees," Stephen interjected, looking at me.

I had been caught completely off guard. Every fiber in my body commanded me to absolutely refuse to agree to such a futile and doomed proposition. Yet I could find no acceptable way to refuse. I knew that I owed a debt to Stephen. The room ached with silence.

"Of course she will," Guttman said while I continued to gape. "Miss Millholland is one of Dr. Azorini's oldest friends as well as an attorney for the corporation. She would do anything in her power to prevent a hostile takeover of Azor Pharmaceuticals. Am I right, Kate?''

When I still didn't answer Guttman actually reached under the table and pinched my leg. Hard.

''Yes, yes. Of course,'' I bleated.

My fight with Guttman quickly entered into the legend at Callahan Ross. By the end of the day there was lively wagering on what would be the exact hour of my firing, and the serious jockeying for who would get my office had begun.

I had barely managed to contain myself in the taxi coming back from Morganelli, DeGenova and Rocco. I observed the rule about not discussing a case outside of the physical confines of the office—barely. But the minute we crossed the threshold of Callahan Ross, I crossed a line somewhere inside of myself.

No one had ever talked to Guttman that way before (and lived). Certainly not a lowly associate. But the last few days I had been beaten up emotionally and physically. And Guttman, after all his years of trying, had finally pushed me past the boundaries of restraint.

''What the hell went on back there?'' I demanded as soon as we crossed the threshold. My public anger caught him off guard.

''Not here, Kate,'' he murmured, concerned.

''Not here. Not there,'' I retorted. ''When will you explain exactly what I've been forced to agree to? When we postmortem the takeover, and you need someone to blame for Eichel marching in the front door?''

''Kate. Let's discuss this in my office.''

''No. You might ooze away under some doorway on our way down there, you oily son of a bitch.''

He took my arm, and I shook it off in a fury.

"Don't you touch me!" I snarled.

"What has gotten into you?" he had the audacity to ask.

"You seem surprised that I'm angry," I remarked, wrestling myself under control. For a brief moment I had sounded like my mother. I hadn't liked it at all. "It's hard to know where to begin. Let's just say that I am sick of your making assumptions about what I would and would not be willing to do for this firm and what boundaries I'd be willing to cross for a client. I am not your personal assistant. I am an attorney, and if you can't keep that distinction clearly in your mind, then I suggest you send your secretary to court for you next time you need to have a motion argued."

"I acknowledge that the agreement that was just signed is a bit unorthodox, but that doesn't explain this . . . this . . . premenstrual emotionalism."

I came close to hitting him. "Let me explain," I said with as much calm as I could muster. "Didn't you wonder, with your finely honed legal mind, why there were three people sitting around that conference table who looked like they'd been hit by a train? Last night I was at Stephen's apartment when his brother Joey and his bodyguard, Vito, paid a visit. Joey decided on a spot of fratricide, and it got pretty rough. You think you're some sort of legal genius, but didn't it ever occur to you to ask why Joey, Stephen, Vito, and I all look like we walked out of the same accident?"

"You mean he struck you?" Guttman asked incredulously.

"Only to knock me down. Then Vito kicked me in the face. I have sixteen stitches and a mild concussion. The bruises all over my body would qualify me as the poster child for the national association of victims of aggravated assault. But that's okay, because I would do anything for the firm, right? Walk through fire, use my position as a friend of an important client, go to extraordinary lengths to try to clear someone who might have been involved in the death of his sixteen-year-old and who definitely did try to kill our client and commit aggravated assault against me. All in a day's work, right?''

"There was absolutely no way I could have known," replied Guttman.

"Well, you should have asked, Einstein. You should have asked." I'd blown off all the steam I had. "I'm going to my office now. I have a letter to write," I announced.

As I walked down to my office I had the sensation of heads popping out of offices to stare at my retreating back.

I sat at my desk for a while and took a final look around my office. All the other spaces of my life were decorated by indifference. Empty cans and old newspapers on the floor of my car, the weird hodgepodge of furniture that littered my apartment like driftwood on the beach . . .

But my office was full of the things I loved. There was a Regency writing desk given to me by Aunt Sarah. She was my father's lesbian sister who lived in exile from the family in California. I had a pair of armchairs that I rescued from my parents' house when my mother purged the house after my brother's death. There were the files and documents that constituted the whole of my refuge from the bitterness of the past.

I punched the intercom on my desk. "No calls," I told Cheryl.

I drew a single sheet of my personal stationery from the bottom drawer of my desk. I uncapped the lapis and gold fountain pen that had once belonged to my grandfather. I began my letter of resignation.

I had almost finished when there was a knock on the door. I ignored it, but after a few seconds the door opened and Skip Tillman, the firm's managing partner, peeked in through the crack.

"Kate," he whispered, as if gently waking a sleeping child. "Kate, I'd like to have a word with you."

"I'm just finishing my letter of resignation, Skip. It'll be on your desk in five minutes. Then we can talk all you want."

"No, Kate. Please, hear me out. Guttman is a brilliant lawyer, brilliant. He's an incredible tactician. It's just that he's an idiot when it comes to people. You know him better than anyone. Don't let him goad you into doing something rash. Let's talk this through."

"The time for talking is past," I replied, wondering why it is that in times of crisis I inevitably take refuge in clichés.

"Kate, I've known you since you were a little girl. The least you can do is grant me the courtesy of a few minutes of conversation."

"And if I don't, you'll just stand there dithering in my doorway until I do," I sighed. "You just wear people out with politeness, Skip. I guess that's why they made you managing partner."

Skip insinuated himself into a chair.

"John tells me you were beaten up by Joey Azorini last night. Is that true?"

"Joey and his bodyguard."

"Did you call the police?"

"No. And not because I was trying to protect the interests of the firm, but because Stephen, as a friend, asked me not to."

"When did this happen?"

"Last night, around ten o'clock."

"Did you have to go to the emergency room?"

"No. I have a friend who's a doctor. She came over and stitched us up."

"Did you call John? Tell him what had happened?"

"No."

"And you didn't see him this morning?"

"No. He called me at home from Morganelli, De-Genova and Rocco. I know what you're getting at. You want me to understand that there was no way that Guttman could have known what had happened. I accept that. But he was so obsessed with trapping Stephen and me into this pointless agreement that he didn't even take two minutes to ask what had happened to me, even though it's obvious to anyone that I've been beaten up. It still doesn't change the fact that he's backed me into a corner I don't want to be in."

"I understand," Skip replied reassuringly. "John showed me the agreement. It's certainly not something they prepared you for in law school."

"You can say that again."

"But you do have to admire John's ingenuity."

"Yes," I replied grudgingly.

"He took a catastrophic situation for Azor Pharmaceuticals . . . What percentage of the company does Joey control? Provided he gets possession of his daughter's shares?"

"Between four and five percent," I answered.

"So Guttman took a situation where almost five percent of the total shares of the company were tendered to Eichel, flushed as it were down the john, and created the possibility that they would be withdrawn from the offering pool."

"They could always have been withdrawn—up to the fourteenth day of the initial offering. Every shareholder has the right to change his mind up to the fourteenth day," I said.

"But Joey has agreed that if his brother apologizes he will withdraw the shares."

"Oh, come on, Skip. This thing is full of holes. Let's assume for argument's sake that Joey was in no way involved. He was holed up in a monastery for the whole weekend with a hundred Jesuit priests as witnesses. And let's say that Stephen apologizes. I'd like to see if this constitutes an enforceable contract."

"I don't see why not. If Joey doesn't withdraw his shares, provided the other terms of the contract have been met, I would assume that Joey would be liable for monetary damages."

"And would you like this firm to go into court to collect? You'd be better off sending Ringling Brothers instead."

"Oh, I think that if Stephen apologizes, Joey will withdraw the shares. The father will see to that."

"And if Stephen doesn't apologize? What if Joey *was* responsible, or that I can't prove that he wasn't? And what if it's a close contest? You know that in a lot of deals it takes a lot less than four percent one way or another to decide who comes out on top. You don't honestly believe that I won't get the blame for letting Azor Pharmaceuticals go down the tubes. And the worst part is that it won't be because I didn't do a good job as a lawyer, but that I wasn't able to do my part as a girlfriend. People will always be thinking, 'If she really had any influence with Stephen Azorini, she would have been able to convince him to apologize to his brother. . . .'

"For Christ sake, Skip. I'm an attorney, not a bimbo!"

"Kate, aren't you just overreacting a bit? No one is

asking you to be a bimbo. We're just asking you to take advantage of your unique position in a complex situation in order to help an important client. A client who happens to be your friend. Wouldn't you, just as Stephen's friend, help to find out what happened to his niece?''

"Of course I would," I said. "That's not what I object to. I object to being summoned blind to a meeting by Guttman and having this whole thing shoved down my throat without even the pretense of having any say in the matter. I object to having the potential outcome of the takeover resting on this.''

"The entire M&A department is going to be working around the clock on an aggressive defense for Azor Pharmaceuticals. With any luck, the outcome of your investigation will have no bearing on the takeover. But, if you do decide to take on the assignment, I can assure you that the partners will be exceptionally grateful.''

"Meaning?"

"Meaning that we've been very pleased with your work for the firm so far, Kate, and—''

"Cut the crap, Skip. What's the bottom line?"

"The bottom line, as you so coyly put it, is that if you agree to investigate the death of Gretchen Azorini, I will propose your name for partnership at the next partners' meeting, and John and I will give you our strongest recommendation.''

"I'm a lawyer, Skip. Not a detective. I wouldn't know how to begin," I replied.

"Hire a private detective. Get all the help you need.''

"And I want a free hand," I said. "The full resources of the firm, no constraints. I want my decks cleared of other work, and I want a list of investigators the firm deals with regularly.''

"You've got it," Tillman replied, being careful not to look too pleased.

"And I want Guttman off my back."

Skip nodded.

"And another thing. I won't be held responsible for what I find. If Joey is responsible, he's responsible. I won't gloss it over, not for Azor Pharmaceuticals or all the corporate clients in America."

"We are honorable people, Kate. We serve the client, but we also serve the law."

"You've already won, Skip," I replied. "So spare me the bullshit."

I carefully folded up my letter of resignation and slipped it into the top drawer of my desk. I thought about what Stephen had said about everyone having their price. I thought about becoming a partner and whether that was truly my price.

Callahan Ross, like most other large law firms, was organized as a partnership. About two-thirds of the lawyers were associates. Their time was billed out at a certain hourly rate, and they were paid an annual salary for their labors. For example, my time was billed to Azor Pharmaceuticals at the rate of $180 per hour. My annual salary worked out to about $50 an hour to me. A fraction of the difference went to pay the firm's overhead, but the lion's share was put into a pool and divided up by the partners at the end of the year. For a lawyer toiling in the vineyards of corporate law, partnership was the payoff.

But the payoff wasn't just in dollars, and for me the bucks certainly weren't the draw. The real bonanza was in power and prestige. When you were a partner, you were a peer, no longer checking over your shoulder to see who might overtake you. It meant picking and choosing your own cases, it meant control over your time and caseload. In my case it meant blowing off Guttman if I wanted to. Fine, I thought to myself. Let him find himself another poor associate to torture.

I took a cab to Stephen's office. The loop was jammed with Christmas shoppers, bundled against the cold and dragging bulky shopping bags into the wind. The steps of the Art Institute were crowded with comers and goers. The two stone lions that flanked them wore Christmas wreaths around their necks tied with enormous red bows. The museum was one of Chicago's great treasures. The last time I had been inside its doors I'd gone with Russell.

The Azor offices bustled like any other work day. The security guard had taken up permanent residence behind the reception desk.

"Kate Millholland to see Stephen Azorini," I informed him.

"Is he expecting you?" he asked politely, inspecting his clipboard.

"No. Just tell him who it is. Tell him it's urgent and personal."

The guard eyed my face and made a whispered phone call.

"It'll just be a few minutes," he replied after he replaced the receiver.

Richard Humanski came out to fetch me. "Hi, Kate," he said. "Stephen's in a powwow with Gould. He says he'll just be a few minutes and I should entertain you."

"I don't need to be entertained, Richard. I know you've got lots to do."

"No, that's okay. I could use the break. Let's stop at the canteen. Maybe there's something left from lunch."

I trailed him down the corridor past large frames filled

with the same modern art you find in every techy corporate office. American business was keeping the paint splatterers and the paper crumplers in business.

"I hope you don't mind my asking, but did the same thing that happened to Stephen's face happen to you?"

"What did Stephen say happened to him?" I asked.

"He said his older brother tried to beat him up. I mean, it's so weird that the two of you both are all banged up."

"Yeah, I happened to be there when Joey paid his little visit."

"Gee, I'm sorry. It looks like it must hurt."

"Yeah, it does."

The little lunchroom that the employees called the canteen was deserted. A much-picked-over deli tray was set on a buffet table on the far wall.

"Would you like a sandwich?" Richard asked.

"No, thank you. Just some black coffee." I realized I hadn't eaten since the breakfast of M&Ms the morning before, but my whole face hurt from the effort of talking. The idea of chewing just seemed way beyond anything I wanted to try.

"I'm going to make myself something," Richard said, setting a cup of steaming coffee on the table in front of me. "I still haven't had lunch."

He pulled up a chair across from me. He always looked so young to me, like a fourteen-year-old wearing one of his father's suits.

"You sure you don't want any?" he asked.

"No, thanks."

"It's awful. I practically feel guilty for being hungry. It's so terrible about Gretchen, I still can't quite absorb it. I didn't sleep at all last night just thinking about it."

Richard did look like he hadn't slept. His face was pale, and there were dark circles under his eyes. Indeed, his grief seemed much closer to the surface than Stephen's. I supposed as Stephen's assistant, he must have come in contact with Gretchen a good deal.

"So there you are," interrupted a young blonde, her arms full of computer printout. "Dr. Azorini says he's ready for Miss Millholland. Is that you?"

"You bet."

Richard got up, too. "I'll walk you back," he said.

"That's okay. I know the way. You finish your lunch."

I found Stephen sitting behind his desk flipping through a stack of phone messages. His face, though it bore the clear signs of the previous night's struggle, looked better than mine. It always did.

I closed the door behind me and took a seat opposite him.

"What can I do for you, Kate?" he asked in the tone I imagined he used with division managers who'd pleaded successfully with Richard for an audience.

"For one thing, you can tell me what the hell is going on," I replied.

"In what sense?"

"Stephen, let's not get into semantic games here. Last night one member of your family tried to turn us both into ground round. This morning, another one of your relations railroaded you into some sort of agreement and me into playing private eye. I want to know what we've been suckered into and why."

"Then you'd better talk to Guttman, or better yet, my father. Because I'm not that solid on the sequence of events myself. Around ten this morning a messenger hand delivered a copy of the letter Guttman showed you at DeGenova's office."

"The one tendering Joey's shares," I said. "How did Joey get to be such a big shareholder?"

"It's a long story."

"That's okay," I replied. "I have the time."

Stephen sighed. "Well, you know how I told you my father always wanted me to go into business with him?"

"Do you mean join the Mafia?"

Stephen laughed at my naiveté.

"It's not like the movies. No, my dad may have started out as a leg breaker for a loan shark, but now he's president of a Fortune Five Hundred company. I'm not saying that there isn't mob money invested in the company. Christ, what company can say where the money comes from to buy its shares? Can GM claim to have no illegitimate investors?"

"You were saying that your father wanted you to go into business with him," I prodded.

"He wanted me to get an MBA from Harvard and go to work for him. But I fell in love with science. Besides, I didn't want to spend my entire life being Anthony Azorini's son. The problem is, my father is pretty used to getting his own way."

"So what happened?" I urged.

"So I started Azor Pharmaceuticals. But you know how hard it is to raise start-up money, and a company like Azor takes a ton of money to capitalize. The normal route is to go to friends and family for the seed capital. I went to the banks and borrowed against money that I had in trust, but I was still nowhere near what I needed. I'd hired people. I was having a hard time meeting my payroll. I went to all of Pop's friends. The rich old men who'd known me since I was a kid. Not one of them would lend me a dime."

"Because your father had told them not to."

"Exactly."

Another silence. Finally Stephen spoke again.

"In the end, Joey gave me the money. One day he

walked into my office and said, 'I heard you were strapped for cash' and plunked down a Marshall Field's shopping bag.''

"What was inside?'' I asked.

"Four hundred eighty thousand dollars cash. He wanted to just give it to me as a gift. I knew where it'd come from. I felt guilty, but not guilty enough not to take it. I insisted that he take the shares in exchange. Now they're worth more than fifteen million dollars, but then, they were just pieces of paper.''

"So how did you manage, exactly, to make Joey mad enough at you to try to kill you last night? I know you told me about his owning the property where Gretchen's body was found, but I want to know what you said or did that made Joey so angry.''

"Exactly?''

"Exactly would be good.''

"When I got back to the office after we identified the body, I started to think about why Gretchen would go all the way to Wisconsin. What for. Then I asked Richard to bring me a map of the area. I was so upset when we flew up there, when we identified the body, I wasn't exactly sure where we were. As soon as I saw the map though, it clicked. Then my dad called, angry that I hadn't called Joey yet. I told him that Joey probably already knew, because in all likelihood Gretchen had gone up there to meet him.

"I probably shouldn't have mentioned it to Pop, at least not that way, while I was so angry. But then, you heard what happened. Pop had some guys pick Joey up. They were pretty rough. Pop was pretty mad. Joey's not mad that I think he's responsible for Gretchen's death, he's mad that I made Pop think so.''

"And so he came to your apartment to kill you.''

"Oh, I don't think he came to kill me. He came

because he was mad, and the only way that Joey knows how to deal with anger is with his fists. If I hadn't been at home he would have taken it out on somebody who looked at him the wrong way in a bar.''

''That doesn't sound like the guy who tendered his shares. That's the sort of thing a smart man does who wants to get even—hurting you where you live.''

''Joey is a lot of things,'' replied Stephen evenly, ''but smart is not one of them.''

CHAPTER

My parents' house looked rainsoaked and deserted. The elm trees wept freezing rain, and the windows were darkened and blank at the front of the house.

Mrs. Mason was in the kitchen, her hair tied in a vivid Gucci scarf, a castoff of my mother's. She was slicing mushrooms and watching a rerun of "Gilligan's Island" on an old black-and-white set.

"Lord! What happened to your poor face?" she exclaimed as I came in.

"I was in a car accident," I replied, hating the lie. "Nothing serious."

"What happened? Were you driving?"

"No, no. I was just a passenger. Nobody was badly hurt. Just cuts and bruises. Where's Beth?"

"Upstairs in her room. I sure was sad to hear that little Gretchen Azorini had passed. Your poor baby sister. I don't know what she's going to do without her friend."

"Gretchen used to stay here quite a bit, didn't she?" I inquired.

"Yeah. She stayed here some. Beth was glad for the company, your mom and dad being so busy on the weekend."

"So what was she like?" I asked. "You're a good judge of people."

"It ain't my place to talk about the folks in the house where I work."

"I know, but Dr. Azorini asked me to find out some things about Gretchen's death, and I really never had a chance to get to know her. You probably saw her much more than I did."

Mrs. Mason drew up her vast bosom and perched her ample seat on the tall kitchen stool she kept for 'resting her poor, weary, working feet.' Mrs. Mason had worked for my family since I was a little girl, but somehow I had no recollection of her ever having been any younger.

"Well, I'll say this much: Gretchen Azorini was no happy child," she began finally with a shake of the head. "No, ma'am. Quiet. Never looked a grown person in the eye, always sneaking up on a body. So sad and quiet she might just as well be a ghost."

"Why do you think she was unhappy?" I asked.

"Sure beats me. I can't figure why any of you are so unhappy. Look at your brother. Look at Beth. You live in this house, three meals a day, don't need to work a day in your life, ain't known a minute's trouble except what you manage to make yourselves. Maybe if you ain't got enough real troubles, you just got to be imagining them."

"But Gretchen did have real problems," I objected. "She was sick with diabetes. Her mother was dead. Her father was away so much she had to live at school and with her uncle. . . . "

"But her daddy used to call her. He always tried to keep in touch—"

"What do you mean?" I asked keenly.

"Nothing. Just that her daddy called here sometimes.

Really cheered her up. Called her the day before she died."

"He called here?" I demanded.

"Yes, ma'am," Mrs. Mason answered.

"How did you know it was her father? Did he say who it was?"

"Noooo. But when he called the house once, Polly—you know the little housemaid your momma fired for using her perfume—asked him who was calling, and he said he was Miss Gretchen's daddy."

"Did you talk to him the day he called here? The day before Gretchen died?"

"Yes'm. I was giving the girls some cocoa. Lord, you know how your sister eats. Gretchen seemed real nervous, like she was waiting for the phone to ring, but I was standing right there so I picked it up. She almost snatched it right outa my hand."

"Did she talk for a long time?"

"No. She just talked for a coupla minutes, whispering like. When she put down the phone, she had a big grin on her face."

"Do you remember what time she got the call?"

"Well, let me see. I just finished listening to the 'Reverend Paul's Gospel Show' on the radio. That ends up at five, and I had just finished peeling the shrimp for dinner, so probably a little bit after five. What're you asking all these questions for?" Mrs. Mason demanded.

"I told you. Stephen asked me to find out some things. He's very upset about what happened to Gretchen. He was at the office the whole weekend, so he barely saw her. He wants to know what she was up to that last weekend, whether she seemed happy, that sort of thing," I replied, thinking that for a lawyer I was a rather poor liar.

"Well, you tell him she seemed real happy for a change. The last few times she's been by she's been really dragging, depressed like. Seeing her and your sister together was enough to give anybody the willies. But after her daddy called, she just perked right up."

"Mrs. Mason," I replied, "thank you. You've been a big help."

"I'd do anything for Dr. Azorini. Such a handsome, good-looking man. When're you two getting married? Lord knows this house could use some cheering up."

"Is Beth home?" I inquired.

"She's been upstairs in her room since yesterday. That doctor of hers gave her some sleep medicine. I don't hold with that. A person's got to get their grieving done with before they get on with things. Sleeping pills ain't going to help your sister, just slow things down."

In my parents' house the children lived in one wing (above the servants) and the adults in the other. There was more than enough room for each of us—Teddy, Beth and me, and a suite for the nanny. Teddy was dead, I'd moved out, and the last of the string of long-suffering nannies was gone.

All the lights were off in Beth's room. She had pulled an armchair up to the window. She was wearing a worn, flannel nightgown with her knees pulled up underneath. She sat looking out the window at the rain.

"Hi, kidlet," I said, taking a seat on the edge of the bed.

"I was wondering when you'd come," she replied, not even bothering to look at me. There were circles under her eyes like bruises, and she was as pale as I'd ever seen her.

"I'm sorry I couldn't get out here sooner. Things are a mess at work. I couldn't get free."

"Stephen called me," she said, still motionless, "but Dr. Dirt gave me some tranquilizer junk, and I couldn't come to the phone."

"Who?"

"Dr. Dirt. That's what the kids call Dr. Weingart. He's such an asshole." She turned and glanced at me. "Hey, what happened to your face?"

"Fender bender," I replied. "Stephen asked me to say hi. You know someone's trying to buy his company."

"I know. A hostile takeover. Gretchen told me all about it. It's a pretty big deal. She was really worked up. She used to say that she was going to go to work for Azor when she graduated from college so that someday, when Stephen got too old to work, it'd be her company."

"Are you doing okay?" I asked softly.

"I'm going to kill myself," she replied matter-of-factly. She might just as soon have been reporting on the weather. "Life is shit."

"Oh, Beth, that's just not true," I replied, with Mrs. Mason's words about my brother ringing in my ears.

"Life is shit and then you die," she continued. "Gretchen had diabetes, her mother was dead, but she managed to be happy—so she died. I mean, that's what happens to you when you finally stop being miserable. Life's a setup. The only way to win is to not play."

"Beth, listen. What happened to Gretchen is a terrible tragedy. But you owe it to yourself to take a little time to heal. To get things in perspective. You won't always feel the way you do now. . . ."

There was a discreet knock on the door, and Ellen, the housemaid, and Mrs. Mason came in carrying trays.

"I made you girls some supper."

"Take it away, I'm not hungry," Beth announced.

I motioned to the two women to put the trays down. "Thank you," I said.

Having Mrs. Mason bring up dinner was one of the few good memories of childhood. A silver tray lined with crisp linen—steamy tomato soup and a grilled cheese sandwich with the crusts neatly excised—the Royal Doulton children's china with its pattern of Beatrix Potter rabbits, and a tiny Waterford vase with a single rosebud. The message was always clear—mother might be at the hairdresser, but someone in the kitchen cared.

I lit into the food, but Beth, who usually would eat anything, left her tray untouched.

"What happened to her?" whispered Beth after the servants had gone.

"What did they tell you?" I asked.

"Some bullshit about having to wait for an autopsy. Was it her diabetes? She was always so careful about her insulin, I can't believe she'd ever make a mistake. . . ."

"It wasn't her diabetes," I replied. "Who did she go to Wisconsin with?"

"Wisconsin? What do you mean?"

"I mean that they found her body on a dirt road in Mannetuoc, Wisconsin. Some poachers found her. Her father owns some land up there, but there's nothing up there, especially this time of the year. What was she doing up there? Who did she go with?"

"Don't grill me," Beth snapped. "I asked you a question, and instead of an answer I get the third degree."

"Okay. It's true. They're waiting for the results of some tests that were done at the autopsy. But so far it seems likely that Gretchen was raped and then strangled.

That's why it's so important to know who she was with.''

"No," Beth whispered.

"It doesn't matter now if Gretchen cut school," I urged. "It doesn't matter if she was breaking the rules. It doesn't matter if you were breaking the rules. We just need to know what she was doing."

"I don't know anything!" Beth shouted, clamping her hands over her ears.

"What's going on here?" demanded my mother from the doorway. She was wearing a black wool skirt and a red Jaeger twin set of cashmere. She held her hands up, away from her body—she had obviously just had a manicure and didn't want to unintentionally bump her crimson talons.

"Kate was just leaving," Beth announced, studying her knees.

"I was just asking Beth some questions about Gretchen," I reported, not moving.

"Dr. Weingart has given strict orders that Beth is to have complete rest. No visitors," snapped Mother. "It's very important that she not be upset."

"Mother, her best friend just died. It's only natural for her to be upset."

"If my memory serves me correctly, I paid for you to get a degree in jurisprudence, not psychiatry. I think we'll just let Dr. Weingart decide what is best for Beth."

"Mother, this is important. Gretchen was cutting school the day she died. She drove up to Wisconsin. No one knows why—"

"Let me just remind you," Mother said, tapping her Gucci-shod foot with irritation, "that your first concern should be with your own family. I will not have your sister pestered against doctor's orders."

"But Mother—"

"Don't you 'but Mother' me," she paused, really looking at me for the first time. "What ever have you done to your face?"

"I was in a car accident."

"Well, I hope none of it is permanent," she said, waving vaguely at my bruises. "Anyway, I have spent enough time on this already. Your father and I have to be dressed and downtown in an hour and—"

"Stop it!" shrieked Beth, bolting from her chair and knocking over her untouched dinner tray, causing a riot of tomato soup and spilled tea to bleed into the rug. "Stop it! Stop it! Stop it! I can't bear to hear you. Go away." She sobbed convulsively. "For god's sake, just go away and leave me alone."

"Oh, Beth. I'm so sorry," I said kneeling next to her chair. "I know that this is a terrible time for you."

"Just leave me alone," she hissed while Mother rang the bell furiously for the maids to clean up the mess.

"Of all the thoughtless, irresponsible things," Mother raged. "This carpet is less than two months old!"

Ellen appeared at a trot with Mrs. Mason wheezing up the stairs behind her. Mother fired off orders as the two women gathered up the crockery and mobilized for sponges and buckets. Under the cover of the chaos Beth slipped, barely noticed, into the bathroom. I heard the faint click of the lock.

Once the servants were sufficiently terrified, Mother checked her watch and announced that there was no way she could manage to be ready on time. With a toss of her perfectly coiffed head, she stalked off toward her bedroom. I followed.

"Mother, I need to talk to you for a minute."

"Kate, you have done quite enough talking in this house tonight."

"It's important."

"I have to get dressed."

"Mother, Beth told me she wants to kill herself."

Mother wheeled around, furious. "If this is some sick way to get my attention, you have certainly succeeded."

"Mother, please. Just now Beth told me she wants to kill herself."

"I don't believe it. She's just depressed because of this Gretchen Azorini thing. She'll snap out of it."

"Maybe," I said, "but I don't think she should be left alone."

"Well, what do you suggest I do? I can't exactly post a guard." She gave her watch an impatient glance.

Part of me wanted to argue, to rail against her for leaving for yet another trivial party, yet another self-indulgent vanity fest while her sixteen-year-old daughter wept and wrestled with the loss of her best friend and the cruelties of life. But part of me, the grown-up part, had learned the hard way to choose my battles with care. So, reluctantly, I let it go.

I waited until my mother was safely primping in her lair and then crept back up the servants' stairs and tapped at Beth's door. I peered inside and found her back in the chair by the window, hugging her knees in the dark.

"You okay?" I asked from the doorway.

"I don't want to answer any questions. I don't want to talk about it."

"Fine," I replied. "I just want you to know that I'm going to spend the night. This house is enough to depress anybody. I remember after Russell died I didn't want to be with anybody, but I hated being by myself."

"Sometimes I forget about Russell," mused Beth. "Mother took down all your wedding pictures. She said she was redecorating."

"I never forget," I answered truthfully, "not ever, not even for a second. Just like you'll never forget Gretchen. But after a while you do manage to live with the hurt, to find a place for it so that it doesn't control your life."

"I just took one of Dr. Weingart's pills," said Beth with an enormous yawn.

"Just one?"

"Just one. I think I'll go to bed."

"I'll be in my old room if you need me."

I hid like a thief in my old bedroom until I heard the scrunch of my parents' car on the drive as they left for their party. I spent the time thinking about Gretchen and Stephen and Guttman and why I had somehow managed to fill my life with people who were ciphers to me. Maybe that's why I found the mystery of Gretchen's death so depressing and disturbing. She was another enigma, albeit a peripheral one, and my life was already too full of unfathomables.

I slipped downstairs and moved my car to the servants' side of the house so that my parents wouldn't see it when they came home. Then I went into the library, helped myself to some of my father's Scotch, and tried to figure out what to do next.

Beth had seemed genuinely surprised at the mention of Wisconsin. Worse, I was certain that Beth did know things that might be helpful—even if she herself had no understanding of their relevance, but between Mother and Dr. Weingart, whatever Beth did know was not going to be quickly and easily forthcoming.

I was back at the beginning—lots of questions and no answers.

Why did Gretchen go to Wisconsin? Did she go to meet Joey? If so, did he strangle her? Did someone else? And if Joey really had been involved in some way, why all the indignation? Why burst into Stephen's apartment with fists flying?

I knew that on some level when I allowed Skip Tillman to talk me into taking on this unorthodox investigation, I was hoping that I had stumbled on the lawyer's equivalent of a get rich scheme—a fast and easy road to partnership. I was taking a gamble, though I acknowledged it was one with a low probability of success. I had hoped I would drive out to my parents' house and just ask Beth what Gretchen had been doing in Wisconsin. "Oh," she would answer sorrowfully, "she was giving one of the boys from Country Day a ride so that he could collect specimens for the science fair. He's a little creepy, but I never thought he was actually dangerous. . . ." I would tool off, tell Guttman, and live happily ever after in my new corner office.

Life is full of gambles that don't pay off.

CHAPTER

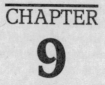

I spent a fitful night filled with bad dreams in the single bed of my childhood. The labyrinth of empty rooms in my parents' house seemed to hang over me, cavernous and vaguely frightening. I padded down the hall during the darkest hours of the night to make sure that Beth was in bed, alive, and asleep as opposed to doing something foolish—like bleeding into the bath. But Beth didn't move all night. She slept pale and motionless in the sleeping pill's thrall, hands folded across her chest like a young corpse.

I was exhausted past the point of rest. I fretted and twitched, finally nodding off into troubled and exhausting dreams of Gretchen's muddy hair tangled in Joey's hands. He tried frantically to free himself while John Guttman sat impassively making notes on his legal pad.

Before the sun rose I gave up even the pretense of sleep. I crept into Beth's room for one final look. Then I sneaked into her closet to find some clothes to go running in. She moaned as if in protest as I rifled through her things, but didn't wake.

I changed into a pair of Beth's sweat pants, a T-shirt and a heavy, hooded sweat shirt. Her shoes were a little big for me but were serviceable with two pairs of socks.

Downstairs I paroled Rocket from his kennel in the mud room and together we slipped out the back door into the dark.

From the front you'd never know that the house sits on the lake. But it, and the dozen or so other estates like it, sit on a small bluff that overlooks Lake Michigan. The bluff erodes a few feet every year, so that from time to time men with bulldozers have to come in and rebuild the back lawn to stall the houses' slow progress lakeward. From the front it looks like any other palatial house; from the back, via a twisted wooden stair, there is a boathouse, cabanas, and a stretch of beach. It is the private use of a public resource that only a lot of money can buy.

I always loved the beach. It was just down the stairs but completely removed from the house. It held wonderful memories for me as well. Teddy and I playing beach football, burying each other in the sand, Tucker Sweet slipping away from one of Mother's garden parties to teach me to fly a kite on this beach. . . . It was a world away. From there, even the city was just a glimmering mirage in the distance.

In the darkness I picked my way down the precipitous wooden stairs that led to the beach. Rocket, rheumy and wheezing, rattled ahead of me, much more certain of the way.

The lake lapped cold and inky in the predawn darkness. The cold wind blew fresh across the water. Gulls screamed and wheeled above me. Clouds hung low, blotting out the distant lights of the city.

I headed north toward the Hendersons' boathouse, about three miles distant. I heard the faint clink of Rocket's license and collar as he trailed behind me. My face throbbed, a monotonous reminder of Joey Azorini and the mess I found myself in.

But at some point my strides became easy and automatic. I began to shake off the paralysis that had seized me between the discovery of Gretchen's death and the debacle in the law offices of Morganelli, DeGenova and Rocco. I still couldn't quite grasp the tragedy and the twisted strands of human behavior that had put me in the position to investigate it. But finding out how Gretchen Azorini came to meet her death was at least a concrete problem. The mechanism of my lawyer's mind switched on at last.

Back in the house I went upstairs and slipped into my mother's closet. Mother's closet is bigger than a studio apartment. It has two doors, one that Mother opens when she wants to go in and find something to wear, another, at the back, that her maid uses when she wants to hang up clothes without disturbing my mother. I used the maid's door.

I helped myself to a pair of black wool Yves Saint Laurent trousers and a cashmere turtleneck of soft gray. Mother would have accessorized the outfit in some original and eye-catching way so that she'd look like a fashion photo come to life. On me, they would just look like clothes.

After a quick shower in my old bathroom, I dried and dressed, and, after a quick look at my sleeping sister, I was ready to return to the working world.

I was torn about Beth. I didn't want to leave her alone, nor did I feel she had told me everything she knew about Gretchen's last days. But there was no telling when she'd wake up and no guarantee once she awoke that she'd be more forthcoming than she'd been the night before. There were other balls I needed to get rolling, I reassured myself; talking to Beth could wait until I had some other things more under control and she was more ready.

Traffic was light moving into the city. The sun was not up yet, and there were just a few other cars on the road—for the rest of the world it was Sunday, a day of rest.

But Edgar Eichel had set a fast clock for his takeover attempt, and I could practically feel him (and Guttman) breathing down my neck. As I drove, I dictated the day's agenda into the tiny tape recorder I kept in my glove compartment. It was a trick I'd learned from Guttman. And while I didn't like to admit it, it was just another sign that he'd rubbed off on me.

The elevator delivered me to the forty-second floor before 6:00 but the M&A department, Sunday notwithstanding, was already in full gear. I felt a pang knowing that I was not going to be part of their efforts that day.

I found Cheryl crouched behind her desk, stripping off her gym socks and sneakers—trading up to her daytime heels.

"Ugh, your bruises are getting worse," she said by way of a greeting.

"Thanks," I replied, flipping the cassette tape onto her desk. "I need this first. Then get us a pot of coffee and I'll fill you in on the interesting turn our careers are taking."

"Right," she answered with raised eyebrows. "The newspapers are on your desk. And Guttman called from home this morning. He's been trying to reach you. He wants you to call him as soon as you get in."

"He can fuck himself," I replied with more feeling than I expected.

Normally during a takeover my first order of business every day is to scour the business press to see what kind of coverage we're getting. It may not be the truth, but it's what the shareholders are reading. Today I was only interested in any stories about Gretchen Azorini's death. But the *Tribune* and the *Sun-Times* were full of a story about a Schaumburg man who had poured brake fluid on his pregnant fifteen-year-old daughter and set her on fire. The rape and murder of yet another sixteen-year-old, no matter whose granddaughter, was relegated to a two-paragraph mention at the back of the metro section.

I spent the rest of the morning getting my act together. I had my calls held at the switchboard. I spent an uninterrupted hour with Cheryl laying out the strange particulars of the past few days.

Then I called one of the assholes I knew from law school. His name was Aaron Horvitz, and in the five years since graduation he had parlayed his special combination of aggression and abrasiveness into a highly successful divorce practice.

"Is this business or pleasure?" he asked me once Cheryl managed to get the busy man himself on the line.

"Business," I replied.

"Too bad. I was hoping you'd called to suggest we get together to talk about the good old days."

"They weren't all that good."

"True. Sorry to hear about Russell. He was a nice guy."

"I need to hire a private investigator," I replied. "I thought you might have some names."

"What kind of problem?"

"It's a wrongful death case."

"I'm surprised. I didn't think you guys at Callahan dirtied your hands with wrongful death cases."

"We aren't litigating. It's a personal matter for an important client. Still, I need someone smart and well connected. Someone who can get results in a hurry and keep his mouth shut.''

"You don't want much, do you?''

"I'll pay for the best.''

"I know someone who might be good for you. Sharp young investigator from the D.A.'s office who's just starting his own shop. Very smart, well connected. His dad's a cop. He might be just the guy for you. His name is Elliott Abelman.''

"A P.I. named Elliott? Will wonders never cease.''

"If you want a flatfoot, I can send you to a hundred guys named Gus. Elliott's a class act.''

"Does he know anything about business?''

"Might. D.A.'s hot to prosecute white-collar criminals. He wants to be governor some day. So this is for a corporate client?''

"No,'' I lied. "I'm calling for an associate in trusts and estates. When I suggested he call the great Aaron Horvitz himself, he got the vapors.''

"As well he should. Okay, here's the number. . . .'' He gave me two, one for the office, another for home. "And remember, if he's fabulous, I'm the guy who recommended him. If he fucks up, I never heard of him.''

I buzzed Cheryl and told her to get in touch with Elliott Abelman and set up a meeting as soon as possible. Then I checked the list of private investigators that Skip Tillman's secretary had left on my desk that morning. Elliott Abelman's name was not on it. I was glad. This was private business, and I wanted to keep it private. At Callahan Ross office gossip was transmitted at the speed of light. I wasn't taking any chances.

Next, I called another law school friend who was married to an editor at the *Sun-Times*. He put me in touch with the city desk editor, who got me on the line with the metro reporter who covered organized crime.

She in turn told me that the person I really wanted to talk to was one Detective Cancasci of the twenty-first precinct, who supposedly knew everything that was worth knowing about the Azorinis.

I called Cancasci and explained who I was. I asked if he might, in exchange for dinner, be willing to spend an hour telling me about the Azorini family.

"You pretty?" he asked.

"Just okay," I replied, "but now I've got stitches, a black eye, and the rest of my face is pretty banged up."

"How'd that happen?"

"Joey Azorini's bodyguard kicked me in the face."

"Vito kicked you? You are one lady I've got to meet. You like good food?"

"Yes, I like good food."

"Meet me at a restaurant called Taglieteri's. It's in a brownstone on the corner of Taylor and Twenty-third Street. I'll be there a little after six."

"See you then."

Cheryl buzzed to say that Elliott Abelman would be there in a half an hour. I had Cheryl call a paralegal into the office to get me anything and everything they could lay their hands on about the Azorini family. Then I summoned a first-year associate and sent him to get a copy of Joey Azorini's criminal record. I also wanted a copy of the police report and the doctor's findings from Wisconsin. He wanted to know when I needed it. By yesterday, I told him. He reminded me that it was Sunday, but promised he'd try.

I called my parents' house on the servants' line. I didn't recognize the voice of whoever answered, but that came as no surprise. Astrid Millholland was no Mother Teresa, and besides Mrs. Mason—who cooked like an angel and was shockingly overpaid—Anna, my mother's disagreeable maid, and Raoul, the incompetent gardener, the rest of the staff had roughly the same half-life as plutonium. I asked to speak to Mrs. Mason.

Mrs. Mason reported that Mother was out until 4:00, when Dr. Weingart was expected.

"Your mama called us all together this morning and told us that we aren't allowed to let anybody talk to Miss Beth without her permission, and that included you."

"That's okay. I won't get you into trouble. I just wanted to be sure she's okay. Will you just tell her I called?"

"I'll tell her," replied Mrs. Mason, "but I don't know what good it'll do. Things are going bad around here," warned the old black woman. "Bad like they were before Mr. Teddy did go and hang himself. I can't say I ain't worried about it. . . ."

I didn't usually receive unannounced visitors at the office on Sundays, but when I'd agreed to investigate Gretchen Azorini's death, I had ventured way beyond the pale of the usual.

Vince DeGenova was a thin man. Handsome. With a carefully groomed look and a leanness I usually associate with distance runners. He wore a black Armani suit, and his wing tips positively gleamed. He had the look—Type A all the way.

"I hope you'll excuse the intrusion." He wore a white shirt with wide-set maroon stripes and a white French collar. The collar had eyelet holes, one on each side, to accommodate a gold pin that peeked out from beneath his subdued silk tie. "I'm sorry to drop in on you unannounced. . . ."

"Not at all," I replied. "Anyone who can stand the mess is welcome in my office."

"Oh, it's not that bad," replied DeGenova, setting

himself carefully into one of my wing back chairs. "I once had a professor who said that a messy office was the mark of an organized mind."

"I assume his office was a mess," I replied.

"Just atrocious. My word. Does your face hurt?" he asked sympathetically.

"It throbs a little. Sometimes I forget about it, but it certainly looks worse than it feels."

"I know that you promised Stephen that you would help with the arrangements for the funeral, and I hope you won't feel that I've been forward. But since you so generously took on the more difficult task of investigating what happened, I took the liberty of making some preliminary arrangements, with your approval, of course."

"Thank you," I said. "I really haven't had a chance to think about it."

"I quite understand. You've had enough other things to do. The body was brought to Chicago this morning. There'll be a wake tomorrow evening and then the funeral is set for Tuesday morning. There will be a mass at nine-thirty at St. Bonaventure's, followed by the burial at Lakeview Cemetery."

"That's fine. Thank you."

"In terms of your investigation. Anthony Azorini wanted me to be sure to offer you whatever assistance I could."

"I'll need to know how to get in touch with Joey Azorini."

"If you have a piece of paper, I'll be happy to write it down for you."

I handed him a piece of From the desk of Katharine Millholland from the pad on my desk. As he wrote he said, "The first number is his apartment in the city, the second is the number of a nightclub he owns on Rush

Street, the third is his place in the suburbs. If you strike out at all three places and you need to reach him in a hurry, call me and I'll make sure he gets in touch with you. I'll put my home and office numbers here as well.''

''Like you found him the day after Gretchen Azorini's body was discovered?''

''Pardon?''

''Joey said he was in bed with a girl and some guys came and dragged him out of bed to see you.''

''His father wanted to see him right away. We found out where he was and picked him up. Stephen had been trying to reach Joey to tell him of Gretchen's death, but he was having no success. So he called his father. You can imagine how distraught Anthony Azorini was, first to learn that his granddaughter was dead and naturally, I suppose, by Stephen's accusations.''

''And what did Joey say?''

''He appeared genuinely upset at the news of his daughter's death, definitely surprised, if that's what you're getting at.''

''Can you get me the address and phone number of the girl he was with?''

''Of course.''

''What's Joey like?'' I asked.

''Joey?'' Vince DeGenova stretched out his legs and drew in a deep breath. ''First off, you have to understand that I work for his father, Anthony Azorini. My dealings with both boys have only been through him, so I guess my opinion is highly reflective of the senior Azorini's. . . .

''What is Joey like?'' he began again. ''Joey is certainly a criminal, but I'm not sure that he's a monster. He's a drug dealer, a violent man in a violent business. He certainly has less control over his impulses than most people operating in civilized society. He also believes that the rules don't apply to him. Considering his experience, I would say that they don't.''

''You mean the fourteen-year-old girl who died in the car accident and his wife's death?''

''Yes, among others.''

''It's pretty clear that Joey Azorini is capable of murder,'' I mused.

''Oh, I think we're all capable of murder. Every one of us,'' replied Vince DeGenova.

''Then Joey is certainly more capable of it, or capable in more situations than most of us.''

''True. But why would he want to kill his daughter? What would be his motivation?''

''Does there need to be one for him to be responsible?'' I asked. ''The girl who died in the car accident wasn't meant to die; neither, I think, was his wife. The first was an accident caused by recklessness, the other, an accident, if you will, of Joey's temper.''

''From what Stephen says about the circumstances of Gretchen's death—found raped and strangled in the woods—what kind of accident does that sound like?''

Elliott Abelman looked more like a banker than a private eye. He probably checked in at around six feet with a head of soft brown hair going thin at the top. He had a pleasant, classic profile and a pair of horn rims. He wore a gray suit, carried a black briefcase, and had a firm, dry handshake. The only thing out of the ordinary about him was his smile. When he turned it on, it lit up the whole room.

I told him everything—about the takeover and Gretchen's murder, about John Guttman and Anthony Azorini maneuvering me into investigating her death, and about Joey Azorini being a drug dealer. Well, there were a couple of things I skipped. I didn't tell him that

Stephen and I sometimes slept together. I figured that it was none of his business and that if he were any good as a P.I., he'd find out for himself.

While I talked, Elliott took notes.

I told it chronologically, starting with the police officers waiting for Stephen at his apartment and ending with my agreeing to look into the matter for the Azorinis.

"Nice family," remarked Abelman when I'd finished. "What do the police think?"

"From what the pathologist says, they're assuming it's a rape/murder until somebody shows them otherwise. I don't know whom they suspect, if anybody. I don't know how they're conducting their investigation. That's one of the things I need you for. I have no idea how to keep open lines of communication with a rural sheriff's department. The few times I've had contact with them so far all I've done is piss them off."

"I'm sure they don't much like pushy lady lawyers from the big city up there," replied Abelman, flashing his terrific grin. "Tell me, you said you knew Gretchen Azorini. What kind of kid was she?"

"I didn't really know her. She was my little sister Beth's friend. In the few times I was with her, I don't think she said ten words. She was either very shy or just preternaturally quiet."

"Was she a good student?" he asked.

"According to Stephen, she made the dean's list every term."

"Do you know if she was popular?"

"I'd say she almost certainly was not," I replied. "She and Beth were the class outcasts. Up until Gretchen went to Chelsea Hall, Beth literally had not one single friend. She just went to school, did her time there, and then came home."

"And when Gretchen came to the school she and Beth became friends?"

"Yes. Gretchen was thirteen when they met. She came from a completely different kind of background than any of the other girls. You have to understand what a school like Chelsea Hall is like. There are six hundred girls from nursery school through high school. About seventy percent are lifers—they start when they're four, and they graduate when they're eighteen. Their parents are all friends, they all belong to the same clubs, do the same things, go to the same places on vacation. Whereas Gretchen Azorini . . ."

"Was the daughter of a former porn queen, now deceased, and a vicious but successful drug dealer. I'm surprised the school was willing to accept her."

"Some strings were pulled. I'm an alum. I asked a friend of my family's, Tucker Sweet, who is a trustee of the school, to lobby on her behalf. There was a substantial contribution involved as well."

"So what does your sister say about her friend?" asked Elliott, sensibly enough. "If they were best friends, she must have some idea of what Gretchen was into."

"I'm sure she does. The problem is, I haven't been able to get her to tell me. Beth is, well, emotionally screwed up is probably an understatement. She's angry, she's depressed, she's suicidal. I know this sounds horrible to say about one's own sister, but of the two girls, Beth is definitely the one you'd expect to run away from school and end up in the woods somewhere."

"Usually teenagers run in a pack. What one of them is into is what the others are into, to a greater or lesser degree. If your sister's into trouble, chances are Gretchen was into it too."

"I don't think that Beth's into trouble," I replied. "I

think she's into unhappiness. I think she's lost and miserable and depressed.''

"How's she taking Gretchen's death?"

"Not well," I replied in a grand case of understatement. "She fainted when she heard the news. When I went to see her, she said she was going to commit suicide. Her psychiatrist has her so doped up she can't or won't answer any questions. On top of all that, my mother has forbidden the servants from allowing me to speak to her.''

"Forbidden the servants, I like that," mused Abelman. "Then maybe I should have a go talking to her."

"I'd like to try one more time. I thought I'd go to see her at Chelsea Hall tomorrow morning. I thought I could talk to some of Gretchen's teachers and maybe the school psychiatrist as well, while I was out there. Who knows, maybe when the freshness of it wears off and she's away from my mother, she'll be able to tell me something.''

"So what do you want me to do?" inquired Elliott.

"I'm not exactly sure," I replied. "I'm not very experienced at investigating a possible murder. I thought you might be able to offer some guidance.''

"Well," said Elliott Abelman, setting his notebook down carefully on the edge of my desk, "the way I see it, there are two, possibly unrelated problems that you could choose to tackle. The first is, where was Joey Azorini when his daughter was killed? If you find that he was having breakfast with the mayor and Cardinal Bernadelli, then the issue of Joey's involvement can be settled to the satisfaction of his father and brother.''

"But then we won't know who killed her," I said.

"You could leave that to the police," answered Abelman.

"And will they find out who killed her?"

Elliott raised his eyebrows and shrugged his shoulders. "Maybe," he said. "Eventually. Probably. But this is the kind of case that is usually either solved right away, within the first week, or drags on for years."

"What do you mean?"

"Either they get a break up front—she had a fight with her boyfriend the night she disappeared and there were witnesses. They find a piece of physical evidence that links her death with an identifiable perpetrator. Someone walks into the police station and confesses. Those are all ways that cases like this get solved quickly.

"But let's say this is a stranger abduction," continued Abelman. "Let's say she was waiting at a red light and a man with a gun climbs in the passenger side and puts a gun to her head and says 'drive.' Those are the cases that lie, gathering dust, on detectives' desks until they retire."

"We don't have that long. We have only ten business days," I reported.

"Why only ten days?" asked Abelman.

I explained about Joey tendering his shares and how he would have to elect to withdraw those shares before the close of the offering pool.

"Which, of course, raises a third possibility," said the private investigator.

"And what's that?"

"That it's Edgar Eichel that's responsible for Gretchen's death."

"Don't be ridiculous!" I retorted.

"Ridiculous? What do you think Eichel will net if he buys Azor and sells off the pieces—twenty million?"

"That's absurd. Eichel may not be a gentleman, but he's certainly a successful businessman. I can't believe he'd stoop to murder."

"Well, there are a lot of people at the D.A.'s office

who wouldn't blink at the thought of Eichel stooping to murder. Randy Harrigan, the D.A., has had his eyes on him for years. He played very rough with the union back when he was in the muffler business. Two key people who were trying to derail his contract negotiations ended up dead. He's the kind of guy a corrupt town like Chicago breeds. There've always been whispers about Eichel playing dirty.''

''But why would he want to kill Gretchen?''

''Look at the situation with Joey's shares. It looks like the only winner in this situation is Edgar Eichel.''

''I must confess I find the whole setup with Joey tendering his shares to be suspicious. It happened so fast. Where did he get the idea? Who drafted the tendering letter? But even if the shares were a setup, Eichel couldn't know that Stephen would react the way he did and accuse his brother of being responsible for her death. It's too bizarre to have predicted.''

''Oh, I don't know. Maybe that was a setup, too. Maybe Eichel chose to have her killed on Joey's property, knowing what that would make Stephen think.''

''And the rape?''

''Maybe Eichel's hired help got a little carried away, decided to have some fun. I'm not necessarily suggesting that Eichel killed her himself.''

''I think this is getting pretty farfetched.''

''I agree. But you have to admit there's a lot in this for Eichel. During a takeover a tremendous amount is resting on the shoulders of the CEO. If the executive's sharp, lucky, and keeps his eye on the ball, there's a chance he'll succeed in wriggling out of Eichel's grasp. But what if he's struggling with a personal tragedy—the unsolved murder of his sixteen-year-old ward? That would certainly tip the odds in Eichel's favor.''

"I still can't believe even Eichel would stoop that low," I replied.

"In my time, I've seen people go a lot lower," remarked Abelman. "But we still haven't resolved where we go from here."

"As I see it," I said, "we have no choice but to pursue both lines of inquiry. If we can find that Joey has a provable alibi for the time of his daughter's death, wonderful. But the truth is, if Joey could produce one, I think he already would have. And if we can't prove without a reasonable doubt that he didn't do it, we're left with trying to prove who did it anyway. We might as well try to find that out in the first place."

"Do you have any idea what it costs to run a private murder investigation?"

"I don't know. Why don't you educate me?"

"I charge five hundred a day plus expenses. To tackle a job this big, I'm going to have to use a lot of help. I'll take on some free-lancers whom I use, some moonlighting cops. They cost maybe three hundred a day. In the end we're talking about a pretty steep tab."

"Fine," I said. "As long as you're able to submit a fully itemized invoice, there shouldn't be any problem."

"Good," Elliott Abelman said. I got the distinct feeling that this was a really big assignment for him, maybe his first.

"So who's the client?" he asked.

"What do you mean?"

"Well, whom will I be working for? Stephen Azorini? The Azorini family? Callahan Ross? Who'll be paying the bill?"

"I will," I answered.

"You personally? Why?"

"Because I'm in the middle of enough trouble as it

is without having to answer to anyone else,'' I replied.
"I can't risk having the firm decide it doesn't want to
pay for the investigation because it doesn't like where
it's headed. The same for the Azorinis.''

"We're talking about a lot of money. . . ." continued Abelman incredulously.

"Will a five thousand dollar retainer be sufficient?''
I asked, pulling out my checkbook and writing him a
check. I used the same lapis pen I had used to draft my
letter of resignation the day before.

"That will be fine. Since you're the client, do you
want a report every day?''

"More than that," I replied. "I've been freed from
my case load until the investigation is over. Besides, I
think that I'm probably in a unique position to find out
some things. Like I said, I'm going to go out to Chelsea
tomorrow morning. I think that my sister will probably
talk to me sooner than to a stranger.''

"Well, then, I'd suggest that I get a team working on
checking Joey's alibi.''

"He claims he was in Colombia on a business trip.
That he returned on Wednesday morning. Stephen says
that his father heard he was in town, seen on Rush
Street.''

"Fine. I'll have some operatives get started on that
issue. Then I think the next step will be to get up to
Wisconsin and see what the local authorities have turned
up so far. Who knows, maybe they've solved it by now
and they're grilling some poor dumb redneck under the
lights.''

"I'm not optimistic.''

"In any event, I'll report back to you tomorrow.''

"Make it in the afternoon, I'll be at Chelsea Hall
during the morning.''

"I hope you don't think I'm being impertinent," began Elliott Abelman as he headed toward the door, ''but what happened to your face?''

''I got in the middle of a fist fight. When Joey found out that Stephen had told their dad that he thought Joey was responsible for Gretchen's death, he went immediately to Stephen's apartment and tried to kill him.''

''How come he didn't succeed?''

''I hit Joey over the head with a statue and took his gun away,'' I replied, trying to make it sound matter-of-fact and feeling rather embarrassed.

''I'm impressed, Miss Millholland,'' Elliott Abelman said, flashing his smile.

''Please,'' I said, ''call me Kate.''

CHAPTER
10

Taglieteri Restaurante was a few blocks west of the University of Illinois Circle Campus in a garbled neighborhood teetering on the verge of gentrification. It was a weird hodgepodge of old houses with deep stoops, discount stores in urban renewal strip malls, tenements, and freeway turnarounds. There were enough restored town houses to make a difference during the day, but after dark I gave the cabby an extra five dollars and asked him to wait until I was safely inside before he headed down Dearborn toward Greektown and his next fare.

The restaurant occupied the ground floor of a dilapidated brownstone that was wedged between a laundromat and an all-night Korean grocery. Inside, it was a tiny place, with about ten tables and a hostess with jet black hair and a build like a refrigerator. A mural of an Italian street scene, obviously painted by an amateur hand, covered one wall. It was bathed in the reflected light from the Coke machine.

Detective Cancasci stood when I walked into the restaurant and waved me over to a table for two at the back. He was a short, powerful man with a bull neck and a beer belly. He had a thick brush of salt-and-pepper hair that looked like he trimmed it himself—after he'd had a beer or two too many.

"Vito did a good job on you," Cancasci remarked after we'd exchanged introductions.

"I'm sure he'd be glad to hear you say that," I replied. "I'm sure he's proud of his work."

"You hungry?" he asked.

"I'm always hungry," I replied truthfully.

"You don't look it."

"You mean I look well fed?"

"No, just the opposite. You look thin, in good shape, not like you eat all the time."

"I don't eat all the time," I said. "That's why I'm always hungry."

Cancasci grinned. "Well, the food is pretty good here. It's gotta be, otherwise no one'd come into this crummy neighborhood to eat it." He motioned a waiter over. I asked for an order of gnocchi with gorgonzola sauce. Cancasci ordered in Italian. The waiter hurried back with hot and crusty rolls and a bottle of Valpolicella.

"So, you wanna know about the Azorinis?" began Detective Cancasci, ripping a piece of bread in two.

"They say you're the expert."

He nodded in acknowledgment. "You know how some people like to keep up on what Prince Charles and Princess Di are up to? Well, cops like to stay current on the crime family gossip."

"Sort of like 'Dynasty' with live ammunition," I quipped.

Cancasci laughed. The sound was somewhere between a gurgle and a snort.

"My hobby is the Azorini family," he said as he poured another glass of wine. It was fairly rough stuff, but the second glass went down easier than the first.

"But I gotta say I was surprised when you called and said you wanted to hear about the Azorinis, seeing as you've been Stephen Azorini's girlfriend pretty much since you were kids. I mean, what is this? You finally thinking of tying the knot, and you want to know what you're getting into?"

"I'm not Stephen Azorini's girlfriend," I replied. The term girlfriend implied a level of ease and intimacy that had never characterized Stephen's and my relationship.

"Then what are you? Your pictures are in the paper every coupla months, smiling at each other for the camera."

What were we? That was a good question. Old friends? A lawyer who slept with her biggest client? Busy yuppies engaged in recreational sex . . .

"I've known Stephen a long time," I replied. "It's true, we met in high school, at a dance. We dated for a while. But when we went away to school, I married somebody else."

"I didn't know you were divorced."

"I'm widowed. My husband died of cancer. Stephen was a good friend to me during my husband's illness. Now I'm one of the attorneys who represent his company, Azor Pharmaceuticals."

"The company that Edgar Eichel wants to take over. I know all about that little greaser."

"You mean Edgar Eichel?"

"My kid brother used to work for him, as a foreman down at his muffler plant. Eichel sold it off a coupla years ago, when he decided to make his move uptown. But my brother used to come home with stories. . . . Jesus, he said that Eichel was as crooked as they come. Used to have a big business buying defective parts from his suppliers—stuff they'd usually put in the dumpster. He'd get guys to stay after closing, weld the parts together, and sell the defective mufflers to countries in Latin America for double what the real thing would sell for here. My brother said Eichel'd do anything for a buck.''

"What other kinds of things would he do?" I asked, interested.

"When they were trying to unionize the plant, it got very, very rough. You know, these union guys aren't so gentle, but Eichel, he's got rough friends of his own. For a while there, down on Cicero by the plant, it was like a combat zone.''

"Did they ever unionize?"

"Nope.''

"Stephen will be thrilled to hear these stories.''

"Your friend Stephen grew up on stories like this. His old man and his friends wrote the textbook guys like Eichel learned from.''

"What do you mean?"

"I mean that Anthony Azorini might be some grayhaired captain of industry now, but ten, twenty years ago, he was one guy you didn't want to cross—not if you cared about not ending up dead. He is one crafty individual. Tough. Smart. Absolutely ruthless. Started as a small-time leg breaker. Now he's been to dinner at the White House—Nixon invited him. He's been courted by every politician in Illinois. Didn't your good friend Stephen ever tell you about how his old man got his start?"

"I guess he never got around to it.''

"Anthony Azorini started out working for a loan shark when he was just a young kid. He was a tough punk like a lot of other tough punks, but he was smarter than most and probably more vicious. There was a guy who owned a business. His name was Tony Bako, and he owned a little company called Bako Industries that made arcade games, you know, pinball machines and those scales that give you your weight and your fortune for a nickel. Anyway, the company was in trouble. I don't know what the problem was. Maybe Bako drank or gambled or he was just a crummy businessman. Well, genius that he is, he makes matters worse by borrowing from Anthony Azorini's boss, the loan shark. He gets in pretty deep. I don't know how he swung it, but somehow, Anthony Azorini tells the loan shark that he'll make good on Bako's loan if he lets Azorini have the business. Well, it doesn't surprise anybody now, but Anthony Azorini had the company in the black inside of six months.

"Now, of course, Bako Industries makes slots, video games, even exercise equipment. Big company, big profits. Sure, the poor schmuck who owns the corner tavern gets his legs broken if he doesn't put Bako pinball machines in his joint, but mostly the company's legit. That doesn't stop the old man from being a hood. He's just a hood in a limousine."

"Whatever happened to the guy?" I asked.

"What guy?"

"The guy who owed money to the loan shark. Bako."

"Dead," Cancasci said, his mouth full of bread, "definitely dead."

"Do you think that Anthony Azorini killed him?" I asked.

"Shit, yes," the detective replied. "One thing I'll say for your future in-laws, my dear, they're very good at killing."

"I didn't think Stephen's dad was that involved with organized crime," I said.

"The most successful mobsters are the most anonymous ones," Detective Cancasci instructed. "No one knows how much the old man has. He must be worth a billion bucks. But that's why he wants Stephen so bad—to make his money legitimate. His dream is to make the Azorini family the next Rockefellers—the next Millhollands maybe.''

''And Joey?''

''And Joey? The White Duke has all the old man's balls but none of his brains.''

''What did you call him?''

''The White Duke. That's Joey Azorini's street name.''

''Why do they call him that?''

''They say it's because he's the John Wayne of cocaine. Personally, I think that Joey made up the nickname himself.''

''So how long has Joey been dealing drugs?''

''I don't know, ten years, probably more. He timed it just right. Got into cocaine right when the market for the stuff went through the roof.''

''That should make his father proud,'' I commented.

''Nah, the old man's past that. He's made his money. Now he wants what money can't buy—respectability. The last ten years Azorini has been concentrating on building a legitimate business empire, letting the illegal stuff go.''

''Has he been turning over the illegal operations to Joey?'' I asked.

''I don't think so. I think Anthony Azorini is just dying for Stephen to come into the business. I think he'd just like Joey to fall off the face of the earth.''

''So what's Joey like?''

''Your face looks like it does, and you don't know what Joey Azorini is like? Joey is a psychotic punk. A loser. A sociopath. The worst kind of scum there is. If his old man wasn't always there to get him out of trouble, he'd be in jail for life or have bled to death in some alley gutted like a fish.''

"What do you mean, he's a sociopath?"

"You don't know what a sociopath is?"

"I know what a sociopath is. I want to know what Joey Azorini's done."

"Killed Manny Epstien by stuffing handfuls of cocaine down his throat. Shot Ed Gossett in the balls and then pissed on his face after Joey found him in bed with his girlfriend of the moment—at least that's the story Gossett tells, and I see no reason for him to lie. Killed his wife. Joey thinks with his dick, that's his problem."

"Did you say he killed his wife?" I asked.

"Yeah. That's the story. The way they tell it, Joey and his wife fought all the time—"

"What about?" I interrupted.

"All sorts of things, I guess. The wife did drugs, she was a slut, Joey cheated on her, rumor had it he was making moves on his teenage daughter. No shortage of material. Anyway, one day they have a fight and Joey's slapping the missus around, but things get a little out of hand and he cools her. She goes down the stairs on her head. Coroner rules it accidental, and a lot of cops in the ninth precinct buy powerboats that summer."

The waiter brought our dinners. Cancasci's was some sort of veal covered in a thick red sauce. He broke off a hunk of bread, dipped it in the sauce, and popped it into his mouth. I had trouble starting my meal. I was already struggling to digest too much information.

"So the rumor is that Joey killed his wife?"

Cancasci chewed and nodded.

"And that he had been making sexual advances toward his daughter?"

"That's the story. The mom found out he was making it with his daughter, she got pissed, and he bashed her.

What did Stephen tell you when he suddenly got custody of his thirteen-year-old niece?''

"He told me that his brother traveled a lot on business, and now that Gretchen's mother was dead, the family decided that Stephen would be best able to provide a stable home for her and make sure that her diabetes stayed under control," I responded.

"Aren't you going to eat your dinner?" Cancasci asked. "I thought you were always hungry."

"I seem to have lost my appetite," I replied.

I was drunk, and it was raining. After several half-hearted offers of a ride home and other comforts, Detective Cancasci ordered me an espresso and a taxi. I think I slept on the ride back to Hyde Park, because the next thing I remember was handing the driver a twenty dollar bill and stepping out into the icy drizzle and wet street trash in front of my apartment.

Fighting the temptation to just go to bed and forget Joey Azorini, Azor Pharmaceuticals, and the entire Azorini family, I went inside and put on a pot of coffee. I stripped out of my wet clothes, unceremoniously adding my mother's sweater and pants to the ever-growing pile of dirty laundry in the corner of the bathroom. I took a long, hot shower and changed into a pair of jeans and an old button-down shirt that had belonged to Russell.

I called Stephen at the office and got Richard Humanski. He told me to try Stephen at home, but all I got was the answering machine. I left a message. I called the number that Vince DeGenova had given me for Joey Azorini. I didn't even get a machine, just the empty ring of an unanswered phone.

I turned all the lights on in the apartment to help combat my sleepiness. I poured myself a cup of black coffee, stuffed Warren Zevon's "Excitable Boy" tape into the player, cranked up the volume, and parked myself and my briefcase at the kitchen table. Then I got to work.

The first thing I looked at was a fat manila envelope full of information on Joey Azorini that Cheryl had slipped into my briefcase. It was difficult to decipher. The copy was miserable, and the list of arrests was full of abbreviations that I had to guess at. Still, the list was pretty impressive, a constant stream of petty felonies and assaults, beginning as a juvenile and escalating to a couple of incidents of aggravated assault and a charge of manslaughter when he was seventeen. In every case the charges had been dropped.

There was a hiatus in the progression of arrests corresponding to the years that Stephen said Joey had been sent to New Jersey. But then the pattern picked up anew, like the thread of light that streams across an EKG machine, only the peaks were more jagged this time as his arrest record became peppered with drug-related arrests and weapons charges. Joey Azorini had been arrested more than two dozen times. He had never once spent the night in jail. He had never seen the inside of the courthouse. The matter of his wife's death did not appear at all.

I took out all the mug shots and lay them in a line along the length of the kitchen table in chronological order. There was the Joey Azorini album, from young punk to adult creep.

Next I pulled out what the paralegal had been able to pull together on the Azorinis on short notice. The file was slimmer than I had hoped but reinforced what Cancasci had said about a successful mobster being an anonymous one. At least half of the clippings were photos of Stephen and me at various charity functions with a line or two about how we "danced the night away to benefit such-and-such worthy cause." I had never seen half of them, but in all of the pictures Stephen looked wonderful, flashing eyes and wicked grin above the white collar of his tuxedo shirt and the black butterfly of his tie. I, on the other hand, looked like I had just run in from a tough day at the office. Even bad mothers are right a lot of the time.

The few articles there were in the pile chronicled Anthony Azorini's legitimate businesses. He may have started as a leg breaker and an extortionist, but the fact was that Bako Industries was now a Fortune 500 company operating in sixteen states and six foreign countries. I thought about the early Prescotts and Millhollands who had sold opium, busted unions, and smuggled rum. . . .

There were a number of articles on Azor Pharmaceuticals as well. Small clips from the *Wall Street Journal* when the company announced a new product, and several longer stories from around the time that Stephen had taken Azor public. At the bottom of the pile was the article that had run last year in *Business Week* with Stephen's picture on the cover. I placed the picture next to Joey's most recent mug shot, turned the tape over, and poured myself another cup of coffee.

I heard a key in the front door and saw Claudia, white-faced and exhausted, shuffle in. It was almost midnight. I turned down the stereo.

"How's it going?" I asked.

"Two ruptured appendices and a multiple stabbing with an ice pick since dinner. I feel like shit."

"You want some coffee?"

"I'll have a Coke. You're looking colorful," Claudia remarked as we went into the kitchen.

She examined my face under the light. "I do good work, though."

"Thanks," I said.

"How's Stephen doing?"

"I'm not sure. Things are getting weirder and weirder."

"Weirder than my finding you guys sitting in a room full of overturned furniture covered with blood?" Claudia demanded incredulously.

"That was just the beginning," I replied, and explained about Joey tendering his shares and my being railroaded into investigating Gretchen's death.

"I don't get it," Claudia remarked. "They found her in the woods somewhere hundreds of miles from here. Why would Stephen jump to the conclusion that someone she knew was involved, especially her father?"

"I gather that part of the agreement that grants Stephen Gretchen's custody stipulates that Joey only be allowed to see his daughter four times a year with another family member present. Stephen had begun to suspect that Joey had been calling Gretchen recently. But he was busy, and he figured if it didn't bother her . . . Joey also owns the piece of property where Gretchen's body was found."

"I still don't understand why that makes Stephen think that it was Joey who raped and killed her."

"I don't know whether he thinks it was Joey who killed her or that he was just responsible by convincing her to cut school and come up to meet him. The argument being that either on the way there or back she was abducted and murdered, but that if she were safely back at school, nothing would have happened to her. Ergo, Joey is responsible."

"I don't know," Claudia mused. "It sounds a little thin."

"Tonight I heard a rumor that Stephen was made Gretchen's guardian because Joey was sexually molesting her."

"Oh," Claudia said. "That would make Stephen's behavior make a lot more sense."

"Plus," I continued, "Gretchen's body was found Wednesday, but the pathologist puts her time of death at Monday morning. I asked the school why they didn't report her missing. The headmistress said that a man claiming to be Stephen Azorini called Monday morning and said that Gretchen was in the hospital. Nothing serious, but it would be a few days before she was back."

"Doesn't sound like a stranger then, does it?" commented Claudia with a look of mild distaste.

"It seems so disgusting and unbelievable to me," I replied with a shiver.

"You are suffering from incredulity caused by a too sheltered life," my roommate replied.

"Oh, come on," I said. "You have to admit that molesting your own daughter is pretty horrible."

"Horrible, but not uncommon," was Claudia's response. "You can't begin to imagine what goes on in the world. When I did my first ER rotation, I was just numb by the end of it.

"One night it was very late and very quiet. There were only three of us on duty. Two nurses and me. All women. All of a sudden, in come three people. A man, a woman, and a young girl. The woman has been badly beaten, the girl was twelve years old, nine months pregnant, and in labor. It took a while for us to figure out what was going on—finally the girl told us. The man was her father and the father of her baby. The woman who had been beaten was the man's wife and the girl's mother. On the way to the hospital, the woman had threatened to report the father for incest, so he beat her up. I mean, he *beat* her. I remember at the time we didn't know if she'd live."

"How awful," I said.

"We got the mother into surgery and the girl into delivery, and we were left with the man, sitting all by himself in the waiting room. We called him back and tried to get him to tell us what happened. The smug bastard made up some stuff about his wife and daughter both being sluts. They had gotten themselves knocked up and beaten up by their respective boyfriends.

"So the three of us went back to the nurses' station and steamed. There was nothing we could do unless the wife or the daughter would press charges, which seemed unlikely. The man was a monster, and he was sitting in the waiting room eating a bag of Doritos and drinking a Coke while his twelve-year-old daughter was giving birth and his wife was fighting for her life.

"I don't remember who came up with the idea, but somehow we started talking about killing him. It would be easy. Like I said, it was just the three of us. One of the nurses could call him back to talk again. I could inject him with a sedative before he knew what hit him. I could give him an overdose of phenobarb and sign the certificate as a ruptured appendix. No one would know. We would be doing the world a favor."

"And did you?" I asked softly.

"I've always regretted that we didn't" was her reply. "We discussed it quite realistically, but the truth is I think each of us was afraid of taking the responsibility. Taking a life was too far outside the range of what we felt we could do and still live with ourselves, no matter how we could rationalize it intellectually."

"Today one of the lawyers for the Azorini family said to me that each of us is capable of murder, given the right circumstances."

"Oh, I agree," Claudia said. "Like I said, I came very close that night."

"I'm surprised this is the first time you told me about it," I remarked.

"It happened while you were in Kansas City on that really long case. By the time you came back, it had lost its urgency. So," she said, changing the subject, "how are you going to find out what happened to Gretchen Azorini?"

"This afternoon I hired a private detective, and I had dinner tonight with a Chicago police detective—"

"A cop and a private eye?" Her question was cut short by the sharp buzz of the doorbell. We both looked at the clock. It was after 11:00.

"You expecting anybody?" I asked.

"No, are you?"

"No."

I went to the intercom panel in the front hall.

"Who is it?" I inquired in a voice meant to instill second thoughts in would-be burglars and rapists.

"University of Chicago police. We've got a guy out here who says that he's a friend of yours. Says his name's Stephen."

"Stephen who?" I bellowed into the intercom panel.

"He won't say."

"What does he look like?" I demanded.

"Really big, way over six feet, black hair . . ."

I buzzed them in and met them in the building vestibule. Sure enough, it was a campus cop and Stephen Azorini. Stephen was dressed in a business suit, no topcoat, even though it was only in the thirties out. He was soaking wet.

"Stephen!" I exclaimed. "What happened?"

"Nothing," he answered tonelessly. "I needed to take a walk. Think. I didn't realize it was raining."

"I found him walking by himself down Drexel," explained the cop incredulously. "I mean, I know he's a big man, but that's not a neighborhood that I'd ever walk alone, and I carry a gun. At first I thought he must be drunk, but I don't smell any alcohol. He didn't have any I.D. on him, so I was going to take him into the station. That's when he suggested we stop here. Said you'd vouch for him."

"Of course I will," I replied briskly. "I appreciate your trouble, Officer. My friend has recently had a death in the family, and I think the stress has just gotten the better of his judgment."

"You'll make sure he'll get home alright?" inquired the policeman.

"I'll take care of him. Thank you. You've been very kind."

I pulled Stephen into my apartment and closed the door. He was wearing a white shirt and what had, earlier in the day, been an expensive suit. His shirt was so wet it was transparent and clung to his chest. His hair was soaked and curly from the rain. His lips were blue, and he was shaking. The bandage over the stitches in his forehead was soaking wet and half off so that it flopped uselessly to one side, exposing the stitches. No wonder the cop stopped him.

Claudia peered in anxiously, but I waved her away. I thought Stephen was probably embarrassed enough.

"Are you okay?" I asked.

"A little cold," Stephen mumbled, shaking violently. "I guess it was pretty stupid to just walk out without a coat, but I wasn't thinking."

''That's okay. What you need is to get out of your wet clothes and have something hot to drink.''

I led him into the bathroom and turned the shower on full hot. The room filled with steam while I went into the kitchen to put on the kettle for tea. I came back with a cup only to find Stephen standing where I'd left him, still fiddling clumsily with the buttons of his shirt.

I undressed him carefully, like a child, and pushed him into the shower. I sat on the toilet seat and watched through the frosted glass as he stood beneath the spray. I worried about his stitches getting wet.

Eventually he shook his head and ran his fingers through his hair. He rubbed his face in his hands and turned off the water. I stood outside the shower door and held a towel for him, feeling awkward. Strange as it may seem, we had never reached the level of familiarity where casual nakedness was the norm.

He pulled me toward him. I was startled by his quickness, the intensity of his desire, the ferociousness of his need, and the speed with which mine rose to meet it. His hands, his lips, were everywhere—under the loose cotton of my shirt, brushing my bruises, twisting my hair away from my neck, lifting me off my feet and carrying me into my room, laying me gently on the rumpled linens of my unmade bed.

From the very first time there was an intensity between Stephen and me. During the day we were cordial, we were friends, an important businessman and his lawyer, an heiress and her handsome escort at a society event, two old friends who were not always close but had shared a lot of history.

In bed it was different. In bed it was all heat and sweat and desire.

That night had an urgency all its own. We made long and desperate love and then, when I had finally wrested myself free and begun to doze, Stephen turned and reached for me again. By the time we both fell exhaustedly to sleep, pale light was leaking in around the edges of the curtain, falling in weak pools onto the tangle of my discarded clothing on the floor.

CHAPTER
11

I woke tender and trembling from the past night's enterprise. Stephen was already gone. It was 9:00 A.M. Guilty, I realized I had no time for indulgences like last night.

I picked up my shirt from the floor and went into the kitchen. Claudia, who could stitch together the severed ends of an infant's artery, found that simple things, like making breakfast, eluded her. She stood scraping the charred edges of her smoking toast into the sink.

"What are you still doing home? I thought you'd have been at the office hours ago," Claudia asked. She was wearing the top half of a set of surgical scrubs meant for someone much larger, and nothing else. Across the front it read Property of the University of Chicago Hospitals. I realized it had probably been two years since I'd seen her in anything but surgical green.

"Have you seen Stephen?" I asked.

"No. I've been up about a half an hour. He must have gone before I got up."

"I wanted to talk to him."

"Well, I'm leaving, too," Claudia announced.

"I thought you just got off your rotation," I commented.

"Just going in for a little cadaver practice," she replied.

"Don't you get enough practice cutting up live people?" I asked.

"You know what they say, 'a woman's work is never done . . .' "

Before I left I called Joey Azorini. I tried the number that DeGenova had given me for his apartment first. I let it ring for a long time. Just as I was about to hang up and try another of the numbers, a groggy voice answered.

"Whaddya want?" demanded Joey Azorini unpleasantly. I guessed that drug barons worked by night and slept during the day. Like bats.

"This is Kate Millholland," I said, "I need to talk to you."

"So talk."

"Not on the phone. I want to meet in person."

He took such a long time to answer I thought he might have fallen back asleep.

"I'll be at the wake tonight. Meet me there. I'll fix someplace private where we can talk."

"I'll see you then," I replied, suppressing an inward shiver at the thought of being anywhere private with Joey.

The women in my mother's family had always gone to Foxcroft, a horsey boarding school in Virginia where the children of the very, very rich were sent to have their characters developed in the Spartan tradition of the St. Midas schools—conveniently out of their parents' way.

But my father, whose family tradition had run along the same lines, had cried himself to sleep every night for four years at Andover. It was he, in a rare incidence of defiance against my mother, who refused to allow any of us to be sent away to boarding school. Mother, who felt that this was a shocking victory of sentiment (which she had little use for) over principle, reluctantly agreed to Chelsea Hall for my sister and me and Country Day for my brother. Both schools offered the option of boarding during the week.

Chelsea Hall School for Girls was a series of gloomy Tudor buildings set in the damp woods about twenty minutes northwest of Lake Forest. The campus was set well back from the road, accessible only by one arched gate and completely encircled by an eight-foot stone wall.

Every generation of girls wove their own fable about the wall. One said that the school had once been an insane asylum and the wall had been erected to prevent the inmates' escape. Another held that it had once been the compound of a rich and eccentric scientist who had kept wild animals and allowed them to roam free around the grounds within the confines of the wall. I suspected that the wall had been built in the days of cheap labor and even cheaper limestone to keep out poachers, prowlers, and would-be boyfriends.

As I parked my car in the visitors' lot and made my way up the wide stone steps to the massive oak door of the main classroom building, I realized that I always dreaded returning to my alma mater. I had done my time there with loathing and had left its finishing school claustrophobia with relief.

I always felt strange coming back to the place as a grown-up, in the protective armor of my high heels and business suit. The vaulted ceilings, the oak beams, the well-scrubbed girls with their starched white blouses and their dark green kilts—the school never changed.

It still gave me the creeps.

The headmistress's name was Mrs. Bigham. She was a poised woman with short blond hair, not many years older than myself. When I was a student, the headmaster had been a portly wheezer named Fitzroy with a sneaky temper and a secret drinking problem.

But while the occupant had changed radically, the head of the school's office hadn't altered one bit. There was still the same ominous paneling, the same stern portraits of past benefactors, the same leather couch on which I had perched miserably more times than I cared to remember to listen to clipped lectures about standards of behavior and living up to one's station in life.

Mrs. Bigham informed me that my little sister was in gym class and would meet me after she had showered and changed. In about forty minutes.

"I've also arranged for you to see Mrs. McMurtry, Gretchen's class adviser," Mrs. Bigham said cordially. "I know you'd asked to see our school psychologist, Caroline Meek, but when I checked our records I don't think that Gretchen and Dr. Meek had ever even met. I thought you might prefer to speak to someone who knew Gretchen well."

"Thank you," I replied. "I was wondering if you might be able to answer a few questions for me. We're very curious about the phone call you received telling the school that Gretchen was in the hospital."

Mrs. Bigham folded her hands on top of her desk and fixed me with a steady and inquiring gaze. It had the same effect on me it undoubtedly had on the girls in her charge—it made me want to explain myself.

"It wasn't Dr. Azorini who called," I began. "And Gretchen didn't die in the hospital."

"I gathered as much," replied Mrs. Bigham.

"Until Sunday night she was staying with Beth at my parents' house in Lake Forest."

"And then?"

"And then we don't know. That's one of the reasons I want to talk to my sister. Gretchen's body was found on Wednesday, but the coroner says that she probably died sometime late Monday morning."

"And in the meantime, nobody looked for her because everyone thought she was in the hospital," mused Mrs. Bigham.

"You thought she was in the hospital. Dr. Azorini thought she was in school. The first inkling he had that she was missing was when the police contacted him Wednesday night."

"How did she die then?" the headmistress asked softly.

"They think she was strangled. They're waiting for some test results to come back before they rule on a cause of death. I'd rather you not tell anyone until the family knows for sure."

"Oh, how horrible."

"What was Gretchen like, Mrs. Bigham?" I asked. "Was she in any kind of personal trouble? Do you know who she was hanging out with?"

"Gretchen?" Mrs. Bigham echoed with a sigh. "The only person Gretchen hung out with was your sister. She was an unbelievably quiet girl. Very closed with adults. A good student, always polite, but she kept her distance from everyone, faculty and students alike. I'm sure it's no different from when you were here. In every class there is the fast set, the girls who experiment . . ."

"You mean with drugs," I said.

"With drugs, with sex . . ." answered the headmistress. "I would never put Gretchen or your sister in that group. Those girls would never even condescend to speak to them.''

''Because they're so uncool.''

''Gretchen was uncool. Your sister is, well, she's just too unhappy for them. Too moody. But just because Gretchen didn't hang with that crowd doesn't mean that she didn't do what they did. We had a girl here my first year as headmistress. Mary Holzheimer. A very quiet, plain girl, much like Gretchen. An excellent student and a championship rider. She had to leave school in her sophomore year because she was pregnant. She'd been sleeping with a boy she'd met working in the stables. It came as a complete shock to everyone.

''I've worked with adolescents for nearly twenty years,'' Mrs. Bigham continued, ''and the one thing it's taught me is that teenagers create their own closed society. They do not let adults in.''

I took Beth back to the dormitory to talk. I told myself that she would probably be more open with me in a less authoritarian setting than the headmistress's office. But the truth of the matter was that the place was getting on my nerves.

We walked, coatless, across the wide stone terrace and over the frozen athletic fields toward the dormitory. In the warm days of spring and fall, Friday lunch was served on the terrace to the whole school. Everyone from jaded seniors to fresh-faced primes sprawled on the grass, eating bacon, lettuce, and tomato sandwiches and warm brownies, and drinking milk from the carton—a weekly reprieve from the etiquette imposed in the dining room. But today the grass was crisp with frost, and the only witnesses to our chilly passage were a flock of enormous crows who flapped away in protest as we approached.

The dorm was deserted and possessed with a queer, after-hours stillness. The ticking of the grandfather clock in the front hall seemed unnaturally loud. There was a chubby little Christmas tree decorated with ornaments that looked suspiciously like the ones we'd had when I stayed in the dorm.

I led my little sister into the morning room, a pretty alcove with a view of a half-frozen creek through French windows. Beth sat sullenly in a wicker chair, her face half-hidden by a hank of unwashed chestnut hair. Her uniform looked like she'd slept in it. She probably had.

"How are you doing?" I asked.

"You don't give a fuck," she replied matter-of-factly. Her choice of language, especially in that setting, was meant to shock.

"I'm wondering whether you do," I replied, having just that moment decided to take a different tack.

"What do you mean?" Beth snapped.

"I just wonder whether you care how your best friend died, or whether you're too into your own little miseries to care about anybody else."

"How dare you—" she began, pulling the hair trigger on the dark emotions that always roiled for her close at hand.

"Save it for Dr. Weingart," I replied, remaining deliberately calm. "He gets paid to listen to that shit. This isn't about you. This is about Gretchen. She was murdered a week ago today. I need to know what you can tell me. If you don't want to that's fine. The police will be here in my place, and I know for a fact that they don't care about your feelings or anybody else's for that matter."

Beth grew pale and very still, and I worried that I had gone too far. Her eyes filled with tears.

"The police think that maybe it was a stranger abduction, someone whom she didn't know who just chose her at random. They don't know about the phone call to the school on Monday.''

"Phone call?" Beth sobbed weakly.

"The man who called and said he was Stephen Azorini and that Gretchen was in the hospital for a couple of days. You had to know. You're the first person who would have wondered where she was. I bet she didn't even go back to school on Sunday," I said, venturing a bold guess.

"No, she didn't," whispered Beth, crying. "She dropped me off at the dorm a little after six. We knew Mrs. Milnickel would be glued to 'Sixty Minutes.' I just signed the two of us in."

"Where was she going?" I asked. "To meet her father?"

"Her father?" was Beth's startled response. "No, she had a boyfriend."

"A boyfriend! What's his name?"

"I don't know."

"Oh, Beth, I'm not in the mood for this. Just tell me his name."

"Honest. I don't know. She'd never tell me."

"There isn't a teenage girl born who could have a boyfriend and not tell her best friend all about him."

"She did tell me all about him," Beth answered defensively. "She just didn't tell me his name. She said she couldn't. It was too dangerous. She said if her family knew about him, they'd have him killed."

"You can't be serious," I said. But I could tell from the look on my sister's face that she was.

"So what do you know about him?" I asked.

"That he was nice, handsome, rich. He was older than her."

"How much older?"

"I don't know. I think he'd already graduated from college."

"Where did she meet him?"

"I think she knew him from before she came here."

"From before she was thirteen?"

"I guess so."

"So what else do you know about him?"

"He had a real important job, and he traveled a lot, so they couldn't see each other very often. That and the fact that it had to be a secret. A lot of times they only saw each other every month or so."

"Did he do drugs?" I asked.

"Drugs? No way. He was way too mature. He took her to restaurants. They drank wine," replied my sister, clearly envious of her friend's mysterious romance.

"Did he ever call her?"

"Sometimes. We're not allowed to have phones in the dorm, and she was always too scared to use the community phone, so a lot of the time she called him from my house on the weekends."

"Do you know where he was when she called him?"

"I don't know. Different places. I told you, he traveled a lot."

"Did she call collect?" I asked, vainly hoping for some clue from the phone records.

"No. He gave her his phone credit card number so that she could always call him." Beth was obviously impressed.

"Did you ever hear them talk on the phone?"

"I never eavesdropped or anything, but yeah, sometimes she'd talk to him while I was in the room."

"What did they talk about?"

"Nothing much. How are you, I really miss you. It was very romantic. They even had pet names for each other. She called him 'Papa Bear' and he called her 'Baby Bear.' ''

"Jesus Christ," I said silently to myself. Out loud I said, "And Gretchen and her boyfriend arranged that she would pretend to be in the hospital for a couple of days so they could spend time together? Weren't they worried that she'd get caught?"

"It didn't really matter if they got caught," Beth replied. "They were running away to get married. All that mattered was that no one found out in time to stop them."

I only spent a few minutes with Gretchen's class adviser, Mrs. McMurtry. She was a prim woman in her fifties who wore a crisp white blouse, a watch-plaid kilt and flats. She carried a purse that looked for all the world like a tiny picnic basket painted to look like an even smaller New England town. She seemed truly shocked and grieved by Gretchen's death and was eager to cooperate. However, within the first five minutes of conversation it became glaringly obvious that no teenager, not even a dorky one, would ever confide anything in Mrs. McMurtry.

Her portrait of Gretchen was not surprising, though it stood in stark contrast to the scenario my sister presented of Gretchen running off to elope.

According to Mrs. McMurtry, Gretchen was a quiet girl, very tidy and careful about her appearance. Not like some of the girls who'd go all day with their shoes untied or use a stapler to fix the hem of their uniform. Very responsible about her diabetes, too. Meticulous about her diet, never had to be reminded about checking her blood sugar or taking her insulin. The school nurse often commented on her maturity.

She never spoke in class meetings, participated in no

extracurricular activities except the business and investment club, which generally attracted the participation of only one or two girls each year.

Gretchen was an excellent, but not a natural, student. She was always on the honor roll but not without a great deal of hard work. According to Mrs. McMurtry, Gretchen had taken diligent notes in class, then copied them over by hand, and then summarized them. Finally, she typed the notes and the summaries to study for the test. Mrs. McMurtry had obviously approved. No wonder most of the girls in the class wouldn't have spoken to Gretchen. . . .

I stopped back at the headmistress's office on my way out to thank her for her help.

"I'm afraid I told Beth what the police suspect. I told her not to tell anyone until we know for sure. You still might want to reinforce the message."

"I'll speak to her. I'd like the excuse to talk to her anyway. I must confess I'm more than a little bit concerned about your sister."

"I'm not surprised. From what everyone tells me, Gretchen was her only friend. I confess that always surprised me. They seemed to have so little in common."

"They were the two outcasts in their class," answered Mrs. Bigham frankly. "I worry about Beth now that her friend is gone. I have spoken to your mother briefly on the phone and tried to urge her to come in and speak to me and the school psychologist. I think we all need to work together to help Beth through this. Unfortunately, your parents seem to be very busy people." The rebuke was polite but unmistakable.

"My parents have always dealt with misfortune by ignoring it," I said. I didn't tell her that three days after my brother's funeral my mother and father went island hopping in the Caribbean. Mother honestly thought that not changing their vacation plans was an act of stoicism.

"I'll try to speak to her about it, and I'll try to check up on Beth myself," I said instead. "There is also one other thing I wanted to ask you. Do you think I could look through Gretchen's room in the dorm? Maybe there is something there that could shed some light on what happened to her."

"I'm afraid I've already had Mrs. Milnickel and Mr. Lawicki, the janitor, pack it all into boxes over the weekend. We felt that it was healthier for the girls staying in the dorm than leaving things as they were. I thought that when Dr. Azorini was ready, I'd approach him about having her things sent to him."

"I'd be glad to bring them to him myself," I offered.

Russell and I had purchased a bright red Volvo station wagon right before we were married. The plan had been to fill it with kids. I pulled it up to the service entrance of my old school while the janitor loaded up the back with box after box containing things that had belonged to Gretchen Azorini.

I spent the drive back to town trying to remember what it was like to be a teenager and not having any particular success. My adolescence had been a turbulent blur. The things I recalled most, my brother's suicide, battles with my mother, seemed indigenous to my teenage years. I didn't feel comfortable extrapolating from them to Beth, much less to Gretchen.

Still, I couldn't help but wonder about what Beth had told me about Gretchen and her boyfriend. The story was so improbable. I wondered whether it was all a figment of a lonely teenager's imagination. A rich, sophisticated lover with whom to drink wine. Gretchen's assertion that his identity had to be kept secret because her family would have him killed seemed especially like it had been plucked directly from Romeo and Juliet.

But what if that lover were her father? What if the story of the secret lover were in some way a rationalization of that relationship? What if it were just a way for Gretchen to be able to talk about it in some way? Could Joey have lured her up there on some other pretext, made physical advances, and been rebuffed?

I parked my Volvo, crammed with boxes, in the underground garage at the office and slipped the attendant my last five dollar bill to keep an eye on it. Then I joined a covey of gaily chatting secretaries carrying bags from McDonald's in the elevator and rode up to the forty-second floor suddenly feeling weak from hunger and craving French fries. I got back to my little piece of Callahan Ross to find Cheryl, Tucker Sweet, and lunch waiting for me, in that order.

"How did you know I'd be back and I'd be starved?" I asked Cheryl, swiping a French fry smothered with cheddar cheese from her desk.

"Hey, those are mine," she replied with a token swat at my hand. "I called Chelsea Hall and had the headmistress's secretary call me when you left. I knew you'd be hungry because if I don't feed you, you don't eat."

"Is that true?" Tucker asked.

"Well . . ." I stalled.

"Did you have breakfast this morning?" Cheryl demanded.

"Does coffee count?" I asked.

"I rest my case," Cheryl replied, and began unpacking the rest of my lunch. Two grilled Polish sausages with onions, an order of cheddar fries, a chocolate milk shake, and some onion rings.

"How do you stay so thin eating this stuff?" asked Tucker, who was very careful about his diet.

"When you only eat four times a week, you can eat whatever you want," I joked.

"Well, I hope this doesn't put you over your quota, because I dropped in to invite you to dinner. I thought we might grab a quiet bite somewhere before the wake this evening. Then we could head over there together."

"That would be nice. How about going to the University Club?" I said, suggesting my club, much more famous for its squash courts than its dining room. "Monday night, rib special . . ."

"Please, be serious," Tucker replied with mock alarm. "I've made reservations for us at seven at the Mid-Town." The Mid-Town was one of Tucker's many clubs, this one for rich men who wanted to eat their lunch or dinner in the company of other rich men. The chef was Swiss and the wine cellar renowned.

"Seven o'clock then," I replied with a smile. "I'll meet you there."

We said our good-byes, and I retired to the privacy of my office to eat my lunch. A Swiss chef was one thing. A real Chicago Polish sausage was quite another. The guys at the Mid-Town Club didn't know what they were missing.

I was noisily sucking up the last of my milk shake when Elliott Abelman called to report in from Wisconsin.

"Hi, there," I greeted him, cheered by my lunch.

"Well, hi," he replied. "You sound cheerful. Have you solved the mystery?"

"Are you kidding? It's only gotten more mysterious."

"You want to tell me about it?"

"No. You first, what have you come up with?"

"I've just gotten up here. This place is a bitch to get to. I'm at the sheriff's office, waiting for Whittle. But my guess is he's going to make me wait for a while. It seems the Azorini family has a lot of political clout, and they're not afraid to use it. I heard that Sheriff Whittle received a phone call from the governor himself telling him to mind his p's and q's and stay away from the press. Whittle is pretty steamed.''

"Great."

"But some of my operatives have reported in. So far it seems likely that Joey was not in Colombia as he claims to have been. It's true that he was in Latin America on a buying trip for a couple of days, but we've turned up three disinterested witnesses who say that he made the rounds on Rush Street that Saturday night. Two waiters say he closed down Donatello's at four A.M. Sunday, which, if you calculate flying times, etc., would give him just enough time to make it to O'Hare, fly to Colombia, turn around and fly back, provided it was a private plane. The commercial flights all leave late in the day, and there'd be no way he could make a round trip.''

"Plus, why would he fly to Colombia and then just turn around and fly back?''

"Why would he lie about where he was on Monday?''

"Because he's hiding something.''

"So what's he hiding?''

"You're the detective, you tell me.''

"We're working on it. Of course, for every witness I have who claims to have seen him in Chicago, I have a dozen wise guys swearing on their mother's rosaries that they were on the plane back with him. I figure Joey paid them off, but again the question presents itself—why bother?''

"The problem,'' I mused, "is that Joey has a credibility problem. If he was having an audience with the Pope, nobody would believe him.''

"Well, I'm still checking out the Colombian angle. I've got operatives checking passenger and customs lists and showing Joey's picture—Vito's, too. It's more likely that he'll be the one that people will remember.''

"What's to say he wouldn't have left Vito at home?''

"Word is that Joey doesn't go to the john without Vito. Anyway, you can be pretty certain that Joey is not going to be happy about all the questions we've been asking.''

"Tough,'' I said.

"You've already had him mad at you once and look at what it got you.''

"He wasn't mad at me, he was mad at his brother. I was just an innocent bystander.''

"If that's what innocent bystanders look like, you might want to think about what happens to guys who really get in Joey's way.''

"Is that a warning?'' I asked.

"Just some unsolicited professional advice,'' Elliott replied. "I'm sure you're smart, and you obviously have guts, but I don't think you've had a lot of experience dealing with guys like Joey and Vito.''

To change the subject I told him about my talk with my little sister.

"So she had a boyfriend,'' he said. "Do you think it was Daddy?''

"I don't know,'' I replied.

"Well, we knew the little lady had a secret life. It'll just take some doing to find out what she was into.''

"I don't have the first idea how even to begin,'' I lamented.

"I'll get started up here. It's more than a coincidence that her father owns property in this neck of the woods.

Maybe she knew someone from the area from when she lived with her father. I'll ask around.''

"Good. I'm going to talk privately with Joey Azorini tonight," I reported.

"What are you going to ask him?"

"Whether he was molesting his daughter, what he was really doing on Monday morning. You know, the obvious.''

"Promise me you'll be careful."

"I promise," I said.

Leon, the mail clerk, loaded all the boxes from the back of my car onto a dolly and brought them up to the big conference room on the forty-third floor. He deposited them silently in one corner, slit the tops open with his pocketknife, and then retreated, pulling the double mahogany doors closed behind him.

I shook off my reluctance for the task with an effort and forced myself to begin my grim sorting. There were nine boxes. I chose the one closest to me and dumped it out on the conference table.

At the end of an hour I had made one hell of a mess. The only things I had managed to learn were that Stephen had been very generous with his ward's clothing allowance and that Gretchen had, indeed, been compulsive as well as compulsively neat. She owned every item in the J.Crew catalogue in every color. There were T-shirts, polo shirts, rugby shirts, cotton sweaters, cashmere sweaters, jeans, khakis, cords, boxers, skirts, shorts, sweats, and sweat shirts, all folded with military precision and arranged by color.

Guttman opened the conference room door.

"Bringing your laundry to the office?" he asked with his unerring instinct for saying exactly the wrong thing.

"From Gretchen Azorini's room at Chelsea Hall," I

replied, wishing I had been able to think of a snappier comeback than the truth.

"I came to see if you could spare an hour for Bill Faller. He's working with Morgan Stanley to prepare an independent valuation that Stephen can take to the bankers if he has to leverage assets to raise the money to keep fighting Eichel if this thing drags on. You're probably the most hands-on expert when it comes to the financial implications of Azor's antitakeover provisions. I told him I'd ask if you would be able to bring him up to speed."

I should have been the one presenting the documentation to Morgan Stanley; instead, Bill Faller was doing my job, and I was sifting through underwear.

"Sure," I replied, "but I thought Stephen was leaning away from leveraging corporate assets. He told me he didn't want to take on a crippling debt load to fight off Eichel."

"We'll see how he feels when it comes time to make that decision. For now, I think an independent valuation could have many uses. Maybe they'll conclude that Eichel's asking price is much too low. Maybe it'll help us convince some of the pension funds that hold big blocks of stock that they're better off hanging on to it."

In any type of merger, whether it be hostile or friendly, the central issue is always: What is the company worth? Valuation of something as complex as a multimillion dollar corporation, especially a pharmaceutical corporation on the verge of a major research breakthrough, was open to a wide range of interpretations. There was book value, value based or multiple of earnings valuation, discounted cash-flow analysis and, of course, the most important valuation, the value that Edgar Eichel had placed on the company when he'd made his offer of forty-eight dollars a share.

An independent valuation was always a gamble. If the conclusions suggested that Azor was worth substantially more than forty-eight dollars a share, that added ammunition to the defensive strategy against Eichel (at least until he upped his offer). If the valuation came in lower than what Eichel was offering, it could potentially do us a lot of damage.

"So what's the status of your investigation?" Guttman asked, taking a seat and stretching out his legs so that his skinny ankles protruded absurdly above his heavy wing tips.

"It's hard to tell," I replied, not really wanting to get into it. "I've hired a private detective. We're trying to find out what happened to Gretchen Azorini. I have no way of knowing whether we'll be able to find out whether Joey was involved or not—especially given the time constraints. How important do you think Joey's shares will be?"

"This is going to be very, very close. Eichel has filed to have the ESOP shares tendered." The ESOP was Azor Pharmaceuticals' Employee Stock Option Plan, under which Azor employees were granted company stock as part and parcel of their compensation package. There had been a trend in recent years for the courts to rule that, based on the ESOP's fiduciary duty to the employees, the plan had to tender their shares to a raider if the price offered was at a substantial premium over the price quoted in the public stock market.

"We're going to fight like hell," continued Guttman, "and maybe we'll get lucky. Who knows? The latest Thirteen-D amendment shows about thirty percent of shares tendered. The guess is that most of that is pension funds, but Eichel is courting the scientists who own big blocks of shares very fiercely. It's just a crap shoot. Some of those shares might be pulled out of the pool before it closes, other shareholders might be waiting until closer to the end of the offering period in the hopes that Eichel is going to up his price. We've had Tucker Sweet buy a couple of shares of EIC, Eichel's holding company, so that we have access to whatever information he's sending out to his shareholders and, of course, we're keeping tabs on what Eichel is saying to ours. Tucker plays polo, of all things, with Bud Lipson, who's on Eichel's board, and he's been trying to establish a back channel on what Eichel's intentions are.

"Gould's been trawling for a white knight, possibly a cosmetic or hospital supply company that might want to expand into pharmaceutical." A white knight is a person or, more often, a company that comes in and rescues a takeover target by negotiating a more palatable deal than that offered by the hostile raider, usually one that keeps existing management in place. "Merridan, the Swiss pharmaceutical giant, has expressed some interest, but I'm afraid there'd be too many antitrust obstacles."

"So on a scale of one to ten," I asked, "how are we doing?"

"Four and a half," replied Guttman as my stomach churned. I was used to pressure; God knows, you don't survive in M&A unless you thrive on it. But this sort of pressure, a multimillion dollar deal riding on my being able to accomplish an impossible task that I had no skills for, was different from the normal guerrilla warfare between companies. I had agreed to tackle a longshot investigation, but I had never intended it to become Azor's principal defense.

"So you can give Faller an hour?"

"I'll try," I replied. "Have him call Cheryl."

"Your face is looking better," Guttman said as he rose to go.

"Thanks."

"You should take a picture so you'll remember what you looked like."

As the door shut behind him I reflected on the fact that that was just the sort of stupid and incomprehensible comment that set Guttman apart from normal men.

I buzzed Cheryl to bring me some coffee. I needed to wash away the bitter taste that these encounters with Guttman were leaving in my mouth of late. When she came back I told her that when Bill Faller called she should try to schedule a meeting for first thing in the morning, and to try to track down Stephen Azorini and tell him I would see him at the funeral home later that evening. I also gave her my ATM card and sent her to the cash station in the lobby to get me some money. Then I got back to the boxes.

The picture of the dead girl that emerged as I sorted raised more questions in my mind than it answered. Her clothes were all unisex and casual. Her panties looked like they'd been pressed and had been elaborately folded into meticulous squares. There were no party clothes, nothing that suggested it would be worn on a date. There was no makeup; her sponge bag contained a white plastic soap case with a bar of Ivory soap inside, toothbrush, dental floss, a box of baking soda, a bottle of baby shampoo, a container of baby powder, a tube of hand cream, and a disposable razor. The sight of her brush, with its tangle of long red strands between the bristles, shook me to the core. I felt like I was committing the most ghoulish invasion of privacy.

I opened up another box.

This one looked as though it had come from her desk.

There were pencils, erasers, a wooden ruler, two very high-tech HP calculators, a heart-shaped tin stamped with yellow rosebuds that contained paper clips, three markers—the kind used to highlight textbooks—all chartreuse, 3 x 5 note cards, a packet of notebook paper, three empty spiral notebooks. There was a steno pad that looked like it contained notes for a business course and a small spiral notebook that contained all of her homework assignments for the preceding semester. Each assignment had been ticked off in chartreuse marker, presumably after it had been completed. There were six other identical notebooks in a neat stack wrapped in a rubber band—one for each semester she'd been at Chelsea Hall. She had the loopy handwriting of a schoolgirl, very neat, and she had dotted her i's with little circles.

There was a calendar, a big one, spiral bound at the top, with a different photograph of teddy bears, seasonally attired, for each month. I sat down in one of the leather swivel chairs that ringed the conference table and studied it with interest.

I opened the calendar to November and looked immediately at the twenty-seventh, the date of her death. The box was empty. I looked at the boxes for the preceding days. Friday was marked "trigonometry test" in her tiny and meticulous script. For Saturday she had noted "weekend at Beth's." On Sunday the box was blank again.

I turned back to November and went methodically backward. There were no mysterious entries, only notes like "Stephen's for weekend," "business club meeting," "English paper due." At least once every month, often twice, there appeared an appointment with "Dr. Lawrence," who I assumed must be her endrocrinologist. She had seen him on November 2.

I flipped forward to December. The only date of any interest was December 22, which was marked "Richard's birthday." I made another note and set the calendar aside.

There were a couple of photos in the box, in Lucite frames, that must have stood on her desk. One of Stephen, another of a pretty woman—probably her mother—and a much younger Gretchen. A snapshot of Gretchen and Beth, this time both in their ugly Chelsea uniforms, sitting next to each other and eating popcorn in the dorm living room. The last framed photo was bigger than the others and struck me as a little curious. It was a group portrait of all of the directors of Azor Pharmaceuticals. I recognized it from the company's most recent annual report. Indeed, it looked as though it had been cut out of the report and framed. It showed Stephen and the six corporate directors standing on the front steps of the new Hematology Research Facility. I remember Richard complaining about Stephen's incredible pickiness. They had originally taken the board photo at one of the meetings, all of them just standing in front of the Azor corporate logo in the lobby of the main office, but Stephen had vetoed all of those shots when he'd seen the proofs. He was at least a head taller than anyone else in the photo and complained that it looked awful. Hence, Richard had to schedule a retake—this time with the group arrayed on different stairs. I knew that Gretchen had been very interested in the company. Stephen had been proud of her desire to someday join him at Azor. Still, it seemed a strange thing for the keeper of the teddy bear calendar to have on her desk.

There were other things in the box that I pulled out one by one and set on the conference table. A music box with tiny teddy bears dressed as ballet dancers that twirled to the tinny strains of *Swan Lake*. A small electric teapot for heating hot water; two pink mugs; tea bags; a china box with a picture of a teddy bear on skis painted on the top, which contained packets of Sweet'n Low; nine packs of sugarless gum; a box of sanitary napkins; rubber bands; a box of stationery with, surprise, surprise, an Edwardian teddy bear in the corner; a rubber ducky; Band-Aids; a bottle of jasmine-scented bath oil, unopened; an expensive 35 mm camera; more Band-Aids; film; a small leather case containing nail scissors and emery boards; a jar of Vaseline; a box of Kleenex; a radio alarm clock; batteries; and a small, pink, heart-shaped pillow.

The next box was filled with the paraphernalia of a diabetic. Blood testing kit, a bottle filled with strips used to test urine for sugar, syringes, needles, cotton balls, little foil packets that contained squares of cotton soaked in alcohol, which I presumed she used to clean the skin before injecting herself with insulin. There was a neat stack of small spiral notebooks in which she had recorded her blood sugar level each of the six times she checked it every day going back a year and a half. There was also a tube of K-Y jelly, and a three-month supply of birth control pills. The doctor's name on the prescription label was Conlin. I wrote it down.

The last box was of school work. Textbooks, notebooks, returned tests. I flipped through, casually noting that Gretchen appeared to have been taking trignometry, French, chemistry, and English this term. Her grades were good, especially in chemistry and trig. In English they were reading Jane Eyre. She had gotten as far as chapter 12—that's where the chartreuse highlighting stopped.

At the bottom of the box there was a manila envelope. On the front in labored and shaking print was written: "I found this between the mattress and the box spring—K. Lawicki, janitor."

As I opened the envelope I sank back into a chair. Inside were photocopies of Azor documents. Each was a draft copy, and every one was marked at the top "Confidential—for internal distribution only." I spread them out on the table in front of me. There were computer printouts that looked to be sales projections for the various corporate divisions, as well as a set of correspondence between Azor and the FDA discussing the likely approval date for the antischizophrenia drug that Azor was pushing to get on the market.

The third document was a final draft of Azor's first quarter 10-Q, the financial statement that all public companies file with the SEC. Azor's fiscal year ended May 31, so that its first quarter 10-Q covered June, July, and August. The SEC requires that the 10-Q be filed within ninety days of the end of the quarter, and typically it is filed on the ninetieth day. The draft I was looking at had passed over my desk ten days before for my final review. It was scheduled to be filed, and made public, three days from today.

I had no idea what Gretchen Azorini was doing with confidential corporate documents. Did Stephen give them to her? Did she filch them from his desk? Why? Why were they hidden in her room? I looked at the piles of Gretchen's things on every available surface of the conference room and realized that while I had set out looking for clues, all I had ended up finding were more questions.

CHAPTER

12

I tried reaching Stephen before I left to meet Tucker Sweet for dinner, but he had already left the office. According to Richard Humanski, Stephen was having dinner with his father, something neither Richard nor I could ever remember happening before.

The Mid-Town Club is on the top floor of the Deerfield Building. A discreetly marked private elevator whisks members and their guests away from the unattractive strains and dangerous disappointments of the world of commerce.

Tucker belonged to a dozen such clubs and loved them all. He loved the comfortable chairs, the real silver, the "good" pictures in the reading room, the silly drawings in the men's room. I found myself wondering, not for the first time, whether it bothered him that it was Eunice's money, not his own, that purchased all his pleasures.

"Good evening, Miss Millholland," said the porter as I went into the dining room. "It's been almost a year, hasn't it?"

"Too long, Frederick," I replied absently, spotting Tucker across the high-ceilinged, large-windowed room. Tucker rose as I approached his table and beamed at

me as if the sight of my battered face was the best thing
that had happened to him that day.

Knowing that I detested social kissing, Tucker shook
my hand warmly instead. He had a head of salt-and-
pepper hair and bushy eyebrows that licked up above
his eyes in elfish peaks. He had the square jaw of an
Irishman and the strong hands of a man who is good
on a horse. He was less handsome than charismatic,
but no society photographer left a party before getting
his picture.

"I'm sorry it took such a somber occasion to get you
out to dinner with me," Tucker said, always charming.
"When was the last time we dined together?"

"A long time ago. It was probably the summer I
clerked for Barker and Seidel," I answered, unfurling
the elaborate tulip folds of my white linen napkin and
putting it in my lap.

"It can't have been that long. I distinctly remember
dining with you one night at the Whitehall Club. I remember you wore a red silk dress with a princess neck.
You even raked out some of your jewelry. You looked
stunning."

"I thought we were only counting you and me alone.
That was the night you took Russell and me out to dinner right before we announced our engagement."

"It was a happy night," Tucker said gently. He had
obviously not meant to bring up Russell. "We've had
some memorable meals together. Do you remember that
night at Le Français?"

"I remember. I ate until I thought I was going to die.
Guttman was there, too. He wanted you to meet Stephen."

"You did, too. There was the matter of getting
Gretchen into Chelsea Hall midterm."

"And you ended up a director of Azor. . . ."

"Eunice ended up investing a million and a half in the company. I even threw in a few pennies of my own. Stephen cleverly appealed to my ego as well as Eunice's checkbook and made me a director.

"He was raising money for the drug infusion pump project," Tucker reminisced. "Stephen showed up at the house on a Sunday afternoon to make his pitch. Eunice, as usual, had completely forgotten the appointment and was out in the garden transplanting some rose bushes. Stephen just rolled up his sleeves and helped. Two hours later the bushes were moved, and Stephen and Eunice were both filthy. Then Eunice went inside and wrote the check. Stephen got a million and a half out of two hours of gardening."

"As I recall, you and Eunice both got a pretty generous deal in terms of shares and warrants," I pointed out. "I'd say your investment has paid off handsomely."

"Eunice's investments usually do," Tucker mused. "Still, how many guys raise that kind of money doing manual labor? What a charmed life!"

"Not recently."

"No, not recently," Tucker concurred gravely. "These days he's getting crucified."

"I don't know whether we should be talking about this here," I suggested.

"What are you worried about?" Tucker queried. "The waiters?"

I *was* worried about the waiters, but somehow Tucker made me feel foolish saying so.

"I think what's happening to Stephen is horrific," he continued, my warning notwithstanding. "Eichel plays very, very hard ball. I think he's gotten a lot of the scientists that Stephen was counting on to think seriously about tendering."

"How's that?"

"Money, of course. I know that Stephen is counting a great deal on their personal loyalty, but for many of the scientists their entire wealth is tied up in their Azor shares. The problem is, you can't spend stock. Eichel's had people making personal visits to everyone who holds more than a certain number of shares. They're saying: 'We will write you a check for X dollars in twenty-five days.' For a lot of those guys, that's more money than they make in five years. That's the carrot. Of course, they're also using the stick."

"How?" I demanded.

"Telling them that in the process of trying to avoid being taken, over, Stephen's going to have to load the company with so much debt that he'll end up in financial trouble and their shares will be worthless."

"Well, I knew this wasn't going to be a happy evening," I groaned.

"The world's a hard place," Tucker Sweet said, one of the few people I knew for whom that statement didn't seem to be true. "I wonder myself whether Stephen is right in putting up a fight."

I took a quick look around the room. This was the sort of thing that, if overheard, could do tremendous damage. But I was just being paranoid. All the other tables were set quite a distance from us, and the neighboring diners were bent over their salads, intent on their own conversations.

"It frightens me to hear that coming from you," I said with a sinking feeling in the pit of my stomach.

"I know it's unfair, but Eichel is right. Look at the number of companies in the last five years that leveraged themselves to fight off raiders and then couldn't service the debt when interest rates went up. If I were

Stephen, I might rather live to fight another day rather than go down with the ship.''

"I think you're being prematurely pessimistic," I said with feeling. "This is the first one of these you've been involved in. Whenever you're fighting a raider, there are low points like this when it seems better just to give in. But then the tide turns the other way."

"Yes, but how many CEOs have to fight off a raider the same week someone in their family has been found raped and strangled? A lot of people have to be figuring that under the circumstances Stephen's not going to have what it takes to pull it off. How could he? Did you see what Azor closed at today?"

"Forty-seven, twenty-five."

"Forty-seven, twenty-five," Tucker repeated for emphasis. "The arbs are putting their money on Eichel."

The arbitrageurs, arbs for short, are the traders who make their living betting on the direction of individual stocks. They buy up shares of companies rumored to be on the move, companies involved in mergers or raids, bankruptcies and breakthroughs. They try to buy low and sell high, trying to beat the market by anticipating where a particular stock is going before the rest of the pack. In a major takeover like Azor, the arbs were substantial players, and the more certain they were that Eichel was going to be successful the closer the stock was likely to trade to the offering price.

The waiter came and asked us what we would like. I ordered a hot duck and mixed green salad and the poached salmon. Tucker chose clear soup and a small steak.

Once the waiter had retreated toward the kitchen Tucker asked, "So how is your investigation going? Are you going to be the one to turn the tide against Eichel?"

"I'd like to be," I replied honestly. "Stephen told you what they've asked me to do?"

"Yes, a pretty steep undertaking if you ask me."

"I know. I've pretty much decided to focus on trying to find out the circumstances of Gretchen's death. I think it's going to be too hard to convince Stephen of any sort of alibi for Joey as long as there are questions about what happened to Gretchen. I've hired a private investigator, and I think we're making progress. The trouble is that there are only ten days left until the offering pool closes."

I stopped talking and noticed Tucker sitting motionless across the table from me, staring off into the middle distance. I'd never known him to lapse into any discourtesy.

"Are you okay?" I asked, concerned.

"Oh. Sorry, yes, I'm fine," he stammered, embarrassed at being inattentive. "I was just thinking of poor Gretchen Azorini. What a tremendous waste."

Our appetizers were served, and Tucker seemed to brighten. He seemed to make an almost conscious effort to make up for his slip and was especially entertaining, regaling me with gossip about who was currently being indiscreet or in disgrace.

The funeral home was called Salvadore and Sons, and it looked deceptively small from the front. It was on a side street off of Taylor, winding and narrow like all the crannies of that old Italian neighborhood. We had to park several blocks away, the narrow street was so clotted with cars. The black limousines of the important were parked half on the sidewalk, like dead whales washed up on the beach. Despite the cold, neighborhood residents gathered on their stoops to watch the commotion, to point and murmur.

The funeral home was a white frame house with a gray canopy, a Georgian portico, and potted ferns in the front window. As we walked up the red-carpeted front steps, I wondered how all the people who had come in the cars outside could fit inside the small structure. Then I realized that the house was just the facade, and a larger, more majestic building had been added to the back of the house, not visible from the street.

I had never been to a wake before. Russell, my six-foot, soccer fiend of a husband, had weighed less than one hundred pounds when he died. My brother's funeral had been a rushed and furtive closed-casket affair. Those were my only experiences with death. I was still too young to have developed much expertise at funerals, and I felt reassured to have Tucker enter the funeral home with me. Tucker was a marvel in any kind of group, a kind of social chameleon; he always blended right in, completely at ease and at the ready with the right word, the right gesture.

It was a large, pillared room, hung with drapes of burgundy velvet. At the rear there were double doors flanked by tables laid with large silver coffee urns, pyramids of cups and saucers, and trays of little pastries. In the center of the room were white folding chairs set into rows as if for a garden wedding. As we made our way to the front of the room, we could see a raised platform where the casket stood, open, decked with pink roses.

The family stood to one side. Stephen, a head taller than the crowd, his father, head bent to receive someone's tribute or condolences. There were three old women dressed in black, their white heads covered with scarves of black lace, and Joey Azorini, looking sullen and shifty, as if his black suit itched him, and he longed to be anywhere but here.

We joined the queue of mourners waiting to comfort the bereaved. As we waited, I scanned the room for familiar faces. Richard Humanski was there looking pale and grief-stricken. I was struck again by how intensely he seemed to have been affected by the death of his boss's niece. He was talking to a heavy-set old woman in a shapeless black dress who dabbed helplessly at her face with a lace handkerchief.

My eye picked out Vito, a few feet from Joey, scanning the crowd with the same restless glances you see the Secret Service ply whenever the president works the crowd. He shot me a sadistic leer, and I suppressed a shudder. There was no one else I recognized.

As we approached the mourners, I looked down into the casket. Gretchen Azorini lay there as if asleep, her red hair brushed and arrayed over her shoulders, her gently folded hands clasping a single pink rose. The undertaker had put lipstick on her and painted her nails, vanities she had never indulged in in life. I looked at her a long time, like someone staring at a puzzle straining for a solution, but her artful repose granted me no more insight than had the boxes of her meticulously folded clothes or my sister's hostile silence.

Tucker tugged gently at my arm, and I found myself looking up into Stephen's face.

"I'm sorry," I said, for lack of anything else.

He took me by the hand and pulled me a step closer to him.

"Will you come home with me tonight?" he whispered, head bent down to mine.

"I have to talk to Joey tonight," I replied. "How long will you be here?"

"Until ten." He shuddered. I realized he hated being here as much as Joey. The only difference was that he managed to hide it better.

"I'll try to come back here before then. If I can't, I'll meet you back at your apartment."

The old lady standing beside me pretended not to hear, but the sourness of her disapproval was hard to conceal.

"Mr. Azorini," I said, moving down the receiving line and extending my hand to Stephen's father, "allow me to express my condolences at your terrible loss."

"I was hoping to see your sister with you this evening. I understand from Stephen that she and Gretchen were good friends."

"Your granddaughter's death has been quite a blow to her," I replied, falling back on the comfort of cliches. "I'm afraid she's under a doctor's care."

"I am so sorry," murmured Anthony Azorini, and he passed me along to his other son.

I shook hands with the White Duke.

"I know a place," he said, with a sharp glance at Vito, who came like a well-trained spaniel.

I followed Joey out a side door, assuming we were going to some quiet anteroom. Instead, we went down a long corridor and half a flight of stairs, and I found myself following Joey down the alley that ran behind the funeral home, with Vito bringing up the rear. The cold clawed up my pantyhose and turned my silk blouse icy against my skin.

Just as I was about to protest or at least ask where we were going, Joey ducked into a greasy doorway partially obscured by reeking dumpsters. I followed him and found myself in a bustling restaurant kitchen. We walked through unchallenged and unacknowledged. We went up a dimly lit flight of stairs that ended in a single door with a diamond-shaped window at eye level. The door was padded with imitation red leather and upholstery studs. Joey held it open for me, and I passed inside.

It was a small private dining room with a single table. The walls were flocked with gold and black. There was a huge picture of meaningless fruit in a bowl illuminated by a picture light. The table was covered in white damask and elegantly set for two.

I wondered whether this was Joey's idea of a date.

"Frisk her," he commanded Vito.

"If you touch me, I'll file assault charges," I snapped.

"Tough talk from a broad who's still got stitches in her face," Vito growled.

"Just remember who got dragged out of the apartment that night," I retorted.

Vito was not pleased. He shoved me up against the wall, kicked my legs apart and frisked me. I felt the blood rush to my face.

Joey nodded, and Vito took his position outside the door. I could see the back of his thick neck and his bleached blond head through the little window.

Joey sat down at the table. He unfolded a huge white napkin and tucked it into the collar of his shirt.

"So, whaddya want to talk about, babe?"

I couldn't decide whether this was an act designed to rile me or whether he was really the kind of ignorant low life who had everyone he talked to frisked and called women babe. Either way, I decided to let it pass.

A waiter entered carrying a tray with two bowls of steaming soup. He set one in front of each of us. The waiter put a basket of bread and butter in the center of the table. Joey took up a spoon and began eating noisily. I waited until the waiter was gone.

"I was wondering what made you decide to tender your Azor shares to Edgar Eichel," I inquired.

"You went to law school, and you've gotta ask? I did it to make four million bucks. I'd say that's a pretty good reason."

"But you didn't tender right away. You waited until the day after you paid your little visit to Stephen's apartment."

"I'd been thinkin' about it."

"That's not the reason you gave your father at Mr. DeGenova's office. That morning you seemed to be motivated primarily by anger at your brother."

"Like I said, I'd been thinkin'—thinkin' that four million was a lot of money to lose, especially on account of an ungrateful little brother who thinks his shit don't stink."

"Do you want to tell me where you were last Monday morning until noon?"

"I was sleepin'."

"Was there anyone with you who could confirm that?"

"Yeah. I had some company. I got her name and number right here."

Joey reached into his jacket and pulled out a slip of paper where, written in a labored hand, was the name "Kitty Kaiser" and a phone number.

"When was the last time you went up to your property in Wisconsin?" I asked as I folded the slip and stowed it in my pocket.

"Not for a coupla years. My interest got diverted by some other investment opportunities."

"Any ideas why Gretchen might have gone up there?"

"I don't know. We used to take her up there when she was a kid. Maybe she got nostalgic."

"Have you called her or written her in the last six months?"

"Give me a break. You know the agreement that Stephen and Pop made me sign."

"Stephen said he thought you had been giving her presents."

"No way! Pop woulda killed me."

"So why did you give up custody of your daughter?"

"I travel a lot. In my line of work, it's tough to maintain what you'd call a good home environment for a teenager. Especially with Gretchen being sick and all. I just thought she'd be better off with Stephen—with him being a doctor and everything."

"I heard it was because you molested her," I said matter-of-factly.

"Who told you that?" Joey demanded angrily. He half rose out of his chair, bumping the table and splashing minestrone onto the white linen.

"Who told me? Several people actually. It seems to be common knowledge."

"I'll kill my lying asshole brother."

"Stephen never said anything," I said truthfully. "I heard it from other sources."

"Well, it ain't true," Joey insisted, his eyes blazing.

I didn't believe him. "But even after you gave up custody, even after you agreed not to see her without another member of the family present, you just couldn't leave her alone."

"That's not true!"

"How did you convince her to come up to Wisconsin to meet you, Joey? What line did you use?"

"I didn't see her. I never went up there, I swear."

"What I want to know is, what are you hiding, Joey?"

"Everybody's got something to hide, babe. You, me, Stephen, everybody."

* * *

It was raining as I walked back to the funeral home. I cursed Joey, I cursed the rain, I cursed myself for having agreed to the whole impossible situation. By the time I got back to Salvadore and Sons, I was soaked. Tucker was nowhere to be seen.

I found the ladies' room. I took off my shirt and dried it under one of those electric hand dryers. Then I washed my face and hands in hot water. I took my wet hair down, brushed it, and put it back into its usual French twist. I looked at myself in the mirror. I looked like someone who'd been mugged and left in the gutter.

The crowd had thinned down to some latecomers and the truly bereaved. Stephen was still at his father's side near the casket accepting condolences. I found Richard Humanski by the coffeepot. He looked young, tired, and out of place. I went over to him and poured myself a cup of coffee—it must have been my fiftieth of the day.

We exchanged hellos.

"How are you holding up?" I asked.

"I'm still standing," he replied with a weak laugh. "That's something."

"That bad?"

"Are you kidding? When I leave here I've got to go back to the office. Baker's there right now running off all these weird financials for Gould and his gang. I swear, those investment banker guys are incredible. They never sleep. Gould hasn't been out of the conference room in a day and a half, and I don't think his shirt's even wrinkled. He's like Dracula or something. Anyway, everybody's trying to treat Stephen with kid gloves because of what's happened, so instead they're coming after me. . . . 'Would you mind getting this?' 'What do you think Stephen will think about that?'

'Would you try to find a moment when you think he'd be up to it and just run this past him?' ''

"It must be awful," I said.

"I don't mean to complain, really. I'm just tired." He tried to smile, but the effort seemed too much for him. "The worst thing is that I keep getting the feeling that things are getting away from us. You know, like the takeover is developing a life of its own. I'm so used to Stephen calling all the shots. Now there's Gould and the lawyers and bankers and Eichel. . . .''

"You're right. These kinds of transactions often develop their own momentum. It's hard for a CEO to keep the reins in his hands, especially when so many of the players are acting from motives that have nothing to do with what's best for the company. Some people say that investment bankers like Gould have to have shifting allegiances in order to move from one deal to the next. But the truth is that they have no allegiances. Gould has his sights firmly set on his twenty million dollar fee. His only interest is in enhancing his reputation so that he can up his fees for the next one. . . . I'm sorry." I sighed. "I'm not trying to depress you. I guess I'm just tired, too. I can't imagine how Stephen is doing it."

"Most of the time he's just incredible," replied the young assistant. "He acts as if nothing's happened. He's like robo-boss or something. But then there are other moments when I'll be talking to him, and I just think he mentally slips away. I think this has hit him harder than anyone realizes."

"So he and Gretchen were pretty close?" I felt so strange asking the question. Most people would think that I was the person in the best position to answer it for myself.

"I think they were close. I don't think their relationship was what you'd expect. Gretchen was a funny girl.

Very quiet, but also stubborn and very independent. I think she felt like a much older person trapped in the body of a teenager. She didn't feel like she needed parents anymore. Or maybe she felt as though she'd never had real parents and it was too late to start. I think Stephen respected that. I think she really cared about him.''

"Was she interested in Azor Pharmaceuticals?" I asked.

"Absolutely. She and Stephen had agreed that she'd work for the company this summer. Then, when she finished college and business school, she'd come aboard. I think she got a kick out of thinking about it.''

"Did she ever ask you or Stephen for copies of corporate documents?''

"No, why would she want them? She must have gotten the regular shareholder mailings. She got a ton of stock for her sixteenth birthday.''

"And the car," I added.

"And the car," Richard whispered, his eyes filling with tears. He shook his head, embarrassed. "I'm sorry, it's just that the car was sort of my responsibility. Stephen wanted to surprise her with a car for her birthday, but he wanted to be sure he got something she'd think was cool. So he got the idea that I'd sound her out. She and I always talked a lot on the phone. When she'd call for Stephen and he'd be on another call, we'd chat for a few minutes until Stephen was free. So I told her that I was looking for a new car for myself, and we'd talk about cars. The funny thing is, in the end, I wound up buying myself a new car. . . .''

By the time Stephen and I got back to Hyde Park, the rain had turned to snow. Somewhere in the darkness Hyde Park's other life went on; burglary, prostitution, drugs, and gangs ruled the urban night. Out there people were cruising for a buy, screwing in cars parked by the lake, engaging in domestic violence. A car alarm went off, cold drunks were laughing in the park, a siren sobbed by on its way to the U. of Chicago hospital—the night songs of the city.

When we got upstairs I poured us each a Scotch while Stephen took a shower. I stripped out of my gritty office clothes and slipped into the shower in the guest room. Then, wrapped in a towel, I padded back into Stephen's bedroom and rooted around for something to put on. I settled for a tattered Harvard T-shirt that hung on me like a dress. I looked vainly through drawers of sweat pants and shorts, but everything was much too big. Funny, I had never kept as much as a toothbrush at Stephen's apartment. There was nothing of his at mine either. I reflected that anyone searching through our effects would find almost no physical evidence of our relationship. I toweled my hair dry, fastened it in a knot at the back of my head, and went into the kitchen for coffee.

I came back with two steaming cups just as Stephen was pulling on a pair of sweats.

"I helped myself to one of your shirts," I said. "I hope you don't mind. It was the only thing that fit."

"There must be something of Gretchen's that you could wear."

"I didn't know whether you'd mind."

"No, go ahead."

"Do you really have work to do?" I asked.

"Yes," he replied in a half-smothered voice as he pulled a white sweat shirt over his head. "I'm meeting with the senior scientific staff tomorrow morning to brief them on the takeover—several of them hold big blocks of shares, and I've got to get my presentation together. Then I've got a strategy session with Brian Gould and some other financial types, not to mention the regular work that needs to go on, takeover or no takeover. . . ."

"You also need to get some rest," I said, taking one of his hands in mine. "You can't outsmart Eichel if you're so tired you can't think straight."

"I'll just work a couple of hours, I promise. If I don't get this stuff done, I won't be able to sleep anyway."

"Then while you're working, I'm going to go and have a look in Gretchen's room. Call me if you need me."

The night plays tricks on tired people. In the shadowy silence of Stephen's huge apartment, I felt that mundane objects had taken on a sinister meaning, like poisoned icing on a wedding cake. The teddy bears in Gretchen's room frowned grimly into the darkness like malicious children, the canopy hung over the bed like a shroud, the dressing table seemed a demonic altar bearing the icons of a life cut short too soon.

I switched on all the lights and opened the blinds in a deliberate effort to shake off the creepiness that had overtaken me. I stood at the window for a while, watching the sparse late-night traffic shoot down Lake Shore Drive. In the parking lot of the Museum of Science and Industry, CTA buses turned around to head back toward the city or stood parked while their drivers gathered for coffee and night-shift conversations.

I went through the room quickly. More clothes neatly folded and arranged according to color. White cotton underwear. Socks neatly paired. No makeup. Few cosmetics. A full diabetic's kit in a small cupboard in the bathroom. A drawer full of cassette tapes, mostly top 40. It took me less than an hour and confirmed what

I'd always thought—Gretchen conducted her real life elsewhere. This is just where she stopped over on the weekends.

I was switching off the lights when I thought about the envelope that the janitor had found in Gretchen's room in the dorm and his note saying where he'd found it.

I dropped to all fours by the side of her bed and reached in between the mattress and the box spring. I went the length of my entire arm and groped. My fingers hit something, and I pulled it out.

I sat down on the floor and opened the manila envelope, spilling its contents out onto the carpet.

There were only papers—all of them confidential Azor corporate documents—except for two things: a fax transmission cover sheet, and a photograph of the board of directors of Azor Pharmaceuticals in a hinged brass frame.

CHAPTER

13

On the morning of the funeral the sun shone pale and thin through the December chill. I had lain awake most of the night trying unsuccessfully to make sense of the disconnected nuggets of information that had come my way in the past few days. Who was Gretchen Azorini's secret boyfriend? Why did she have packets of Azor documents? Why did she hide them? What was it that Joey was trying to hide?

While I mentally wrestled, Stephen thrashed and mumbled through a difficult sleep. Finally, at first light, he passed into a calmer slumber, and I slipped out of his bed and hurried back to my apartment. Cheryl had scheduled me for the meeting with Bill Faller at 7:00 that morning. The funeral mass for Gretchen Azorini began at 9:30 and was somewhere I'd never heard of in the western suburbs.

The streets of Hyde Park were disreputable and deserted—like a factory between shifts. As the darkness lifted, the hustlers and street revelers had crawled off to wherever they disappeared to in the daytime, leaving their trail of bottles and wrappers and junk to be dragged through the streets by the breeze. The other Hyde Park—the professors and students, doctors and commuters to jobs downtown—was just beginning to struggle out of bed.

If the doorman on duty at Stephen's building was surprised to see me traipsing out into the predawn streets wearing a Harvard T-shirt, the bottom half of a pair of Stephen's long johns (rolled up at the bottom), and a pair of high heels, he was either too well trained or too jaded to show it. Out on the street, I probably looked like just another early-morning hooker hobbling home after a long night's work.

Gretchen Azorini's funeral was a standing room only affair. The church was enormous, a vaulted expanse of gray marble with harlequin splashes of stained glass. Every pew was filled, and mourners crammed the back of the church and chancery aisles. Most were people who had probably never known her, people who came because she was Anthony Azorini's granddaughter. But her entire class from Chelsea Hall was there, including the girls who had considered themselves too cool to speak to her. They took up two full rows in their uniforms, their clean hair shining.

As we walked slowly up the center aisle, the statues looked down on us with their sad eyes, and I was reminded of the teddy bears in Gretchen's room the night before. The air was thick with incense.

The altar was decked with red roses, and they were mounded, blood red and sickly sweet, over the white coffin that held the mortal remains of Gretchen Azorini. An enormous crucifix hung over it all. Christ, bigger than life, bled from his wounds, and the crown of thorns dug cruelly and eternally into his flesh.

The mass seemed very long. The priest in his black skirts and white vestments, the altar boys swinging their incense burners, the strains of Bach from behind a carved screen made me tremble with sorrow and fatigue. Stephen, beside me, was rigid, his face a basilisk of suppressed emotion. I heard quiet sobbing from the back of the church and knew it was the girls from Chelsea Hall.

At the conclusion of the mass, the pallbearers rose and shouldered the coffin. Joey's face was twisted with grief, his cheeks wet with tears. Did murderers cry at the funerals of their victims? I was sure that Elliott Abelman would insist that anything was possible.

As they loaded the coffin into the back of the waiting hearse, I scanned the crowded steps for my sister and caught the eye of Detective Cancasci, half concealed by one of the huge pillars of the church. He was wearing a crumpled raincoat, a toothpick protruding from his satisfied grin. I wondered whether he was there in an official capacity or if he was just amusing himself on his day off.

For the trip to the cemetery, Joey rode with his father. I followed Stephen into the back of another waiting limousine. To my surprise, John Guttman climbed in right behind me, followed by Brian Gould, the investment banker from First New York.

"Eichel has just raised his asking price," Gould announced, "he's upped it to fifty-two dollars a share."

All investment bankers in M&A are complete adrenaline cases, and Brian Gould was no exception. In their world, takeovers are "deals" and the top producers are "players." At forty-three, Gould was definitely a player, a hired gun who made his living in the white-hot crucible of the major league. Brian Gould was a mercenary, a warrior clad in an Alan Fusser suit, form-fitted Turnbull & Asser shirt, Bulgari watch, and a Hermes silk tie, no doubt purchased at a discount at the duty-free shop at Orly Airport.

To my parents, the Brian Goulds of this world represented the worst of the new order, men who made enormous fortunes and insisted on displaying them at every opportunity. They were men who gushed to the press about what they had paid for their houses and what they and their young "trophy" wives had spent redecorating them.

"Not only has Eichel raised his offering price," exclaimed Guttman, "but the judge in Delaware handed down his decision this morning that the ESOP will have to be tendered. That's six hundred sixty thousand more shares into the pool!"

"At that price we're certain to lose a fair number of the scientists who've been hanging on to their shares. A lot of them are just going to cave in," Gould intoned. "If you're not willing to entertain the notion of taking Azor private—"

"I'm not willing to take on that kind of debt burden," Stephen replied wearily. "I'm not going to leverage the company, only to end up unable to carry the debt load. I'd rather lose the company to Eichel than bankrupt it myself."

"Then I think it's time to take a serious look at some of the potential white knights I've been feeling out."

"Brian has set up a lunch meeting with Harry Rumstead at United Hospital Products," panted Guttman. "Not only that, but Phil Dryden at Allied Medical Technologies called me this morning. He wants to meet in his office in one hour. He's ready to talk about a deal."

"United and Allied are two of my main competitors in the hospital service markets. Of course they want to *talk* about a deal. They want to go through my books and see what I've got in the pipeline.''

Stephen was right. Any kind of negotiations with a potential white knight is risky. White knights are usually companies with businesses that overlap or compete with the targets. In order to make a decision about whether to enter the bidding, a white knight needs a lot of information about the target company, and fast. The problem is, if the deal doesn't go through, you've just laid bare all your secrets to your competition.

''It's a risk you'll have to take,'' Gould said. ''It's either that or going private.''

Stephen looked out the window as the car wound its way slowly into the heart of the cemetery. His face was a battleground of conflicting emotion, but his pale blue eyes burned with the same cold fury that I had seen the night that Joey burst into the apartment and tried to kill him.

''Get me a set of projections for taking it private,'' he said finally, spitting out the words. ''And stall Allied and United for a couple of days.''

We pulled up to the grave site, and Stephen, Guttman, and I climbed out of the car. Gould was left behind with his cellular phone and portable fax machine.

It would be a beautiful spot in the springtime, shaded by a willow tree. Now the schizophrenic December weather had allowed the ground to thaw just enough so that my heels sunk deep into the moist earth, and with every step, tiny drops of mud splattered up onto my stockings. As we made our progress to the open grave, the other mourners joined us in somber clutches of one or two.

The girls from Chelsea Hall came in their own cars. Jeeps and Land Cruisers seemed to be in fashion, but several had more expensive sports cars. The teachers drove battered Fords. I could see them in a cluster around Mrs. Bigham. The Chelsea Hall contingent came up to the grave and stayed in its own group. When Tucker arrived, he paid his respects to Mrs. Bigham and took up his place beside her. He also shook hands with several of the teachers and girls. He must have decided that he was attending the funeral as a trustee of Chelsea Hall as opposed to a director of Azor Pharmaceuticals.

There were more prayers at the graveside. Many of the girls from Chelsea Hall were weeping, their arms around each other. I was reminded how close to the surface the emotions of teenagers were and how easily they could be tapped.

Finally, the priest said the benediction, and the casket was lowered into the grave. The crying of the girls grew louder and more ragged, an awful soundtrack to Gretchen Azorini's descent into the earth. The priest sprinkled holy water into the grave, and Anthony Azorini took up a silver trowel. He filled the small shovel with earth and threw it onto the lid of the coffin. Then he passed it to Joey, who did the same, and so on through the mourners. Stephen hung back; I assumed he wanted to be the last. I walked a little distance away from him to give him space but had no intention of leaving. I watched the girls from Chelsea Hall approach the grave to take their turns shoveling earth onto the casket.

Two girls I did not know had taken up position on either side of Beth, each one taking an arm as if to assist someone very frail or very ill. Mrs. Bigham put in the first scoopful and handed the shovel to Tucker Sweet. I remember thinking how strange it seemed that they had managed to put themselves into a hierarchical order: headmistress first, trustee, chief mourner. . . .

Tucker spilled his trowel of earth onto the casket and turned to my sister. As he handed the trowel to her, she stopped her progress toward the grave as if stung, her hand stopped in mid-reach for the trowel, and her knees buckled beneath her. Her two classmates struggled under the sudden weight, and for half an instant I thought the entire trio would tumble into the gaping grave. It was Richard Humanski, who had been standing with a group of Azor people behind the girls from Chelsea Hall, who shot out his hand and helped Beth and the other girls back from the brink.

Stephen rushed up to Beth and in his doctor's voice ordered everyone away from her. He lay her down on the ground, quickly checking for pulse and respiration. "She's fainted," he told me. "She'll come around in a minute." The funeral director produced a small ampule from his pocket and handed it to Stephen.

This must happen all the time, I thought. Stephen snapped it open and waved it over Beth's ashen face. Her head rolled from side to side and then she regained consciousness with a start and a disoriented cry.

Stephen and I helped her sit up as the funeral director tactfully guided people in the direction of their cars. Beth's classmates resisted the funeral director's efforts and hovered anxiously.

"Beth," Stephen asked, "can you hear me?"

She nodded. He held up three fingers.

"How many fingers am I holding up?"

"Three," she whispered.

"Watch my finger," he ordered gently, and moved it from one side of her peripheral vision to the other while he watched that her eyes tracked its progress in unison. "Did you hurt anything when you fell? Any bumps or bruises?"

Beth shook her head. She looked up frantically at all

the people gathered around her and tried desperately to scramble to her feet, but she wobbled unsteadily halfway. I thought that she was just disoriented and embarrassed at finding herself at the center of so much attention. Yet something about her manner, the purposefulness of her gaze as she scanned the crowd struck me as odd.

John Guttman appeared behind Stephen, bent down, and whispered something that I couldn't hear.

"I have to go, Kate," said Stephen. "Can you stay with her? She should just sit still for a few minutes. If she starts feeling weak, she should put her head between her knees. Richard'll give you a ride."

"No problem," I replied, giving my little sister's hand a squeeze. "I'll take good care of her."

In the end I had Richard drive us to my parents' house in Lake Forest. It was the straightest shot from the cemetery. Besides, I didn't have the temerity to bring her back to school and just dump her at the dorm. Beth made the trip curled up like a fetal shrimp on the backseat of Richard's sea green Honda. I found myself wondering whether a person could go into emotional shock the same way as physical shock and if so, how one managed to recover.

"Slow down here," I directed Richard as we approached the drive. "It's coming up soon on the left. There, just past that little sign."

We drove down the driveway, and as we cleared the trees Richard gave out a small whistle.

"Don't say it," I groaned. "It's embarrassing growing up in a house roughly the size of Versailles."

"I bet you get used to it after a while," replied Richard, but without malice.

"Come on, Beth," I said as we pulled up at the side entrance, "you're home."

"I don't want to go home," she whispered.

"Come on, kidlet," I replied, "I'll get you tucked up on the couch with a good movie to watch and a cup of cocoa. You'll feel much better."

She didn't reply but got out of the car, walking very slowly like a sleepwalker.

Richard blinked when he got into the house, like someone accustomed to the dark who suddenly finds himself in the light. I left him to wander around downstairs while Beth and I went up to her room, with Mrs. Mason clucking and fussing as she brought up the rear.

I led Beth into the sitting room on the second floor, where the TV and stereo in the children's wing live, after she had changed into a turtleneck and a pair of sweats and Mrs. Mason had gone to fetch the cocoa.

"You okay?" I asked.

Beth just nodded.

"Did you just faint? Was it the sight of the casket?"

"Stop asking me questions," she retorted. "You're like the fucking Gestapo."

"I only want to be sure you're okay."

"I'm fucking terrific."

When Mrs. Mason came in with the tray I left.

I found Richard in the kitchen, sitting at the servants' table with a cup of coffee and a plate of home-baked cookies in front of him, a sign that he had managed to get around the right side of Mrs. Mason.

"Is your sister alright?" he asked.

"One thing's for certain, my presence isn't going to do anything but make her worse."

I helped myself to a cup of coffee from the big staff coffeepot. While Richard finished his, I sat down at the little desk by the window and wrote a note to leave for my mother.

"So," Richard said when we were back in his car heading back to the city, "that's where you grew up?"

"Yeah."

"Pretty cool."

"I guess. I don't want to do my 'poor little rich girl' thing, but I don't think stuff like that matters when you're growing up. I think it's better to have a family that has a big heart rather than a big house."

"That's easy for you to say."

"You're right. I mean, my parents aren't very good parents, but there are plenty of crummy parents who are poor and uneducated to boot. . . . Do you know there are support groups for people with inherited wealth, just like for children of alcoholics or people who were abused as kids?"

"My father was an alcoholic," Richard said, keeping his eye on the wheel.

"I'm sorry," I said.

"I guess if I had the choice I'd rather struggle with the burdens of inherited wealth." There was no bitterness in his voice, only a touch of wistfulness, and I knew he was thinking of Mrs. Mason's huge, well-scrubbed kitchen. "It's one of the reasons I always felt close to Gretchen."

"Is Joey an alcoholic?" I asked.

"I don't know. Probably borderline, but he does drugs, too. It's not so much what you're addicted to but the pattern of dysfunction the family falls into. My family situation was screwed up, but it couldn't hold a candle to Gretchen's."

"She talked to you about it?"

He nodded his assent, keeping his eyes on the road.

"Stephen would have probably been furious if he knew.

I don't think he would have liked my knowing about it. I think that Stephen and I are pretty close and that he trusts me, but he's the sort of person who likes to keep his life compartmentalized, separate. He knew that Gretchen and I talked on the phone. There were times that she'd come downtown to meet him for dinner and something would come up and I'd take her instead. He knew that we were friendly, but I don't think he realized how open she was with me.''

Intimate, I found myself thinking. He knew they were friends, but he didn't realize they were close—intimate. Beth's words in the morning room of the dorm of Chelsea Hall came back to me. Gretchen wouldn't tell who her boyfriend was because she was afraid Stephen would kill him. They were friends but how intimate? Out loud I asked: ''So you and Gretchen became friends. Did it go any farther than that?''

''No,'' Richard replied quickly with a strange look on his face.

''I'm sorry, I know her death has hit you pretty hard. It seems strange, but I didn't know her very well. I'm trying to figure her out. That's all.''

''I don't think it's all that abstract,'' Richard replied in the kindly tone of condescension that must come naturally to a person who enters college at sixteen. ''Here's a girl who'd had a hellish life—father an abusive drug dealer, mother a junkie, she's got a chronic illness, her mother dies in a freak accident . . . finally, she manages to get out of her bad home situation, she's rescued. It's not Ozzie and Harriet, but things look good—she's happy, she's thinking about college and about going to work for the company when she graduates and boom—dead.''

''Do you think she might have been going to meet her father in Wisconsin?''

"Joey?"

"Stephen said he thought Gretchen had been having contact with her father recently, that they'd been writing, talking on the phone. Do you know if that's true?"

"Oh, I don't think so," Richard replied with feeling. "If she never saw him again it was too soon."

"Why?"

"Didn't Stephen ever tell you?"

"No. Like you said, he likes to keep things compartmentalized."

"Promise you won't say that I told you?"

"Promise."

"I don't know for sure, but I'm pretty sure that her dad had been sexually abusing her."

"Oh," I replied, "so that's why she went to live with Stephen."

"Well, it's not exactly the sort of thing that anyone will talk about, but yeah, that's the reason."

"So you don't think she'd have driven up to Wisconsin to meet her father?"

"Not unless someone was holding a gun to her head," Richard replied.

CHAPTER
14

When I got back to the office, Cheryl was waiting for me with the news that Elliott Abelman had called no fewer than five times. He hadn't left a number, but said he would call again at 1:00 P.M. I looked at my watch; I still had twenty minutes.

"Did he say what it was about?" I asked.

"No," replied Cheryl, "but it's obvious he's got his boxers in a bunch about something."

"I wonder what," I said, vexed at having to wait to find out.

"Well, if you'd turn on your goddamn car phone from time to time you'd know already, wouldn't you?" Cheryl snapped.

It was no use explaining that I had gotten a ride back into town with Richard Humanski. It had been nine days since Edgar Eichel had launched his takeover attempt. It was clear that the mergers and acquisitions department had entered the cranky phase of the takeover. The standard progression after the initial adrenaline rush was from cranky to hostile to belligerent to psychopathic. I could hardly wait.

"Would you please get us both a cup of coffee?" I

asked as sweetly as I could manage, "and then come into my office. I need your help with a problem."

In my office I quickly exchanged my mud-stained pantyhose and wet shoes for clean, dry ones. Cheryl returned with the coffee while I was brushing my hair. I quickly twisted it up and out of the way.

"You know," Cheryl said, while I stuffed bobby pins into my French twist, "you should wear your hair down. It's very pretty."

"Thanks, but it's a pain. Then I have to brush it all the time, and it falls in my face while I work."

"You'd get used to it."

"I'm used to wearing it up," I replied testily. Growing up with my mother had made me thin-skinned when it came to grooming tips.

I opened my briefcase and pulled out the two packets of Azor documents I had found among Gretchen's things. From the one I'd found in Stephen's apartment I extracted the fax cover sheet and passed it to Cheryl.

"Gretchen Azorini had this," I said. "It's a cover sheet for sending a fax, isn't it?"

"Yes," Cheryl answered.

"I've never actually physically sent a fax," I continued. "Is there anything special about this one?"

"Not really. The form we use is a lot different. It looks like a piece of Callahan Ross letterhead on the top. The bottom half is like a form. There's a line for putting in where the transmission is coming from, where it's being sent to, the person it is going to, who sent it, the number of pages being sent including the cover sheet, and a number to call in case all the pages weren't received properly. This one doesn't identify the sender at all," she said, examining the piece of paper in her hand. "The space for a phone number to call in case the transmission wasn't properly received is blank. All this one tells me is that thirty-seven pages were sent to 347-9109. There isn't even a date.''

''Is there any way to find out who lives at 347-9109?''

''You don't know anything, do you?'' Cheryl asked. ''I honestly think all the secretaries in this firm should go on strike. Then you'd see what a helpless bunch of babies you lawyers all are.''

''I think finishing law school is a higher percentage strategy,'' I quipped.

I followed her down the hall to the little room where the copy machine, the fax, and the coffee pot lived. On the wall above the copy machine someone had hung a picture of the Three Stooges, but they had replaced Curly's picture with that of a bald, cigar-chomping Edgar Eichel.

''Do you care if the people on the other end know who we are?'' Cheryl asked, standing in front of one of the fax machines that served the mergers and acquisitions department.

''Since I don't know who they are, I guess I'd rather they not know who we are.''

''Okay, then, I'll just send a blank piece of paper.''

She activated the machine, slipped a blank piece of paper into the feeder, punched in the phone number from the cover sheet that I'd found in Gretchen Azorini's room, then pressed the transmit button. The machine beeped, we waited a few seconds, and the machine beeped again.

''Most fax machines are programmed to talk to each other. When the two machines connect, the sending machine displays the name of the firm that it's transmitting to.''

Our fax machine beeped again, on cue.

''I don't understand it,'' Cheryl remarked with a puzzled frown. ''By now the destination should have been displayed on this little screen.''

She pointed to an LCD display that remained a cipherous gray blank.

''I just don't get it,'' Cheryl said again. ''Maybe the machine on the other end is programmed to not transmit its identity.''

''I don't know,'' I said. ''But if you can find out where that fax is, it's worth a shopping trip.''

''A shopping trip?'' Cheryl asked, rising to the challenge. ''To Neiman Marcus?''

''Anywhere you want. My treat.''

''You know I won't let you down,'' replied my ambitious and hardworking secretary.

''You are one hard lady to get ahold of!'' exclaimed Elliott Abelman somewhat breathlessly.

''Where the hell are you calling from?'' I half shouted. ''I can barely hear you.''

''I'm at a pay phone on Route Eight just north of Lee-High, Wisconsin.''

''I've got some things I want to talk to you about,'' I said. ''I found something out this morning. I'm not sure how it fits in.''

''What?'' bellowed Abelman as what sounded like a semi roared past him.

''What?'' I hollered back.

''I can't hear you,'' he screamed.

''I don't think this is a great way to discuss this.''

''Do you think you could come up here? There's some stuff I want you to see and somebody I want you to talk to.''

''Who?''

''I'll tell you when you get here,'' he answered.

"If you think it's necessary . . . It'll take me all day to drive up there—"

"I've got a friend who flies one of the traffic helicopters for WCNV; he said he'll bring you up. Here's his number. He's waiting for you to call him."

It was midafternoon when the helicopter deposited me on the frozen baseball field of a bedraggled park on the outskirts of Mannetuoc, Wisconsin. Kirk, the pilot, patted my hand and waved good-bye. During the trip up north Kirk explained to me that while Elliott Abelman looked like a pencil neck, the two men had met during their tour of duty in Vietnam as helicopter pilots, flying into enemy fire to pluck the wounded from the battlefield.

Elliott was waiting for me. I shook his hand with renewed respect, and he flashed me his megasmile. He was dressed for the country, in khaki pants and a cream-colored turtleneck. I couldn't help but noticing that he'd obviously put in some time at the gym.

"I think I've found the place where Gretchen Azorini spent the night the Sunday before she died. Plus, I got the pathologist who did the autopsy on Gretchen Azorini to agree to meet us. He's going to give us a copy of his preliminary medical report."

"I can't believe he got Sheriff Whittle to agree to that," I exclaimed.

"He didn't."

"Then how did you manage to convince him to talk to us?"

"I showed him what a charming guy I can be."

"He was pretty scared of Whittle when I talked to him. You must be able to charm a nun out of her habit," I remarked.

Elliott Abelman lit up the afternoon with a big grin.

He looked me up and down in my black funeral suit and white blouse.

"I don't know," he replied with a twinkle in his eye. "You should let me try."

Much to my amazement, I actually blushed.

"Wherever did you get this car?" I asked, climbing into a puke green Chevy Nova of indeterminate age. It reeked of cigarette smoke.

"I rented it from the owner of the only gas station in Mannetuoc. Fifty bucks a day."

"What a deal."

"I'm glad you think so, since you're paying for it."

"Are we going far?"

"About thirty miles. Dr. Yarbrough is very nervous about being seen with us. We're going to meet him at his wife's office. It's four miles past the intersection of Route Eight and Standish Road," he said, handing me the map.

"What's this?" I asked.

"You navigate," he replied.

"I'm not good at map reading," I said.

"You're kidding."

"No, I'm not kidding. Either I drive and you navigate, or you check out where we're going before we start. Otherwise there's a good chance we won't make it there before dark."

He looked at me quizzically.

"Why do you look so surprised?"

"I'm just impressed that you'd admit to such a stereotypically female weakness as not being able to read a map."

"I'm a good lawyer and a bad map reader," I said. "I can live with that."

Abelman took the map from me and opened it up

across the steering wheel. A few minutes later we pulled onto a greasy two-lane road. Pine trees grew thick and close to the tarmac. The sky was gray, and there was a thin dusting of snow. Every couple of miles we glimpsed some sign of life, a ramshackle trailer set back from the road, bearing a single strand of Christmas lights, a darkened roadhouse, a dilapidated frame house with a sign that read: CABINS FOR RENT—FREE HEAT, TV.

"From what I gather, this area has mostly seasonal businesses," Elliott explained. "In the spring and fall there're hunters. In the summer there's some spillover of fishermen from Lake Lewanda, about twenty-five miles south of here. In the winter it's just dead. Some year-round residents, but not many."

"And you found out why Gretchen came up here?" I prompted.

"I think so," Elliott said, keeping his eyes on the road, "but I don't want to tell you. I want to show you. I want to see if it strikes you the same way as it struck me."

"I can't say I'm not curious," was my reply.

"We'll go there right after we see Yarbrough. You said you had something to tell me."

I explained to him about the envelopes of Azor documents that Gretchen had hidden in her rooms. I told him about Cheryl's and my experiment at the fax machine.

"Do you think Gretchen Azorini was sending Azor documents to someone?" Elliott asked once I'd finished.

"I don't know. Maybe, though I can't see why she would."

The sign read: JANICE YARBROUGH, D.V.M. The building looked like a small red barn. There were pickup trucks parked out front and bales of hay stacked up against a small storage shed.

We walked inside into a dimly lit passageway covered with straw and lined with animal pens. Dark shapes moved and mooed around us. A tall woman in dirty overalls was wiping her hands on a rag and talking to a worried-looking man in a grimy John Deere cap.

"Excuse me," Elliott interrupted, "but we're looking for Dr. Yarbrough."

"I'm Dr. Yarbrough," the woman replied. Then she noticed me in my city suit and heels. "I bet you want the other Dr. Yarbrough. He's waiting for you in the office. Third door on the left."

We thanked her and, with our eyes getting used to the dim light, found our way.

It looked like the office of a muffler repair shop. The walls were covered with fake wood paneling, and the floor was cracked linoleum. There was a battered metal desk with a filing cabinet to match. In one corner was a small refrigerator with a Mr. Coffee and paper cups on top. One wall was covered with veterinary degrees and a calendar sporting a picture of a steer.

The other Dr. Yarbrough was sitting at his wife's desk reading something in a file. He was a small man, with a fringe of black hair that looked like it had been cut with an inverted soup bowl to show the way. He wore a blue button-down shirt with a plastic pen protector (with pens) in the breast pocket, and a pair of tan corduroys.

Elliott made the introductions, and we shook hands all around. Elliott told him how much we appreciated him meeting with us.

"Whittle would try to have me fired if he found out," he answered simply, "but it's his own fault. He's been sheriff of Meechum County for the past nineteen years.

The most interesting thing that's happened in all that time is a couple of domestic disputes that ended with the husband or the wife in a body bag. But now he thinks he has a rape/murder in his jurisdiction, and he's like a dog with a bone. I guess it's my fault, too. I should have kept my mouth shut, but it never occurred to me that anybody could be so stupid.''

''I'm not exactly following this,'' Elliott said good-naturedly.

''Of course not. It's because I'm not making any sense,'' the pathologist continued worriedly. ''I guess I should start at the beginning. But I wasn't called in at the beginning. That's the main problem. I never saw the body *in situ*. By the time I got the call, Whittle'd already had the body brought to the hospital.''

''That's not exactly standard procedure,'' interjected Elliott.

''This isn't exactly a place where they have much grasp of standard procedure. Whittle called, and I wasn't in. He had me paged, and when I didn't pick up right away, he decided he didn't want his boys waiting around in the cold so he had the body photographed and brought into the hospital.''

''No forensics investigation?'' Elliott asked.

''You've got to be kidding. By the time they got her out of there, anything worth looking at had been trampled into the mud by the sheriff's boys. Homicide detectives have a saying: 'The victim dies but once, the crime scene can be murdered over and over again.' Whittle is a homicide cop's nightmare.

''They found the body lying in the underbrush about ten yards from the road. She was dressed, but not for the weather. Just a shirt and a pair of pants. The body was found facedown. When they turned her over, the officer noticed petechiae—her eyes were bloodshot, and there were broken blood vessels in her face.

"When I examined the body, I found scratches on her neck. So far it looked like a textbook case of rape/murder. Almost all young dead females found in a rural area like this are rape/murder victims. Almost all of them are strangled. That would explain the petechiae and the marks on her throat.

"I'd gotten about that far when Whittle showed up and demanded to know what I'd gotten so far. I was pretty P.O.ed that he'd moved the body, and I told him as much. I'm afraid I wanted to make him feel like a jerk, so I really laid it on him. Told him that it was probably a homicide and that he'd been on the case less than an hour and had already screwed it up irrevocably by moving the body. He stormed out, but the damage had already been done.

"By the time I started the autopsy, things were looking much less clear-cut. Her nose was broken and there were bite marks on her lower lip and tongue. The bite marks are a sign of seizure. I did a month at the Dade County Medical Examiner's Office. Down there you see a lot of the same characteristic bite marks in cocaine overdoses. The broken nose might fit with that as well. She might have broken it when she fell, but it might have broken easily because of a weakened septum from cocaine use. Then I noticed the subcutaneous scarring on her thighs, which I assumed were from frequent injections. There! I figured she's a skin popper."

"She was a diabetic," I interjected. "The needle marks were from her insulin injections."

"I know that now," Yarbrough answered sadly. "But I tested the eye fluid and urine for glucose, and both came up negative. When you see that kind of seizure in a diabetic, it's usually from hyperglycemia, and you'd find a high sugar content in the eyes and in the urine.''

"But you didn't find any," I said.

"None. I checked for cocaine in the urine. Negative, but we use a test kit at the hospital with a fairly high false-negative rate, and we don't do that many of them, so I sent out a sample to check for cocaine metabolite, especially since I didn't know for how long the body had been around.

"I did a rape kit—combed out the pubic hair. I found several that didn't belong to the victim. I did swabs of the mouth, anus, and vagina. Mouth and anus were negative. She'd had vaginal intercourse. I took a sample of the semen and had it typed. It was A negative, a fairly rare type.

"Then I performed the autopsy. I made a copy of my preliminary report for you, but, in a nutshell, from the location of the sperm, assuming average motility, I'd assume she'd had intercourse twice within the previous twenty-four hours. Probably once twelve to sixteen hours before death and again within four to six hours. She'd probably been lying down both times.

"There were scratch marks on other exposed parts of her body—her hands and her ankles. While the scratch marks were worse on her neck, the trachea was not damaged. There was no blood or skin under her fingernails. Her stomach was empty. Really empty. Her gall bladder was distended. Other than that she was a perfectly healthy girl. I sent my samples off to the Illinois Reference Laboratory, including the semen and a control sample from the girl's liver, and I attached a note to please expedite.''

"So what killed her?" queried Elliott.

"At this point I'm really confused," the pathologist confessed. "On first glance it looked like rape/murder, but there are no clear signs of rape—which doesn't necessarily mean she wasn't—and no conclusive signs of murder. The petechiae could very easily have been caused by the body lying facedown. The scratches could have been made by small animal activity. If she'd been strangled, I'd have expected her windpipe to be crushed. It's possible that she was asphyxiated—somebody put a pillow over her face—but that would be complete speculation. At this point I'm leaning away from rape/murder and toward friendly intercourse followed by cocaine overdose.

"There's nothing I can do but wait for my toxicology results. The next morning Whittle deigns to call me and says he's I.D.ed our Jane Doe, and she's some mafia heiress from Chicago. I told him the problems I was having determining a cause of death, and he went crazy. There was a TV crew on its way up from Chicago to interview him, and there I was telling him I didn't necessarily believe his sexy murder victim had been murdered."

"A TV crew?" I asked. "There's been almost no media coverage."

"Whittle says the family's got a lot of juice and they put the kibosh on it. Didn't do much for Whittle's state of mind, I can tell you. I issued a pending certificate so that the body could be buried. Then a couple of days later you called me, told me that the girl was an insulin dependent diabetic. I called her doctor, and then it all fit together. Right now my best guess is that she died of hypoglycemia." Dr. Yarbrough paused for breath.

Elliott and I waited.

"It's just a theory," the good doctor continued. "But it's the only theory that explains all the facts. It explains no blood sugar in the urine and the eye fluid, it explains the subcutaneous scarring, the distended gall bladder, it even explains the empty stomach and the bite marks.''

We looked at Dr. Yarbrough expectantly until he continued his explanation.

''Okay. Introduction to endocrinology: When a person who doesn't have diabetes eats and digests food, the nutrients in the food are absorbed into the blood, causing an increase in the blood sugar level. As the blood passes through the pancreas, insulin is produced. Insulin is necessary for the cells of the body to be able to absorb the sugar and use it to function. People with Type II diabetes, which is what the deceased suffered from, don't produce enough insulin or, in her case, don't produce it at all. They have to inject themselves with insulin in order for their body to be able to break down and use food. If they don't, or if they don't inject enough insulin relative to the amount of food eaten, their body produces two toxic by-products, ketones and acids. These get dumped into the blood, and the person goes into ketone acidosis, which, if left untreated, causes coma and then death.''

''So Gretchen Azorini died from ketone acidosis?'' asked Elliott.

''No,'' answered Dr. Yarbrough. ''But that's the cause of sudden death we see most typically in diabetics. That's why we routinely screen the eye fluid and urine for glucose. But remember, there was no glucose in either sample from the Azorini girl. If she'd died of hyperglycemia and gone into ketone acidosis and diabetic coma, you'd expect to see an abnormally high glucose level. My theory is that she died from hypoglycemia. In a case of hypoglycemia the blood sugar is abnormally low, or as in this case, nonexistent.''

''How does someone become hypoglycemic?'' I asked.

''There are a couple of possible scenarios. She could have taken an insulin overdose, though in her case considering the fact that her stomach was completely empty, it wouldn't have to be a very large overdose. It might also be that she took her regular dose of insulin and then didn't eat, or even that she took her regular dose and then couldn't keep down whatever food she'd eaten. For example, she might have had the flu.''

''Any sign that she was sick?'' Elliott asked.

''Her white count was normal, but all that means is that she didn't have a bacterial infection. Flu strains are often viral. There'd be no way to know at postmortem. But in cases of hypoglycemia, the blood sugar falls very rapidly. Often there are seizures, which would explain the bite marks on the lower lip or tongue, which are typical of grand mal seizures.''

''How sure are you?'' I asked.

''Not very sure at all,'' answered Dr. Yarbrough truthfully. ''That's one of the reasons I decided to tell you about this. I've got to wait for the toxicology reports. There's still a chance that diabetes or no diabetes, she died from a cocaine overdose. On the other hand, if the girl really didn't do drugs, then hypoglycemia is the only cause of death that fits all the facts. I guess I'm hoping that since you're investigating her death, you might uncover some facts that would make me more certain that I'm right.''

''And Whittle?'' queried Elliott.

''He's dragged in every known sex offender within his jurisdiction and grilled them. He's probably questioned every male that could possibly have spoken to Gretchen Azorini within the last ten years. He's about as subtle as the S.S. It's also just killing him that the family has pulled strings to keep the story out of the press. Whittle would give anything to see his face on the evening news. Right now, he figures the only way he's going to be able to do that is by arresting a killer—any killer.''

"So he's not buying your hypoglycemia theory?" I asked.

"The only song that Whittle is singing is rape/murder. If evidence from the contrary fell from the sky and hit him on the head, I still think he'd look the other way."

After our meeting with Dr. Yarbrough, Elliott Abelman drove me to the edge of nowhere. We drove through a thick pine forest and then turned on a narrow dirt road crusted with ice and full of deep ruts. Every once in a while there was a rusted NO HUNTING sign tacked to a tree. Quite a few of them had been perforated by buckshot. Other than that, there was absolutely no sign of life, human or otherwise.

"This is all Joey Azorini's property," explained Elliott, endeavoring to keep the Nova on the road. "According to the county records, sixty thousand acres are owned by the Duke Realty Development Corporation of Chicago, Illinois, but that's just a front company for Joey Azorini."

"He wanted to develop it into a sort of high rollers' hunting lodge, with a little prostitution and gambling thrown in," I explained.

"Who'd want to come all the way up here? Why not just fly to Vegas? At least it's warm."

"Can you shoot a moose in Vegas?" I asked.

"I'm sure it can be arranged."

The car was slowing down. At first I thought we'd run out of gas, but then I realized that we'd come to the end of the road, literally. Through the trees I could see a cabin.

The building was dilapidated but not old. It had a wide front porch meant for sitting on during a summer evening, and a shingled roof. There was no walkway, no grass. Joey had obviously just had a small clearing hacked out of the woods, put a rough road to it, and put up the cabin. It was, I remembered, meant to be the command center from which the building of his resort was to be supervised. From what I could tell, it looked like the cabin was as far as they got. Weeds grew wild up to the door. From the outside, at least, it was an unfriendly and abandoned place.

"This is where Gretchen Azorini came?" I asked, ruining a perfectly good pair of Ferragamo pumps getting through the mud to the front door.

Elliott nodded. He handed me a pair of latex gloves, the kind that doctors wear.

"Put these on," he said. "Don't touch anything. When we got here this morning, the front door was open."

Inside the walls were unfinished but dry. There was a faint smell of mildew or maybe it was just of the country. I couldn't tell the difference.

Downstairs there were two rooms. The first was a big sitting room with a massive stone fireplace that held the charred remains of a log fire. There were two Adirondack chairs pulled up to the hearth. The second room was a narrow galley kitchen with modern appliances. Everything looked as if it had been perfectly clean until someone came along and dusted it with talcum powder.

"Come upstairs and meet Lou," Elliott said.

"Who's Lou?"

"A forensics technician with the Chicago P.D. He called in sick today to come up here."

I followed Elliott up a set of narrow stairs.

"There are two bedrooms up here. One appears to have not been used in years. It's the other one that's interesting."

Elliott opened the door to the interesting bedroom.

"Make sure you tell her not to touch anything," barked Lou by way of a greeting. He was a burly guy in his forties wearing a purple satin bowling jacket with "Kinzie Lanes" emblazoned across the back. He wore his pants slung low under his beer belly. He was kneeling on the floor next to the bed with his jeans dragged down low revealing what most people wore underwear to conceal. He grunted to his feet when Elliott introduced us. We shook latex-sheathed hands.

The bedroom was like the rest of the cabin except that somebody had gone to some trouble to cozy it up. The bed was unmade but covered in at least a grand's worth of Laura Ashley linens. Two straight-back chairs had been pulled up to either side of the bed to be used as nightstands. On one there was a Movado clock and a crystal carafe and water glass. On the other was a tortoise shell tissue box and a copy of an Agatha Christie mystery—*The Murder of Roger Ackroyd* in hardcover. On each chair was a small Waterford lamp topped with a crisp linen shade.

I sat slowly onto the bed and looked around, hugging myself against the cold.

"Quite a setup," Lou remarked.

"What have you found Lou?" Elliott asked.

"Not one hell of a lot. The whole place has been cleaned fairly recently, I'd say within the last two weeks. I found a couple of hairs in the bed. A couple long ones come from a redhead, a couple short dark brown ones, a couple of pubic hairs—red and brown. I'm gonna take the sheets back to the lab; there're semen stains and I wanna get a make on the guy's blood type.''

"Prints?" Elliott asked.

"The prints don't make any sense," Lou answered. "The girl's are all over the place. All over the bathroom, the nightstand, one set on every single cupboard and door downstairs. It's like she tried every door in the place."

"And the guy?" shot Abelman.

"None. Zero. Zippity doo dah. It's like the guy was never here."

"Could he have worn gloves?" I asked.

"Not likely. You don't leave prints with gloves, but you do leave a mark. I didn't find nothin' like that. It looks like this guy was real careful."

"Anything else?" inquired Elliott.

"Not yet. I have about another half an hour's worth to do up here before I lose the light."

"We'll wait downstairs," Abelman replied.

I pulled up one of the Adirondack chairs and wrapped my Burberry around myself.

"So where did they find the body?" I asked.

"About thirty feet off the side of the dirt road, about two miles from where it turns into the paved county road. It's rained twice since they found her. According to the sheriff's deputy I talked to, the boys in blue did a pretty good job of messing up the scene. The sheriff's department vehicles did a pretty good job on the road, so there's no way to cast for tire prints."

"Did the sheriff come up and check the cabin for prints?"

"Nope. According to the deputy, Whittle said, 'hands off.' It looks like even if Joey isn't going to go ahead with his development plans up here, he's still pretty well connected."

"Why?"

"Probably because he's bought Whittle. It wouldn't make sense that he'd go ahead and buy all of this land unless he knew he could control the cops."

"But if Joey controls the cops up here, why is he letting Whittle run around howling about rape and murder? It would make more sense for him to pressure Whittle to hush it up."

"I don't know. Nothing about this case makes any sense. What do you think of the setup here?"

"I think it's a love nest. I think that Gretchen furnished it, or at least chose the stuff. She has similar linens in her rooms at home and in the dorm. And I think it's safe to say that it's been used more than once. If it were just for a night, why bring up the lamps, the water carafe. . . ."

"But why come all the way up here? The sheriff's department has been looking hard for some local boyfriend, but so far they've turned up zip."

"Beth said that Gretchen told her that if Stephen found out about the relationship, he'd be furious. Would Stephen be that upset to find out that his niece was sleeping with some backwoods yokel?"

"Maybe he'd go crazy if he found out she was sleeping with anybody," Elliott said. "She was only sixteen."

"Stephen got into plenty of trouble when he was sixteen. I don't know if he'd be handing out congratulations, but I can't see him killing anybody."

"Okay. Let's say it's probably not a local boy. Who is he? Why would he and Gretchen come all the way up here to sleep together? Maybe it's somebody from Chicago. Someone who's afraid of being seen with her."

"Maybe," I mused out loud. "But we're looking at

this all wrong. We're looking at this from an adult perspective. Where did you screw around when you were in high school, Elliott?''

"Nice Jewish boys from Highland Park didn't screw around," Abelman replied virtuously.

"Please, let's be serious," I replied. "The correct answer is that high school kids screw around whenever and wherever they can. The problem is, they don't have very much freedom and even less privacy. You don't have an apartment; the car is uncomfortable. When you're a teenager, privacy, real adult privacy, is hard to come by.''

"So hard to come by that it's worth driving five hours up to the Wisconsin boonies?''

"When you're sixteen?" I asked. "Think, Elliott. Would you have driven five hours to get laid when you were sixteen?''

"Does Popeye eat spinach?''

Lou came lumbering down the stairs carrying the sheets in a plastic bag and a large canvas duffle.

"All done?" Elliott asked.

"Uh-huh," Lou grunted.

"Find anything else?''

"Just this," answered the forensics technician, dropping his case and handing me a plastic bag containing an empty syringe and a needle broken neatly in two.

CHAPTER
15

When we got back to Chicago we were hungry, muddy, and weary of Lou. Twenty years of visiting crime scenes and vacuuming corpses had left him with a collection of on-the-job stories that would set anyone's teeth on edge. We gratefully waved good-bye to him on the wet tarmac of Meig's field and discussed logistics. We were, I explained to Elliott, about the same distance from my office or my apartment, but I had enough dry socks for both of us at home. We both agreed the choice was clear.

On the way, we stopped at the Harold's on Fifty-third Street to pick up fried chicken. Elliott, who seemed surprised to learn that I lived in Hyde Park, was truly amazed by Harold's. From the moving neon sign of an ax-wielding chef chasing a running chicken in the front window to the bullet-proof carousel where you slip them your money and they pass you a hot bag of the world's best greasy chicken, I could tell Elliott was impressed.

Back at the apartment, the sound of our voices in the living room woke Claudia. She appeared, rubbing her eyes and wearing a set of bloodstained scrubs.

"Elliott Abelman, my roommate, Claudia Stein," I said. Elliott shook Claudia's hand.

237

"Ah, the cute private detective," she said blearily. "Do I smell Harold's?"

I replied in the affirmative.

"Extra hot sauce?"

"No," I answered. "I ordered plain. It's Elliott's first time."

"Then you're right, it's best to be gentle. If you'll excuse me, I'm going back to bed."

"Interesting roommate," Elliott said once Claudia's bedroom door closed behind her.

"She's a surgeon," I said, as if that explained everything.

"A doctor and a lawyer, and you live like this?" he proclaimed with a sweeping glance around our living room.

"This place has intrinsic charm."

"This place has dustballs," Elliott replied.

"Do you want to have a pair of dry socks, a cold beer, and some fried chicken, or do you want to clean house?" I demanded.

"Socks and a beer, please."

"Wise man."

I threw him a clean pair of gym socks and pointed him toward the fridge. Then I retreated into my bedroom and changed into a pair of jeans and a U. of C. sweat shirt plucked from the semi-clean pile on the floor of my closet. Back in the kitchen, Elliott popped a can of Old Style for me while I unpacked dinner. Each order consisted of three pieces of chicken and a pile of fries resting on two pieces of white bread (to blot the grease), arrayed on a paper plate. For a while our thoughts were only on food, but after about the second piece, Elliott caught me staring off into the middle distance, clutching my second beer.

"What are you thinking?" he asked.

"I'm thinking that it's great to be back in Chicago,"
I replied truthfully. "Wisconsin gave me the creeps."

"Not a country girl?"

"Never. When I was born my parents lived in a big
duplex apartment on Lake Shore Drive. After my little
brother was born, they decided to move to Lake Forest.
I was five. I thought we'd moved into the forest, like
Hansel and Gretel. I cried for a month."

"Is your brother a lawyer, too?" Elliott asked, making conversation.

"No. He died when I was in high school."

"I'm sorry to hear that."

"It's okay."

"I don't mean to pry. I'm just curious about you."

"About me? Why?" I replied, surprised.

"Oh, come on. Your family is as close to royalty as
you can get in Chicago. I just can't figure out what
makes you work at Callahan Ross."

"Why?"

"Because firms like Callahan are meat grinders.
What percentage of starting first-year associates make
partner?"

"About a quarter."

"And how many hours are you expected to bill a
year?"

"Eighteen hundred if you want to stay, twice that if
you're serious about making partner."

"That's what I don't understand. Most of the guys
who are shooting for partner in a firm like Callahan are
really bright and really hungry. They're usually smart
guys from modest backgrounds who see partnership as
their ticket to the big bucks."

"That's true," I confessed.

"I bet you could buy and sell all of the senior partners at Callahan Ross."

"Collectively?"

"You know what I mean."

"You're right. I do know what you mean. What can I say? I don't do it for the money, though I have to say there's a certain satisfaction connected to the money I make. I work because I like it and because I'm good at it. A lot of people at the firm think I work mergers and acquisitions to prove that I can play hardball with the big boys. The theory is that while some rich guys climb mountains to get their thrills and prove themselves, I, in my twisted way, have decided to crash the M&A department at Callahan Ross."

"Are they right?"

"No. Not in the way they think. I went to law school because I couldn't face what was expected of me when I graduated from college."

"And what was that?"

"To date for a year, find some nice guy whom I'd known my whole life who was rich enough to not be marrying me for my money. To settle down, decorate a house, start a family, donate my time to the right charities. You know, live up to my station in life."

"Doesn't sound too bad."

"No, it doesn't. I look around at the world, and I see all the hardships, and my complaints seem very petty. But the truth of the matter is that whenever I thought about coming back to Chicago to start my real life, I felt like I was suffocating."

"So you went to law school."

"And I developed an interest in securities law, especially mergers and acquisitions."

"Why?"

"Who knows? Maybe it's the genes of all the robber baron Millhollands. But it certainly never occurred to me not to go into the field I wanted just because I was a woman and very few women go into M&A. The Millhollands are used to getting what they want.''

"And now that you've got it, is it still what you want?''

"This is getting to be a very intense conversation,'' I said. "What about you? You don't make all that much sense either.''

"Oh?''

"How come an obviously bright Jewish guy from Highland Park ends up flying helicopters, working as an investigator for the D.A.'s office, and striking out on his own as a P.I.? I just can't see you parked in a car outside some hotel, waiting to get photos of some errant husband.''

"Well, I tried being a lawyer, and I didn't like it much.''

"Oh, really?''

"When I got back from Vietnam I went to law school at DePaul. I liked law school a lot, though it was a little funky hanging out with all those pencil necks after being in the Marines.''

"So, what happened?'' I asked.

"Nothing happened. I graduated fourth in my class and went to work for Benish, Carmichael. You've probably never heard of them.''

I admitted that I hadn't.

"It's a forty-man shop on LaSalle Street. Where did you go to law school? Harvard?''

"University of Chicago.''

"Well, there are lots of lawyers who don't graduate from Harvard or Michigan or Chicago, and they go to firms like Benish, Carmichael. Benish does a lot of insurance subrogation claims. I spent my first year settling a big personal injury case. A tanker of toxic gas ruptured when the train that was carrying it derailed.

An entire neighborhood was evacuated for three days while they cleaned it up. There were more than four thousand plaintiffs suing in about half that many separate actions. We represented the chemical company. The railroad had their own team.''

"And you didn't like it?''

"I more than didn't like it. I loathed it. The train went over in a ghetto neighborhood, and most of the plaintiffs had been solicited by their attorneys, so every day I got to go to work to get into screaming matches with ambulance chasers. I was making a lot of money, but it definitely wasn't worth it.''

"So why didn't you make a change? Go to another firm?''

"I did. I went to work for Arlo Standish.''

"That's quite a change,'' I said, impressed. Arlo Standish was one of the city's premier criminal defense attorneys.

"Arlo is a prima donna, but he's the best. If I ever get caught with my hands around somebody's throat, he's the first person I'm going to call. To make a long story short, I did a lot of investigative work for Arlo. After a while I realized I liked it a lot more than the legal stuff that I was doing. I went along for another couple of years with him, and then the D.A. made me an offer. I thought it would be more satisfying working to put bad guys away instead of getting them off.''

"Oh, come on, some of the guys Arlo represents must be innocent.''

"Theoretically. I don't think I ever met one, though.''

"So why'd you leave the D.A.?''

"I wanted to get away from the politics that pervade every city office in this town. I wanted to be my own boss. I wanted to be paid what I'm worth instead of what some civil service pay schedule says I'm worth.''

Elliott polished off the last piece of his chicken, eyed the white bread, and then pushed it away.

"You know, this is all very interesting," he said. "But it doesn't get us any further along in understanding how Gretchen Azorini came to be dead in a ditch in your favorite state."

"I think she was murdered," I said, setting down my beer, "and by someone very clever."

"On what do you base that conclusion?" Elliott asked with an arch of his brow and a challenging smile.

"It's the only explanation for the physical evidence," I replied. "Besides, it's much too elegant to have happened any other way. Think about it. Once the murderer decided that he wanted Gretchen dead, it must have seemed like child's play. The two of them had been meeting at the cabin in Wisconsin, a place that no one knew about, far from help. He already had the perfect place to kill an insulin dependent diabetic.

"They must have driven up separately and met at the K mart parking lot where they switched to his car. I bet there was a bag of groceries in the backseat. Once they got to the cabin, they had sex and went to sleep. Or rather, Gretchen went to sleep. During the night the murderer had to slip out of bed and wipe off all the surfaces where he might have left fingerprints. In the morning they had sex again. Afterward, he said: 'Honey, why don't you go ahead and take a shower. I'll run down and make breakfast.'

"Once he was sure that she'd taken her insulin and was safely in the shower, all he had to do was grab her purse, pick up the groceries, and hit the road. On the way out of town he stopped back at the Jeep, unlocked it, and put the keys in the ignition, hoping that someone would yield to temptation and steal it before it attracted any attention. From his point of view, it's so easy. He's a hundred miles away when she dies.''

Suddenly the image of a man capable of making love to a young girl that he's about to murder turned vivid in my mind. My stomach churned, and there was a taste like cold metal in my mouth.

"But for Gretchen, it is a horrible death. She gets out of the shower, dresses, and goes down to have breakfast with the man she thinks she's going to marry. Instead, there is no one there. She looks for him, innocently at first, thinking that it's some sort of joke. But when she goes into the kitchen, she finds it's empty. Really empty.

"She knows she's taken her insulin, and she has to get some food in her stomach soon. She opens the cupboards and drawers looking for something to eat. . . . She looks frantically for her purse where she keeps her emergency glucose, but it isn't where she thinks she left it. In the meantime, she tells herself that there must be some logical explanation. He'll be back any minute with a trunk load of firewood or the story of having chased a deer. . . .

"But soon she begins to panic. She's already starting to break into a light sweat, the first sign of hypoglycemia. She knows what the progression will be; she knows how little time she has. She starts off down the road— better than doing nothing, she tells herself—maybe she'll catch him as he comes driving back up the road.

"But he doesn't come. Instead she becomes dizzy, and her motor coordination starts to go. She staggers off into the underbrush. Then the seizures start. . . .''

We sat quietly for a moment, swept up in the same horrific imaginings.

"Of course, not everything worked out for him according to plan. I'm sure he never counted on the hon-

est or apathetic folk of Mannetuoc not stealing the car.
Sheriff Whittle also says that it was a just a fluke that
those poachers found her. I'm sure the killer thought it
would be weeks before the body was discovered. By
then the weather and animals would have made the assumption of a rape/murder seem even more likely. Also,
they wouldn't have been able to narrow down the time
of death so closely. But the beauty of the murderer's
plan is that even if his luck had been even worse, even
if the poachers had stumbled across her before she died,
there's a good chance even Gretchen could have been
convinced it was all just a terrible misunderstanding.''

"It's a good theory," Elliott said finally. "But who's
the guy? Are you sure that Gretchen didn't tell your
sister who her boyfriend was? Could she be holding out
on you for some reason?''

"I don't know. I don't think so. My sister is something of a mystery. She's depressed and unstable in the
best of times, and Gretchen's death has sent her into
the deep end. I think we've figured out how Gretchen
was killed, but it's just brought us to a dead end.''

I glumly went to the refrigerator and pulled out the
last two beers.

"When you're at a dead end, you go back to the
beginning," Elliott said. "Let's start with cop 101.''

"What," I asked, "is cop 101?''

"Means, motive, and opportunity. Let's assume
you've figured out how she was killed—the means. Opportunity narrows it down to someone who knew her
well enough to know about her insulin routine and
someone whom she trusted enough to go up to Wisconsin with.''

"Someone with who she was sleeping, you mean.''

"Probably, but not necessarily. Let's not close any

doors just yet. Now, we have the means, and we have the opportunity. What are the possible motives?''

"How come I'm paying you a fortune, and you're the one asking me questions?'' I demanded testily. "I have already cudgeled my brains into a stupor just figuring out how she was killed.''

"Okay,'' Elliott replied agreeably. "When I was at the D.A.'s office, the motives for premeditated murders usually fell into one of three categories—money, sex, or drugs. Those were the murders that had discernible motives, not the ones where two drunks were going after each other with baseball bats because one of them said the Cubs have better pitching than the Sox. But I'm assuming that if Gretchen was murdered, it was a very slick, well-thought-out crime, and whoever's behind it had a very good reason for doing what he did.''

"Joey's unfortunate profession aside, I see no evidence that this was a drug murder.''

"Agreed,'' Elliott said. "Nobody was shot, there's no real evidence that Gretchen was using, so let's start with money.''

"Well,'' I began, "Gretchen had a ton of money, but she couldn't touch any of it—it was all in trust for her. She also owned a big chunk of Azor stock, which, trading at today's prices, would have made her a wealthy young woman. The disposition of the stock is unclear at the moment, but my guess is that her father will inherit the shares as well as the cash. The trouble with money as a motive is nobody's going to get Gretchen's money for a long time. They can't even begin probate until Dr. Yarbrough issues a nonpending death certificate. Even when that happens it'll still take months for the estate to make it through the courts. Besides, the only person for whom money is a motive is Joey, and I can't believe that Joey is the killer.''

"Why not?"

"Because it's not his type of crime. If he'd wanted Gretchen dead, he'd have hit her in the head or shot her on the spot."

"I know you like your elegant murder theory," cautioned Elliott, "but suppose that Joey had managed to resume his physical relationship with the girl. Let's say that Joey was sexually abusing his daughter, but that instead of the girl blowing the whistle on him, someone else did. Stephen became the girl's guardian, but she was not necessarily adverse to continuing her relationship with her father. Gretchen went to live with Stephen, but she continued to see Joey on the sly. Stephen himself suspected that they'd had contact. That would also explain why Gretchen wouldn't tell your sister the name of her boyfriend. She'd be ashamed. The whole secret boyfriend story might have been a way to not only get Beth to act as her accomplice, i.e., helping her cut school, but also as a subconscious rationalization of her relationship with her father."

"It certainly explains why they would go to the trouble of meeting in Wisconsin, even why they would take separate cars," I reasoned. "If Joey and Gretchen were seen together, and Anthony Azorini got word of it, Joey would have real reason to be afraid."

"What about Gretchen telling Beth that she was going to get married?"

"If she fantasized a secret boyfriend, why not a secret marriage? Anyway, it all plays out pretty much as you said, only when Joey goes out to the car to bring in the groceries to start breakfast, his beeper goes off— a drug dealer's office crisis. He forgets all about breakfast, hops into the car to find a pay phone to call Chicago. By the time he gets back to the cabin, it's too late. Gretchen is dead. He realizes what he's done and tries to cover his tracks.''

''What about her purse?''

''He takes it from the cabin so he can have her car keys to leave in the Jeep.''

''What about the fingerprints?''

''Maybe he didn't touch anything. Not everybody makes a good print. Besides, he didn't necessarily have to have been there long.''

''It doesn't make any sense,'' I protested. ''Then why would he precipitate this whole crisis with Stephen by tendering his shares? Why not just lay low?''

''He probably thought that the more strenuously he protested his innocence, the more likely he was to be believed.''

''I still don't buy the premise of Gretchen continuing her relationship with Joey. When I talked to Richard Humanski, he said the only way Gretchen would go anywhere with her father would be if he were holding a gun to her head.''

''Since when is Richard Humanski an expert on what Gretchen would or would not have done?'' Elliott inquired.

''They were phone friends. Richard is Stephen's assistant, so he and Gretchen were thrown together a lot, almost like family.''

''He sounds like a good candidate for the boyfriend. He's young, unmarried, spent time with the deceased.''

''And if Stephen found out his assistant was sleeping with his niece,'' I conceded, ''he'd kill him. Probably not literally, but he'd make darn sure that Richard would feel lucky to be spending the rest of his life flipping burgers at McDonald's.

''I know Richard looks like a good candidate on paper, and if Gretchen wanted to tell Stephen about their relationship, that would be a strong motive. The problem is, when I drove out to my parents' house with Richard after the funeral and I kept trying to imagine him having a physical relationship with Gretchen, it just didn't seem possible.''

"I bet you there're lots of things you can't imagine." Elliott chuckled. "Think of a married couple you've known since you were a little girl."

"Okay, Tucker and Eunice Sweet, they're my godparents."

"Now, imagine them having sex."

I made a face.

"How many kids do they have?"

"Four."

"I rest my case."

"But if it was Gretchen and Richard, why would they have to go up to Wisconsin? Why not just go back to Richard's apartment?"

"Maybe Stephen drops in on him unexpectedly with work from the office. Maybe they only started going up there once he decided he might have to kill her. Tell me," Elliott demanded, as if suddenly seized by a new thought, "how much are Gretchen's shares worth?"

"Stephen gave her fifty thousand shares for her sixteenth birthday. Today they're worth over two million dollars—that figure could go up if Eichel raises his bid."

"Two million is a pretty good motive," Eichel mused.

"For whom?" I snapped. "Certainly not for Joey. I thought that kind of money is pocket change for a drug dealer."

"I was thinking about Edgar Eichel," Elliott replied coolly.

"Oh, come on."

"I'm serious. Why is it that it seems perfectly logical

to you that some punk would knock an old lady over the head for the contents of her purse, yet the thought of some slick fuck like Eichel chilling a teenager for a chance to gain control of a five hundred million dollar company seems farfetched?''

''I'm not saying that Eichel's not a sleazeball, but I do think there are gradations of sleaze. Besides, it only works if you assume that Gretchen was sleeping with Eichel, which we have no evidence of.''

''What if Eichel had been having her followed, discovers she's seeing some local Wisconsin boy, and slips him a couple of grand to abscond with the groceries and just leave her there?''

''Boy, I would just love it if it turned out that Eichel was the bad guy.'' I sighed.

''Maybe we should look a little harder for a mystery boyfriend.''

''Maybe I should take another stab at talking to my sister. I can't believe she's told me everything she knows.''

CHAPTER
16

I woke up earlier than was good for me, but later than I had planned. Elliott and I had parted in the small hours of the morning, each with a long list of leads that needed following. I felt confident that, given time, we would be able to find the evidence that would lead us to Gretchen's killer. The problem was that time was the one commodity that was in very short supply.

I washed my face and forced myself into sweats and running shoes and ran the four miles down the lake shore bike path to McCormack Place and back again. They say that Chicago has two kinds of weather: winter and August. Well, it wasn't August. Icy drizzle clung to my face, melted, and ran off me like freezing sweat. On the plus side, for the first time the parts of me that had tangled with Vito didn't protest with every stride.

I ran out of habit and to clear my head from the troubled scenarios of Gretchen's death that Elliott and I had spun the night before. The whole world felt out of kilter to me. Elliott had me convinced that the world was a place where anything could go on behind closed doors and more often than not did, a dark place with an even darker underbelly, a place where normalcy and kindness were a painstakingly constructed veneer hiding the avarice and pain that were the true nature of things, a place where things are seldom as they seem.

When I got back to the apartment, I was greeted by the aroma of fresh basil and yeasty crust. I found Claudia in the kitchen taking a large Edwardo's deep dish pizza out of a box. It was spinach and sausage, my favorite.

"The breakfast of champions," I exclaimed.

"One of the orderlies on my unit works a second job cleaning at Edwardo's. I take it you would like a piece?"

I went to the cupboard and extracted two plates that would pass for clean.

Claudia served it up. I cracked open two diet Cokes from the back of the fridge. I asked Claudia what was happening at the hospital.

"Not much if you don't count the guy who came into emergency yesterday who'd been shot with a crossbow."

"Nice."

"It was a zoo. I think they paged the whole hospital to come down and have a look."

"Was he alright?"

"Who?"

"The guy with the arrow through him," I said, questioning, not for the first time, the premise that it took brains to be a doctor.

"Oh, him," Claudia replied, helping herself to another piece of pizza. "He died."

"So what's the big deal if the guy was dead?" I asked. "I thought you were supposed to get excited if you managed to save the guy."

"Well, I don't think he died right away. But a crossbow fatality is incredibly rare. Our emergency medicine department is one of the best in the country. More carnage passes through there over a holiday weekend than you'd see in a week in a war zone. But this is the first time they've had anybody shot with a crossbow. They're thinking about putting it in the recruiting literature for the fellowship program.''

''It's a sick and strange world we live in,'' I said, lifting my can of diet Coke.

''I'll drink to that,'' replied Claudia as we clinked cans.

The phone rang, and I answered it. It was my secretary, Cheryl.

''Kate, you'd better get down here quick.''

''Let me guess. Guttman is going into labor.''

''No. Really. Remember you asked me to see if I could find a way of figuring out who that fax number belongs to, the one on the cover sheet?''

''Yeah.''

''Well, I found out who it belongs to.''

''And?''

''It belongs to Edgar Eichel.''

I set a new speed record down Lake Shore Drive, weaving in and out of traffic and leaning on my horn. I found Cheryl, sitting white-faced in my office with the door closed—waiting.

''Tell me exactly how you found out,'' I commanded in the unnaturally calm voice that always rose up in me when I was feeling panicked.

''I came in early this morning to help Bobbi finish up a big brief she's been working on for Jim Hannifin. She had a hot date last night, so I told her she should go ahead and leave yesterday, and I'd come in this morning to help her get it finished. Hannifin wouldn't care as long as it got done.

''So I finished my section, and I was waiting for Bobbi to finish hers so we could merge the two documents and print off the copies. Anyway, I got to thinking about the fax again, so I called the company that made our fax machine. They said that it's possible to program some machines not to reveal their location, to block out that information. So, I figured, if the machine won't tell me, than I have to get the information from a living, breathing person.''

''I got an idea. I made up a phony fax cover sheet from a piece of Azor stationery from the file. I filled in that we were sending seven pages, and I put your office number—not the switchboard, but your direct line—on it. Then I pulled a bunch of old disclosure statements from the Azor file and faxed three pages' worth. Then I sat at your desk and waited. In about ten minutes the phone rang.

''It was a secretary named Trish who was calling to say they hadn't gotten the four pages. So I tried to get her talking by complaining about my demon boss who makes me work all sorts of hours and makes me bring her three meals a day—I was making it all up, of course. She told me that she was new and that her boss was really pissy and she wasn't sure, but she was thinking of quitting. Then she told me his name—Edgar Eichel.''

''Are you sure?'' I asked.

''She told me more than once.''

I didn't answer. After a minute Cheryl said, ''I take it this information doesn't make you happy?''

''You really did great, Cheryl,'' I said.

''Can I get you some coffee, or maybe something stronger? You look like you could use it.''

I looked at my watch. ''Just coffee, then I need you to track down Guttman and tell him that I have to see him right away. Then take this,'' I said as I fished my

Neiman Marcus charge out of my wallet, "and go shopping."

"You were serious!"

"Of course I was serious."

Cheryl took up the card and handled it carefully, as if it might explode, or worse, turn out to be addictive.

"What should I buy?" she asked.

"Anything you want," I replied. "Well, actually, I think you should draw the line on furs. . . . Just go and see what you like."

"Thank you very much," she stammered.

"You earned it," I answered truthfully. She disappeared with a skip in her step. It was fun to be generous. Nice to be able to afford to be.

Cheryl returned in a minute with a cup of coffee and the news that Guttman was at Azor Pharmaceuticals meeting with Stephen, Brian Gould, and a couple of the directors.

I called Richard Humanski and told him that I would be there in a half an hour and that I had something urgent to tell Guttman and Stephen. Then I sent a mail clerk out to get me something to wear.

Thirty minutes later I was in a taxi heading north toward Stephen Azorini's office, dressed in the sort of office nun's navy blue suit that my mother always accused me of wearing, but in reality seldom did. It was the sort of somber, sexless ensemble that was well suited to the bad news I was about to deliver.

Guttman's reaction was quick and savage. I had had Richard pull him out of the strategy session in Stephen's office, and we huddled in a little alcove to speak privately. I had laid out the documents that I'd found among Gretchen's things on the warm top of the copy machine. Guttman countered my quickly constructed theory about Gretchen and the faxed Azor documents by asserting that my reasoning was faulty, my facts mere suppositions, and my behavior totally inexcusable.

As calmly as I could, I walked him through my chain of thought and presented my case as clearly as I would for the toughest jury. When he'd prodded and needled and clawed at my arguments to his satisfaction, he gave my arm a squeeze and said, "Let's go tell it to the boys."

The "boys" were Stephen Azorini, Brian Gould, another stiff in a custom-made shirt from First New York, Tucker Sweet, and Dick Porter, a white-haired captain of industry who was the newest member of Azor's board of directors. They were spread informally around Stephen's spacious office. Brian Gould stood in front of a large grease board, a marker in his hand.

"Sorry to interrupt, Brian. I think you've all met my associate, Katharine Millholland," Guttman said.

Stephen looked mildly suprised. I hadn't seen him since the funeral. He looked awful.

"Kate has uncovered some information I'd like her to share with you. I don't need to remind you that whatever is discussed here this morning does not leave this room."

I didn't go into a lot of detail about how I'd found out. I merely laid out my assertion that someone had been leaking confidential information about Azor Pharmaceuticals to Edgar Eichel. I passed around copies of the documents from under Gretchen's mattresses. The faces in the room turned very grave. "Any idea who sent this material?" Dick Porter asked.

"We have a team of private investigators working on it as we speak," I replied, thinking of the hurried phone message I had left for Elliott. With more confidence than I actually felt, I added, "I'm sure I'll have much more solid information by this time tomorrow."

"So there's no guarantee that this is the extent of the information that's been delivered to Eichel?" Gould asked, waving the thin stack of documents in his hand.

"No," Guttman replied, standing up and taking center stage. "There's no proof that those documents have been sent to Edgar Eichel, either. There might be a completely innocent explanation. The documents might even have been intercepted before they were sent. There's no way to know without actually asking Eichel. On the other hand," Guttman paused for effect, "I think we would be foolish to not take into account the possibility that there is a traitor in our midst."

For two hours they thrashed out the possibilities in Stephen's office, sending out for lunch and sodas, exploring every option from suing Eichel to faxing him bogus documents ourselves. No one told me to leave, so I stayed. I'd never seen Brian Gould up close before, and I relished the opportunity to see his stiletto intellect and instinct for the jugular. But my heart went out to Stephen. He looked like someone had kicked the legs out from under him. I wondered whether he thought that person was me.

After the meeting broke up, I hung back until the others had gone. Stephen asked me where I'd found the documents.

"Gretchen had them," I whispered in the voice of someone trying to soften bad news.

"Why would she have them?"

"I'll let you know when I find out."

Stephen took both of my hands in his and looked down at me.

"Find out soon," he implored. "I don't know how much more of this I can stand."

I stopped in Richard Humanski's office to use his phone. I dialed my parents' number, steeling myself against the sound of my mother's voice, but it was Mrs. Mason who answered the phone.

"They been out of town for the last few days," she informed me. "Miz Millholland thought it might do your baby sister some good to get away, so they paid Miz Prescott a visit."

"Grandma Prescott?" I interjected. "In Palm Beach?" I looked at Richard Humanski, who had just slipped in the door, and wondered what he must be thinking.

"Yes, ma'am. Friend of your daddy's gave 'em a ride on his plane. They'll be back this evening."

"What time?"

"Your mama called me this morning and said I should have dinner ready at seven."

"Dinner at seven? Then why don't you set a place for me?" I asked.

"You sure?" Mrs. Mason asked doubtfully. "You know how your mama hates surprises."

I told her I was sure.

I hung up the phone and rose to go. I was surprised to find Tucker Sweet standing in the doorway, waiting for me. I thought he'd already gone. He feinted a punch and gently chucked me under the chin, something he'd been doing ever since I was six.

"You know, sometimes it's hard for me to remember you're the same little girl who shrieked her way through her christening. Couldn't hear a word the minister said."

"I haven't shut up since."

"You've been busy," he said. "It's an awful business."

I nodded. I didn't know what to say.

"I couldn't help but overhear that you're going out to your parents' tonight. Can I offer you a lift?"

"I'd better take my own car."

"Give my love to your family, then," he said. "And don't worry about all of this too much. It will all work itself out."

As I drove north to Lake Forest, I was filled with a queer, nervous foreboding. I felt as if I were waiting in the dark for someone to turn on the light, but whatever was about to be illuminated was going to be shocking and unpleasant.

There were suitcases inside the back door, and Rocket came clattering and wheezing across the tile to slobber an arthritic greeting. Mrs. Mason was bustling through the last stages of preparing dinner while Gladys and Jewel, two housemaids, prepared to serve the meal and tried to stay out of her way.

"Good evening, Miss Kate," they chorused.

"Something sure smells good. What's for dinner?"

I darted over to the big eight-burner range to take a peek. Mrs. Mason pretended to rap my knuckles with a wooden spoon.

"You keep your hands away from my cooking," she warned.

"Your cooking? It's my dinner!" I teased.

"Until it's out of my kitchen and into your stomach, it's my cooking," replied Mrs. Mason with her part of the catechism. "But just to keep your nosy self out of my hair while I'm earning my living, I'll tell you that it's veal chops with mushroom gravy, wild rice, and asparagus from Mrs. Prescott's garden that your daddy

brought back with him special on the plane from Flor-
ida.''

"Was Mother mad when you told her I was coming
for dinner?''

"She's going to be plenty mad if Raoul doesn't get
his self in here and get those suitcases up to her room.
Gladys, you go find him and tell him to get his lazy
brown butt up here.''

I left the comforting banter of the kitchen and made
my progress to the front of the house. There was a long,
narrow passageway lined with glass-fronted cupboards
and a butler's pantry that led to the dining room. The
dinner table was a dazzle of white linen and Spode. At
the center was an arrangement of orchids. I heard my
mother's sharp step on the marble of the front hall.

"Mother?''

"Where are you, Kate?'' she called.

"Right here,'' I said, joining her beneath the curved
stair where Stephen Azorini had decked Edgar Eichel.
Mother was examining her reflection in a gilt mirror
with an intense and critical eye. I saw my image reflected behind hers and sensed her disappointment at
the comparison. There was no denying that I was her
daughter. But I wore no jewelry, no makeup, and I was
still wearing the boxy blue suit that Leon had selected
for me from Brooks Brothers. I hadn't touched my hair
since I'd pinned it up that morning in the taxi on the
way to Azor Pharmaceuticals. My mother, on the other
hand, had just finished arranging hers upstairs and was
now adjusting it again, following her descent to the main
floor of the house.

"You know, we do have a front door for visitors,''
she remarked. "I sent Raoul to turn on the outside lights
for you, but he said you'd come in the tradesman's
door.'' She paused to reapply her lipstick.

In my whole life I had never known my mother to look less than perfect. Even the night they came home from the Simpson's party to find that my brother, Teddy, had hanged himself, her hair was never out of place.

Beauty, she had lectured me in the more intimate moments of my childhood, was as much a matter of good habits and hard work as nature. I never saw any reason to not believe her. I just never felt particularly motivated to follow her advice.

"Hi, pumpkin!" said my father, coming down the stairs. His ruddy cheeks were already glowing from the tall gin in his hand. "Pleasant surprise, your joining us for dinner like this."

"We're just waiting for your sister, as usual," announced Mother with an impatient look up the stairs. "Edward, pick up the phone in the library and call Beth. Tell her we're waiting for her to go in to dinner."

"I'll go with you, Daddy," I said, not wanting to be left alone with Mother. I mixed myself a Scotch with ice from the bar cart while my father dialed the children's line.

"She's coming," he announced, hanging up the receiver. "I have to tell you, pumpkin, your little sister's having a hard time coming through this thing about Gretchen. We took her down to Palm Beach, but I don't think it did any good. I think it's great that you came out tonight. She needs her family around her now."

Dinner was a gruesome affair. Daddy was half in the bag before the first glass of wine. Mother, who was famous as a gracious hostess and a witty conversationalist, clearly didn't find her own daughters worth the same effort. Through three courses she kept up a cheerful, if somewhat redundant monologue about which of the girls I'd grown up with had recently had babies, or divorces, or liposuction. Beth ate everything in sight and said nothing, sullenly observing the proceedings through a lock of her dirty brown hair.

"I told Mrs. Mason we didn't need dessert tonight," my mother proclaimed with a pointed look at Beth, as Gladys brought the coffee.

"I'm going up to my room," Beth announced, dropping her napkin onto her dinner plate and practically sprinting from the table.

"Your father and I are going to have a brandy in the library. Hopefully, Raoul will have managed to get a fire going. Honestly, he has trouble with the most basic things. Even cavemen managed to build fires. You may join us if you wish, but I imagine that you're anxious to get back to your office."

"I thought I'd run up and have a few words with Beth."

"Very well, but you are not to discuss Gretchen Azorini with her. Dr. Weingart says he's dealing with it in therapy. It is very important that she not be upset. Do I make myself perfectly clear?"

"You are one of the clearest people I know, Mother," was my forthright reply.

I tapped lightly on my sister's door.

"Who is it?" came her anxious voice.

"It's me, Kate."

Beth opened the door and shut it quickly after me. A hash pipe smouldered in a crystal ashtray at the foot of her bed.

"You must be crazy smoking dope in the house!" I exclaimed.

"I do it all the time. It's great stuff. Raoul's brother brings it up from Guatemala. You want a hit?"

"No, thanks, I've got to drive back to the city tonight. How was Palm Beach?"

"About as exciting as watching fish fuck."

I wondered whether her choice of language had the desired effect on Dr. Weingart, or maybe she tried different, stronger tactics on him.

"What did you do?" I asked.

"The parents played golf while I stayed home and watched Grandma Prescott play solitaire and drink herself into a coma. At night they all went out to dinner at the Van Houtens' while I screwed the chauffeur."

"Was he any good?" I inquired, playing it as a joke.

"You know what they say," Beth quipped humorlessly, "once you've had black, there's no going back."

We were silent for a while. I didn't know what to say. Finally I settled on the direct approach.

"Beth, I need your help," I said.

"About what?" Her voice was soft and constricted.

"I think there's a good chance that Gretchen was murdered by someone she knew."

My sister's eyes got wider.

"Nobody who knew her would rape and strangle her," she said.

"I met with the pathologist who performed the autopsy. He doesn't think that's what happened. Did Gretchen ever do cocaine?"

"Gretchen? Never. She never did drugs. She said shooting up insulin every day was enough for her."

"The pathologist thinks that in a way it was her insulin that killed her."

"Gretchen would never make a mistake with her insulin. She was way too careful."

"I know. He thinks that Gretchen gave herself her regular dose of insulin right before she took her shower the morning she died, but that she was unable to find anything to eat. She died of hypoglycemia."

"I don't get it."

"She went up to her father's cabin in Wisconsin and met a man there. He set her up. She went into the bathroom and took her insulin. The only trouble is that when she came out, he was gone. So was all the food. So was the car. He left her up there to die."

"No." Again the constricted whisper.

"Beth, you have to help me figure out who it was. We can't let him get away with this," I implored.

"No, I don't believe it," Beth said, her voice rising like steam in a boiling kettle. "No, no, no! I don't believe you! I won't believe you!"

"Beth, you have to tell me what you know!"

"Mother!" she shouted hysterically. "Mother!"

Mother marched into the room, her eyes flashing.

"Get out of this house this instant," she snapped at me. "I will not have you coming here and upsetting your sister over my express orders."

"Mother, you are only making this worse," I said. "If it's not me, it's going to be the police."

"How dare you threaten to bring the police into this house. Get out!"

I got out. I would make another pass at Beth later. Mother's attention span for parenting was shorter than a mosquito's. There was time to try again tonight.

"I'll just leave you two together," I said, backing out through the closest door.

The handle turned behind me, and I found myself in Beth's bathroom. I saw a bottle of Valium prescribed by Dr. Weingart on the sink and slipped it into my pocket. Then I hastened through the darkened guest bedroom toward the back stairs. My plan was to take Rocket out for a walk until I was fairly certain that Mother would have retired to her room. As long as I had the tranquilizers in my pocket, it didn't matter how long that might be. Then I'd sneak back up to the children's wing and try a different approach.

I was halfway down the stairs when I stopped and considered where I'd been for a moment. Then I quietly made my way back to the empty bedroom I'd just walked through.

The bedroom next to Beth's.

The bedroom where Gretchen slept during the frequent weekends she spent at my parents' house. The bedroom where she spent the night before she went up to Wisconsin to meet her killer.

I could hear Beth's sobs from beyond the connecting bathroom and the rumble of my mother's awkward entreaties. I closed the door softly behind me. I was afraid to turn on the overhead light in case Mother should find me still in the house.

The closet light cast a dim glow through the rest of the room—enough for my purposes. I got down on my hands and knees and reached my arm between the twin mattress and box spring. I groped until my fingers hit the edge of something hard. I grabbed it and pulled it out slowly. It was a manila envelope.

I took it to the closet and there, with the hems of Mother's summer dresses around my ears, I tore open the envelope. I pulled out the contents—a copy of the December issue of *Bride's* magazine, as thick as a small-town phone book. There was also a packet, not quite as thick, of Azor corporate documents. There were current balance sheets and income statements, cash-flow projections, a copy of the summary that I had prepared for Stephen outlining what antitakeover preparations the company should make, the most recent status report—complete with detailed income projections—on a research project aimed at the development of artificial blood. All the documents were photocopies, but it was the front page of the research report that made my breathing come in short, painful gasps and sparked tremors in my hands. Written across the cover in handwriting that I had seen before but could not place was a note:

Edgar—
This should help you set a realistic upper ceiling for the offering price. Dick Porter will be out of the country until Dec. 2nd, which meshes nicely with your plan to make your bid on the 30th!

It was not signed.

I stuffed the documents back into the envelope and, clutching it to my chest, I raced down the back stairs, through the pantry, the kitchen, and into the mudroom. I grabbed a duffle coat that belonged to Beth from a peg by the back door and put it on. I folded the envelope in half and stuffed it into one of the large outer pockets. Rocket came, sniffing hopefully for a walk.

"Come on, old boy," I said as I opened the door.

I strode out into the darkness with my brain reeling. In my pocket was incontrovertible evidence that someone had been giving Edgar Eichel confidential and sensitive information on Azor Pharmaceuticals and that Gretchen Azorini had known about it. In cop 101, that spelled motive. My heart was pounding. I needed to get in touch with Guttman. I wanted to talk to Elliott. But first I had to take another shot at Beth. I was convinced that there were things that she knew but was not telling.

Rocket headed toward the back of the house and clambered down the beach stairs ahead of me. There was a full moon, and it was just light enough to pick out the way. The roar of the waves was reassuring. Gulls wheeled in the frozen air. The city sat, jewellike in the distance.

I never heard him coming.

The first blow was meant for my head but got me on the collarbone—something heavy, swung hard. I heard the snap of the fracture and fell to my knees. I saw the dark shadow of a man rise again in the darkness for a second blow. I tried to get to my feet to run, but he grabbed me by the hair. I kicked him hard in the shins and grabbed for the soft parts of his face but felt a woolen ski mask instead. I grabbed at it, hooked my fingers into the eyeholes and jabbed. He grabbed me by the throat. I tried to scream, but all that came out was a pathetic croak.

I tried to break his hands apart but couldn't. I bit him, surprised at my own savagery, and tasted blood. But it only deterred him for an instant. My attacker was not much taller than me but stronger and heavier. I remembered Dr. Yarbrough saying that most young women who were raped were strangled. I wondered whether he was going to rape me or whether that happened after I was dead.

"No!" a voice commanded from inside of me. "No! No!"

As spots swam before my eyes, I snapped my head as hard as I could up to the underside of his jaw. I heard him grunt as his jaws snapped shut with the impact. I grabbed for his groin with both of my hands but was hampered by the heavy stuff of his jacket. He let go of my throat to grab my hands, but I bit him as he tried to pull me away.

He grunted in pain, and as I turned to run, he caught me by the throat again and squeezed. I felt the strength drain out of me. I willed my legs to kick, but they only responded weakly. I heard what might have been the faint sound of a dog barking in someone else's dream as a soft blanket of darkness fell over me.

CHAPTER
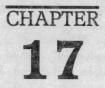

I climbed into consciousness with leaden limbs and the feeling that a great weight rested on my chest. It was hard work to breathe, to force the air in and out. I had a terrible sore throat. I was in a painfully bright room. There was an unpleasant smell that I knew, but could not put a name to. I couldn't move. Somewhere nearby someone groaned weakly, and I wished they would shut up. They were making my head hurt.

"Quick, page Dr. Pollard," thundered a voice somewhere out of my view. Then I slipped back to wherever I had climbed from.

The next time I came to I knew that I was in the hospital. The unpleasant smell was the combination of sickness and disinfectant that I'd learned to loathe during Russell's illness. I knew that the shades were drawn and that the unbearably bright room was in reality only dimly lit. I knew that the person who had groaned was me.

My lips were cracked and swollen. My mouth was so dry it felt as though it was stuck shut. My left arm was in something more elaborate than a cast, and I.V. tubes ran into the other. Everything hurt, but I couldn't localize the source of pain. Breathing was hell.

I had no idea what had happened to me.

There was something that looked like a turquoise plastic remote control on a thick cord positioned near my good arm. I pushed all the buttons on it. The TV flicked on, the head of my bed shuddered up a notch, and a nurse appeared in about ten seconds flat.

"Miss Millholland. We're glad to have you back," she chirped. She pushed another button over my head.

"Call Dr. Pollard and tell him that Millholland's regained consciousness." Then she bent down to me and asked, "Would you like some water?"

I nodded. She poured water with ice from a green container on the table next to my bed into a cup with a top and a straw. The cold liquid clawed my throat. I sputtered and gagged. Water dripped down my chin. With my free hand I tried to touch my throat, but the IV tubes restrained me.

"Just lie still," the nurse admonished gently. She was a middle-aged woman with a frizzy perm of nondescript brown hair and a pleasant face.

"What happened?" I managed to ask. "Why am I here?"

"You've been hurt," she replied.

"How?" My voice was a faint croak. Every word burned.

"It's best not to ask too many questions until you're a little stronger. You've been unconscious for a long time. Dr. Pollard will be here in a little while, and he'll answer your questions."

"How long?" I rasped.

"Oh, he should be along in just a few minutes," she replied.

"No. How long have I been unconscious?" It was getting harder to talk, not easier.

"Let me see, you were admitted Wednesday night. Today is Sunday, so you've been unconscious for—"

"Sunday!" I exclaimed, struggling to sit up, driven by a sense of emergency that I could not identify. "It can't be Sunday!"

The nurse with the pleasant face took hold of my good shoulder and my unencumbered wrist and pushed me back down onto the bed with surprising efficiency.

"You're much too weak to sit up yet," she advised.

I began to protest, but she held me firmly against the sheets.

"If you persist in becoming agitated, I'm afraid we'll have to sedate you," she warned.

I wanted to tell her not to sedate me, that I'd be good and not try to sit up, but all I managed was a pathetic whisper, "Please . . ."

A little while later a white-haired man appeared. He wore rimless glasses and kept a Mont Blanc pen in the pocket of his crisp white lab coat. He was, I learned later, my mother's doctor, none other than Lawrence Pollard, III, M.D.

"It's good to see you've regained consciousness," he said, taking up my chart and looking at it instead of me. "I must confess we've been a bit worried about you."

"What happened to me?"

"What do you think happened?" he asked.

"I don't know."

"You don't remember anything?"

I thought for a minute. Instead of an overwhelming sense of universal agony, I was beginning to be able to identify the individual sources of pain—my shoulder, my arm, my ribs, my throat. Especially my throat.

"I had dinner at my parents' house."

"When was that?"

"I would swear it was just last night."

"What day was that?"

"Wednesday night."

"You know that today is Sunday. Are you sure the last thing you remember is dinner with your parents?"

I thought hard. It made me dizzy.

"That's okay," he said, giving me a condescending pat on the hand. "Memory loss is not uncommon in cases of trauma of this kind."

"What happened to me?" I demanded with growing impatience. It hurt to talk. I was tired of this elliptical bullshit.

"You've sustained several traumatic injuries, but we are not sure how. We were hoping you could tell us. You have a broken collarbone, a broken wrist, four broken ribs, a sprained ankle, and your windpipe has been crushed. A tracheotomy was performed in the emergency room to allow you to breathe. Later, a polyurethane tube was inserted to repair the breathing tube. That's why it's so difficult for you to speak. You have a concussion, also some cuts and bruises. You have a very long, jagged laceration down the left side of your face, which required twenty-nine stitches. You were quite a sight when they brought you in. All things considered, you're a very lucky young lady."

Funny, I didn't feel lucky at all.

I had a busy afternoon, especially for someone in as bad shape as I was in. I was examined by an orthopedist and an internist. A neurologist came and pronounced my short-term amnesia normal.

"Don't try to force it. It may just come back to you," he assured me.

I suppressed a shudder. I wasn't at all sure I wanted it to come back.

The thoracic surgeon who repaired my windpipe came and admired his handiwork. The surplus breathing tube was removed from my throat. Afterward, talking and drinking were even more unpleasant. Food was completely out of the question. I took to swearing at the nurses who periodically came by to urge Popsicles on me.

I was visited by the police.

It was a different kind of Lake Forest detective than the one who had solicitously called on me the day after Stephen decked Edgar Eichel. This was a hard-faced cop in a polyester suit and a crew cut. His name was James Wolfe, and while he didn't exactly come right out and say it, it was clear from the outset that he didn't care whose daughter I was or how much money I had.

I paid attention and tried to answer his questions as best as I could. The trouble was that at the end of an hour—when the nurse came to tell him he'd tired me enough—I had learned more about what had happened than he had.

I also had a stupendous headache.

According to Detective Wolfe, sometime after having dinner with my parents, I went down to the beach for a walk with Rocket, the dog. It was there that I was attacked by an as-yet-unidentified assailant. Around 9:20 P.M. the kitchen staff became alarmed because the dog was barking outside the back door. They were surprised that Rocket was alone and concerned by the persistence of his barking. After a while, the gardener was dispatched with a flashlight. Rocket led him down to the beach where I was found unconscious and covered with blood.

Finally, I thought to myself, Raoul earns his keep.

When asked, I said I thought it was unlikely that I'd taken a purse or wallet with me when I'd gone out to walk the dog. I said I didn't have any idea who attacked me or why. I said that I hadn't been harassed by strange men in the past. I denied having a kinky boyfriend. There was no one I knew who bore me a grudge. I'd never been attacked before, never blackmailed or threatened. I was a hardworking corporate attorney. There was, I assured him, nothing associated with my work that might have provoked an attack.

When Detective Wolfe asked whether I minded having a police guard outside my room for another twenty-four hours I said no.

Later, I asked the nurse whether I was allowed phone calls or visitors. "Only family," she replied. No member of my family had come or called.

I was still on the critical list.

I woke up Monday morning to find Elliott Abelman sitting in a chair next to my bed, fast asleep. My pain medication had worn off abruptly, and I felt like a mass of jangling injuries. I tried to shift myself into a more comfortable position and woke Elliott.

"Morning, gorgeous," he said, grinning and instantly awake.

"Morning," I whispered in the sandy croak that was now my voice.

"You sound awful."

I nodded. "How did you get past the guard?"

"I told him I was your brother. For a nice girl, you sure get beaten up a lot."

I nodded again.

"You scared the shit out of me."

"Sorry."

"One of my operatives thinks he's found out where Joey Azorini was on the night before Gretchen died."

"Where?" I croaked.

"It appears that Joey has a girlfriend."

"So why didn't he just tell us?"

"Because she's thirteen."

"Oh."

"Her name is Shawna. She says that she was with Joey from eleven on Sunday night until five-thirty Monday morning. Her mother says Shawna was home in bed the whole night. Shawna says she waits until her mother is asleep and then she climbs out her bedroom window. Joey waits to pick her up at the end of the street. Do you want to know how they first met each other, Joey and Shawna? It's the best part."

I nodded yes.

"Thirteen years ago Joey used to date Shawna's mom."

We sat silently for a minute, considering Joey Azorini, the king of sleaze.

"It doesn't get us off the hook, does it?"

"No," Elliott replied. "Stephen doesn't strike me as the sort of person who'd take the word of a thirteen-year-old who Joey's sleeping with.

"I talked to Detective Wolfe last night," Elliott continued. "He seems to think you surprised a burglar who's been working in your parents' neighborhood. He said he'd bring a photo array to the hospital later to see if you could identify your assailant."

"I still don't remember anything," I said. "It's awful. I keep on getting this strange feeling that something's missing. It's like I've had something important and now I've lost it."

"Don't force it, and it'll come back to you."

* * *

John Guttman dropped by after Elliott left. I was flattered that he took the time, and then I remembered that he lived about six blocks from the hospital. He was probably double-parked out front, on his way to the office. He immediately plopped down in the visitor's chair next to my bed.

"I thought I should be the first one to tell you," he said in the tone of the newly bereaved.

"What is it?"

"We got a fax from the FDA this morning. You know that Azor was just about to get FDA approval for the new schizophrenia drug?"

"Stephen said it was sewn up."

"Well, it's come unraveled. It appears that one of the commissioners has done a complete three sixty on the thing. Word is he's in Eichel's pocket. It's completely blocked. They've asked for two more years of clinical trials."

"Shit," I muttered, feeling the anger rise up inside of me. If you're trying to buy something there are two ways you can up your bid. Offer to pay more, or keep the same offering price and lower the expected value of whatever it is you're bidding on. Eichel had just done the latter, and considering the fact that once he owned Azor, his pet FDA commissioner would just do another three sixty, I had to admire the guy's balls.

Elliott returned just as the lunch trays were being delivered.

"Take that away," he ordered the bewildered nurse's aide. "This patient is on a special diet."

Elliott kicked the door shut behind him and deposited a paper bag on my bedside table.

"Don't you know that hospital food is very bad for you? I brought you chicken soup from this little deli in Rogers' Park. We'll let it cool off, and then you can drink it with a straw.''

"Thank you," I rasped.

"Remember anything yet?" he asked.

"No," I said. It was getting marginally easier to speak. "But I have this nagging feeling that there's something just at the tip of my tongue. Do you think you could find out what happened to what I was wearing when I was brought in? I keep on thinking it's important somehow."

"I'll find it," he assured me with a smile. "That's what detectives are for. I'll be back before your soup cools."

A nurse appeared with my medication, two Darvocet in a little paper cup. I slipped them into my fist and pretended to take them. I wanted to keep my head clear for Elliott.

Elliott returned twenty minutes later with two large plastic bags marked "personal property."

"It was all packed up for the police, but they haven't gotten around to picking it up yet. I thought we'd just borrow it for a few minutes since you seemed to think it was important."

He began unpacking the bags.

"Some of the stuff is in pretty sad shape," he told me kindly. "Seems they had to cut a lot of it off you in the emergency room."

My black pumps were crusted with mud, and one heel was missing; the blouse that had once been white was stiff with dried blood; the blue skirt of the Brooks Brothers suit looked like it had been filleted. Elliott held up a white silk bra—one cup was soaked with blood, the other was pristine.

The physical evidence of what had happened to me, grisly props from a scene that had played out with its main actor, me, unable to remember what had happened, shook me up. The last thing that Elliott removed from the bag was a navy blue duffle coat that I knew didn't belong to me. The sight of it stirred something in my memory.

"Check the pockets," I said with a sense of rising impatience.

Elliott extracted a large manila envelope folded in half.

"They're Azor documents," I exclaimed, cheered that at least some portion of my memory had come back to me. "They were hidden in the room that Gretchen used to sleep in at my parents' house. I found them right before I went out for a walk."

Elliott slipped the pages out the envelope and read them. "There's a note on one of them," he said, slowly reading.

"Show it to me," I said slowly. I knew that I had read the note and that it had been important, even though I could no longer remember why.

Elliott handed me the sheet and for the second time I held proof that someone had been sending Azor's secrets to Edgar Eichel, and that Gretchen Azorini had known about it.

CHAPTER
18

They cannot make you stay in the hospital, not if you don't want to—not if you are an adult and considered competent. But they try to wear you down with paperwork before you go. As I was laboring through a stack of release forms, Claudia arrived. I had stopped bothering to read them. It was difficult enough to apply a simple signature, encumbered as I was by an airplane sling cast and an I.V. They were all versions of the same thing, mumbo jumbo absolving the hospital from any liability if I died or suffered permanent injury as a result of my early, and they assured me, foolish departure from their care.

I used to think that you couldn't shock a doctor, but when Claudia saw me for the first time that afternoon, she was clearly aghast. The call from Elliott Abelman that morning telling her that I was in the hospital and desperate for her help was her first indication that anything out of the ordinary had occurred. She hadn't thought anything of the fact that we hadn't seen each other in a couple of days. It wasn't at all unusual for our schedules to diverge.

While I explained what I needed from her, Claudia stood at the foot of my bed and read my chart. When she finished, she hugged the metal clipboard to her chest in exactly the same way as every other doctor who had read it. Then she shook her head. "I don't think it's a good idea to move you," she said finally.

"I don't think it's a great idea for me to lie here, either."

"We could have you moved to another service in the hospital under a different name."

"No. I don't want to hide from him, I want to stop him. And I can't find out who he is lying in this hospital."

"You have to realize you've sustained life-threatening injuries. It's not just the trauma to your windpipe or the fractures and lacerations, which are certainly nothing to sneeze at. You have all sorts of internal soft tissue damage, the extent of which I can only guess at. You're scheduled for a CAT scan tomorrow afternoon, which will give us a better idea of what's going on under all those bruises. But there's a very real danger of internal bleeding, especially if you start exerting yourself. I want you to think hard about whether a business deal is worth that."

"This goes way beyond the deal, Claudia," I replied. "You have to believe that. Will you help me?"

"Of course."

While Claudia arranged transportation and the necessary medical support, Elliott was dispatched to pick up Beth from Chelsea Hall. I didn't have a good feeling for her level of jeopardy, since I had been attacked while wearing her coat. There was a good chance that Beth was the one the killer had been lying in wait for.

I wasn't in the mood to take any chances.

It was a strange and somber procession that arrived, via ambulance, at the home of Anthony Azorini. The old man had not demurred when I asked him for a safe place to stay. He hadn't asked any questions either. For that I was grateful.

He lived in one of the old neighborhoods on the southwest side of the city. A quiet place that had fiercely defended itself against the encroachment of the ghetto. It was a neighborhood where old women in black dresses still walked down Cicero from store to store carrying net bags or trailing shopping baskets. There was a bakery on every corner and a knee-high shrine to the Blessed Virgin in front of every third house.

Anthony Azorini may have wanted to take Bako Industries into the nineties as a legitimate company, but he still chose to live in the old neighborhood. It said something about the man and what was important to him.

His house lay at the end of an anonymous cul-de-sac. It was built in the same yellow brick bungalow style as its neighbors, but was five times as large. There were geometrically patterned stained-glass panes in the leaded-glass windows that faced the street, and a wide brick stoop. They had been the rage during the twenties and thirties when these neighborhoods had been built.

The house was set sideways to the street so that visitors were obliged to park and approach the house on foot under the scrutiny of an armed guard at his post on the second-floor balcony. Anthony Azorini came out to the ambulance himself to usher us into the house. He wore a green cardigan sweater over a red golf shirt that gave him an incongruous, yuletide air. He did not seem surprised by my physical condition and didn't offer any comment. Maybe, like a general, he had grown immune to the casualties of his particular brand of war.

When Claudia introduced herself, he seemed genuinely surprised that such a small young woman would be a doctor. The ingrained prejudices of men past a certain age never failed to amaze me. But I always felt sorry for them, too. They had grown up in such a coat and tie world, where women were mothers and teachers and nurses, and men could just relax in the certainty that it was their show. How hard it must be, as you grew old, to see that comfortable order crumble, to discover, on your own doorstep, that this tiny young woman in the down jacket and the tennis shoes is in reality Dr. Stein.

Anthony Azorini led us into the house. The two ambulance attendants carried me on a stretcher while Claudia trotted beside me, carrying the I.V. bag on a pole and looking worried. Waves of nausea washed over me as the paramedics began their unsteady progress up the vast curve of the mahogany stairs. The steps were carpeted in burgundy. The walls were covered in dark paper patterned with poppies the color of old blood. A huge, wrought-iron chandelier of vaguely Moorish design illuminated the way. The pain killers made me feel like I was being carted through a Goya painting.

This was the home of the old man who led the way up the stairs. The man who Stephen claimed had the blood of many men on his hands. The man whom I had turned to to keep me safe from the man with Gretchen Azorini's blood on his.

My room had high ceilings and was dimly lit, with heavy red drapes pulled tight against the pale afternoon light. The furniture was heavy and black and laid with circles of white lace. There was a somber dressing table, its mirror smoky with age, and several armchairs upholstered in dark green baize. If there had once been a bed to match, it had been removed. In its place was a modern hospital bed, so newly delivered that the men from the medical supply company still lingered, finishing up their paperwork.

A private nurse waited for me in my room, a young woman in a crisp white uniform. She had blond hair and a California smile. Her name was Patty. She helped the attendants shift me onto the bed.

"How do you feel?" Claudia inquired while Patty concentrated on taking my blood pressure.

"Terrible," I whispered in all honesty.

"Remember, it was your idea to do this."

"I appreciate your sympathy," I managed to croak.

"Any time," Claudia retorted in her crisp doctor's voice. "With one being a mild headache and ten being the most excruciating pain you can imagine, how would you say you feel?"

"Seven. Seven and a half," I guessed.

Claudia frowned. "I'm going to increase your pain medication. It might make you sleepy."

"No. I don't want to sleep. I need to call Cheryl and have her messenger some documents to me."

"Be serious, Kate," Claudia replied severely. "Just moving you here has pushed this situation to the outer limits of prudent medical practice."

"Please, Claudia, what's the point of leaving the hospital if I can't find out who tried to kill me?"

"I'll make this deal with you. You tell me what you want from Cheryl; I'll call her and tell her to get it together and send it by messenger. In the meantime, I'll give you something to make you rest. I'll make it short-acting. By the time the messenger arrives, you'll be awake again."

"Okay," I reluctantly agreed.

Claudia obediently wrote down my instructions to Cheryl on a prescription pad and then laced my I.V. with something.

"You'd better not croak on me," she warned as she wrote out instructions for the nurse. "Because if you do, I'll be practicing medicine in a storefront clinic in Alaska for the rest of my life, and you know how I hate the cold."

By the time I woke it was almost dusk. While I slept, someone had pulled back the heavy damask that had covered the windows to reveal sheer curtains through which I could see the bony fingers of the naked December trees. The house around me was absolutely still. With consciousness, the pain came back to me as well, a familiar and unwanted companion.

Patty entered the room briskly and snapped on the lights.

"Dr. Stein said not to wake you, but that when you did get up, I should try to make you comfortable. Would you like me to help you get cleaned up?"

A grateful nod was all that I could muster.

Patty washed my face with a warm cloth and combed my hair, plaiting it into a single braid down the back. From somewhere she produced a large white T-shirt, which she slit up the side to accommodate my cast, and a pair of black sweat pants. It made me feel much better to be clean and dressed.

"A Mr. Abelman came by while you were resting," reported Patty. "He said to tell you that he has arranged to stay with your sister at your parents' house and that everything is fine. He also left this envelope for you." Patty laid it on my lap.

I tried to imagine how Elliott had managed to convince my mother to let him stay with Beth at their house. And what was he doing while he was there? Sweet-talking Mrs. Mason? Enjoying Beth's little anecdotes about sleeping with Grandma Prescott's chauffeur?

Playing cards and drinking gin with Daddy? The mind boggled.

"A messenger also delivered a package for you from your office, though, honestly, I can't say that you're in any condition to do any work."

"Will you open the letter from Mr. Abelman for me, please?"

Patty slit it open with a pair of scissors and unfolded it for me. It read:

I had my friend at the phone company check the record of incoming calls to your parents' house for the last night Gretchen stayed there. There was only one call that corresponded to the time that Mrs. Mason talked to the man who said he was Gretchen's father. It was placed from 465-0900.

Elliott

Elliott knew he didn't have to say who that number belonged to. I dialed that number practically every day. It was the main number for the corporate offices of Azor Pharmaceuticals.

I was still clutching Elliott's note, churning through the implications of what it contained, when Stephen Azorini entered the room.

"Oh, Kate," he cried softly as the sight of my battered face drew him into the room. "I had no idea it was this bad. Guttman said you surprised a burglar at your parents' house, but I had no idea you'd been so seriously hurt."

Stephen pulled an armchair up to my bed. He stroked my unlacerated cheek with the back of his hand. He touched my lips with the tips of his fingers. We had known each other for a long time, but our friendship had known few moments of real affection. Stephen looked into my eyes, and I was truly touched. But the paper in my hand sullied the moment as I tucked it awkwardly under the corner of my blanket to hide it from view.

I examined Stephen's face carefully. He looked ill. There were deep circles under his eyes and lines where none had been before. Even his hair, which had once lay thick and black around his ears, now seemed dull and tinged with gray.

I tended to think of myself as a sophisticated woman of the world, but I had, in fact, only had relationships with two men in my life. One of them I had truly loved, and he loved me back. And the other man? The other man was a handsome loner who matched my reserve full measure with his own. I looked at his troubled face.

"What's wrong?" I asked.

"You know," he said, leaning back into the chair, "seeing you like this makes me realize how much I miss the doctoring part of being a physician. Taking care of people. Being needed."

"What's wrong?" I demanded again, alarmed by the defeat in his voice.

"The board has called a special meeting for nine tonight. I was not consulted. I was informed, via letter, at four-thirty today." He was speaking slowly, as if each word was a burden that he was obliged to carry over a long distance. "I tried to call some of my good friends on the board to see what's up. No one returned my calls.

"I did manage to catch my friend Peter Chou at home. Obviously, he hadn't informed his wife about my new status as leper." Stephen's voice was bitter. "He told me that the board is planning to vote to sell out to Eichel. They've invited the largest shareholders to the meeting tonight. They're going to explain their decision and then vote to sell. They've invited Eichel to come and bring his key people. Once they've voted, they want me to sit down with him, face-to-face, and hammer out a friendly deal. . . .''

"Oh, Stephen," was all I could manage to say. It came out between a sob and a wail. I felt as though the force of gravity had been rapidly increased, crushing the wind out of me, physically pulling me down into darkness.

"They must have been planning this for a couple of days," Stephen continued. "They've reserved two conference rooms at the University Club. The Azor group will meet in one. Eichel and his team of sharks will wait for the vote in the other.''

"They can't give in tonight," I protested. "The offering pool doesn't close for another forty-eight hours. They can't even be sure that enough shares have been tendered.''

"It doesn't matter. They obviously have enough votes from the board. Christ, I am angry!" Stephen exclaimed, exploding out of his chair to pace the room. "I could strangle Eichel with my bare hands. No, Eichel I can understand, it's the fucking board that's betrayed me. What the hell can they be thinking? That running a pharmaceutical company is like running a muffler franchise? Do you know what Peter Chou had the gall to tell me? Peter fucking Chou, who would still be a penniless little chemist toiling away as a browbeaten assistant professor in some stinking basement lab if it weren't for me. He tells me that they've decided it's in the best interests of the company to sell out now, before any further revelations like the FDA fiasco come to light. He says the board feels it is their fiduciary duty to negotiate a friendly merger.

"I'd like to kill the bastard. What's best for the company! Shit! What's best for the greedy bastards on the board. They're just trying to protect their asses and line their pockets at the same time. They don't give a damn about the little shareholders or about the public. Peter wants to buy a house in Aspen, and he's got two girls at Smith who are sending home steep tuition bills. He wants to just take the fucking money and sell my company to a man who couldn't understand what half of Azor's products do, even if you explained it to him with flashcards.''

Stephen paced and seethed.

I was no virgin when it came to raging and ranting. Takeovers were emotional pressure cookers for players who, as a rule, prided themselves on controlling their emotions. In every deal, every major participant lost it at least once—usually in front of his lawyer.

You could hardly blame Stephen. The entire process by which Eichel was going to steal Azor Pharmaceuticals from him was a hideous affront. A violation. Stephen had built the company, step by step, decision by decision, gamble by gamble, until by luck and skill and sheer balls he had taken a tiny pharmaceutical company run by a bunch of geeky ex-academics like Peter Chou and made it into a force in the international business community.

And now this manicured little runt of a financier named Edgar Eichel, who knew nothing about science, who knew nothing about research, was going to have his feet up on Stephen's desk. Eichel, with his bald head and his fat cigar, was going to be sitting there while his lovely wife, the former flight attendant, Nadine, and her hateful decorator decided how they were going to redecorate Stephen's office.

But this time I wasn't just watching my client be put through the grinder, I was watching my friend. I was watching him struggle with the fact that in a month, or two, or six—depending on the progress of the negotiations that would be started that night—it would be Edgar Eichel calling the shots at Azor. Eichel who would decide which of Stephen's handpicked staff would be around to hop when the little financier snapped his fingers. And which one of them would be shopping their résumés around town trying to find another job.

And Stephen, who had put every ounce of himself into Azor, he would wake up in the morning and . . . and what? Check how Azor shares were doing in the *Wall Street Journal*? Take up golf? Walk around his empty apartment and wonder what the hell had happened to his life?

The thought that Stephen would have to sit down across the table from that impotent little toad Eichel was unbearable. It was worse than unbearable. It was wrong. It shouldn't happen in a world where the laws of nature and physics still applied. It wouldn't happen. I wouldn't let it.

"We can't let him get away with this," I declared.

"That was my first reaction, too," Stephen replied steadily. "But then I thought about it. If Eichel has enough votes on the board, there's nothing I can do. Especially if they won't talk to me. And what would I say to convince them that I haven't said before? That Eichel isn't qualified to run the company? That he just wants to loot it and load it with debt the way he has with all his other acquisitions? If the board wasn't going to listen to me then, why should they listen to me now?"

"Because I have proof that Eichel is dirty."

"I've told them about the fax. They were not convinced. They said that some of that goes on in every takeover, raiders get stuff over the transom from disgruntled employees—"

"No, it's more than that," I interjected. "Gretchen found out that someone was sending confidential Azor materials to Eichel. I think she was killed to prevent her from telling you. I didn't surprise any burglar; whoever killed Gretchen tried to kill me, too."

Stephen stared back at me, white-faced and thunderstruck.

"Do you know who it is? Can you prove it?" he demanded.

"I might be able to in forty-eight hours. We're getting closer to this bastard every day. I just need a little more time!"

"Time's the one thing the board's being very stingy with. They're afraid that Eichel will be able to pull off more stunts like he did with the FDA, which will depress the value of the company and let Eichel cut an even sweeter deal for himself."

"They have to listen, you're only asking for a short delay!"

"They'll think it's just my grandstanding to satisfy my own ego. I didn't even have an inkling about the meeting tonight. Events have moved out of my control."

"Then you have to let me talk to them," I insisted.

"You've got to be kidding. I bet you can't even pee by yourself. I'll tell you what. Give me copies of whatever proof you have, and Guttman and I will give it our best shot. You never know, we might walk out of there with the forty-eight hours you need."

"No. I'm going to do it," I said. My mind was made up. "Have you ever seen a more eloquent argument than the state of my face? If I drag myself down there in my condition, they have to at least listen to what I have to say. Jesus, this is the second time I've gotten beaten up for Azor Pharmaceuticals. You've got to at least let me get some mileage out of this.''

I was at a dead end. In my twelve-day career as a detective I had figured out that Gretchen Azorini was murdered and why. But I felt no closer to discovering the identity of the killer than I had on the first day. According to Elliott, when detectives are at a dead end, they go back to the basics: means, motive, and opportunity. When lawyers are at a dead end, they go back to the documents in the case. I had asked Cheryl to messenger over the Azor file as well as the packets of documents that I had found in Gretchen's rooms at the dorm and at Stephen's.

Gretchen Azorini had hidden bundles of papers everywhere she had lived. That in and of itself gave them great significance. She had taken the trouble to conceal them. Who was she hiding them from? Why weren't they all hidden in the same place? Did she want to insure that if one of her hiding places was discovered, some portion of her hoard would still remain safe? Why did she leave them hidden once she decided she was going to run off to get married? Were they insurance in case things did not turn out as she had planned? Or did she think that, in and of themselves, they didn't provide enough information to be of much use if discovered?

I arranged the materials that Gretchen had hidden on my lap. Except for the copy of *Bride's* magazine and the framed photo, all of them were Azor corporate documents.

I took up the *Bride's* magazine first. It was the current issue, which might support the premise that Gretchen had not been planning her elopement for months. . . . I leafed through it carefully to make sure that nothing had been hidden between the pages. I looked for notes that might have been written in the margins. I searched for deeper meaning in an ad for china whose page had been dog-eared.

Nothing.

Then I turned to the photograph that had been hidden in Stephen's apartment. It looked as though it had been clipped from the annual report. It was in a hinged brass frame that snapped closed like a book. There had been a similar picture in a silver frame among the things taken from her room at the dorm. Why, I wondered, had she displayed the photo in her room at the dorm and hidden it in her room at home? Why on earth, I asked myself, would a sixteen-year-old girl keep a picture of the directors of a pharmaceutical company at all, much less two copies of the same picture? What was its significance? I slipped the photo out of the frame, hoping that something might have been hidden behind it. The only thing I found was a blank piece of cardboard.

Frustrated, I turned to the corporate documents, examining them one by one. Each was a confidential document, not meant for circulation beyond a small audience within Azor Pharmaceuticals. Each would be of strategic importance to a raider like Eichel who was struggling to put a price tag on as sprawling and complex an entity as Azor. But if there was a pattern, it eluded me. There were financial projections, memos on corporate structure and antitakeover measures, reports on the status of research and development projects—all unrelated.

And then it occurred to me that their very unrelatedness was significant. Only a handful of people in a large corporation like Azor have access to documents beyond their particular division or project. Only a handful of people have access to financial, legal, and product-related material. Only a handful of people at the top.

I thought that one over for a while and reluctantly turned to the transcript of the Azor board meeting, not liking what I was looking for. I had been assuming that Gretchen had discovered who was sending Azor documents to Eichel. But what if she had been sending them herself? Not completely inconceivable if she had a desire to hurt Stephen, or if her boyfriend was in some way involved with Eichel. I knew what Elliott would say. That sort of betrayal might make a fine motive for murder.

The call that Gretchen received from the man identifying himself as her father was placed from Azor Pharmaceuticals. At 5:16 that Sunday afternoon, the board of directors was meeting for the first time to decide what to do about Edgar Eichel's offer. As with every other board meeting, a court stenographer had been present.

The transcript of the meeting had been delivered, as usual, to Cheryl a few days after the meeting. Under normal circumstances, it would languish at the back of the Azor file drawer. A day or two before the next Azor board meeting, Cheryl would frantically struggle to condense the transcript into a page or two of corporate minutes to be presented, amended, and included into the minutes of the next meeting of the Azor board.

The fact that the call to my parents' house was made from Azor was troubling but inconclusive. No doubt there had been many people at Azor headquarters that Sunday while the board met: secretaries and assistants, support staff and number crunchers, all on stand-by should Stephen, the board, or the investment bankers require their services. I think even Guttman may have slid by for a while to hold Stephen's hand. But any of those people could have left the office at any time to make a call from a pay phone. Stephen was one of the few people who, if he had been obliged to make a phone call, would have had to try to slip out of the meeting and call from the office.

But the transcript was difficult to interpret because there was no accurate way to gauge what had been said at what time. I guessed from the time the meeting was called to order and the time at which it was adjourned which portion of the meeting had occurred around 5:00 P.M., but I couldn't pin it down any closer than eight or nine pages of transcript. During that time no fewer than four people may have been out of the room, but none for more than a moment or two: Stephen, to check and see if Richard Humanski had the sales projections from accounting yet; Peter Chou, to use the men's room; Tucker Sweet, to get his glasses from the pocket of his overcoat; and Dr. Carl Swensen to answer a page from the hospital.

I set down the transcript and picked up the framed photograph of the Azor directors that had belonged to the dead girl. The photograph troubled me. It posed so many questions, for which I had no answers. I opened the frame and laid it on my lap. There I sat in a hospital bed in the home of Anthony Azorini. I studied the face of my old friend and client, Stephen Azorini. I stared at it until it was time to leave for the meeting.

CHAPTER
19

I almost fainted on the way there. I had gone cold turkey on the pain medication believing that, now more than at any other time of my life, I needed to have my wits about me. But the pain, undulled by drugs, literally left me breathless. By the time I managed to get into the back of the car, I was shaking and my shirt was plastered to my back with cold sweat.

We rode into town in the back of Anthony Azorini's silver Bentley. The windows were smoked and bullet proof, and the driver looked like he could stop a train with his neck. Stephen's father sat next to me on the leather seat, somber and ramrod straight in his navy pinstripes. He stared straight ahead as if his hawk's profile had been chiseled in stone. Patty, the pretty blond nurse, rode up front next to the driver, which seemed to please him.

The Dan Ryan took us into the tangle of highways that webbed the loop. Then the city came into view like a giant, jagged jewel set against the night. Chicago never failed to speak to me, especially when she was lit up for the night.

We got off on Dearborn and made our smooth and silent progress past the darkened storefronts of the western loop. Scavengers pawed through garbage cans, and the homeless crouched silent and practically invisible in doorways while Christmas decorations winked and glittered in the light of the street lamps. Finally, we passed under the El tracks and glided to a stop in front of the anonymous, forest green awning of the University Club.

When the driver opened the door to let Anthony Azorini out of the car, the cold swept in fast and dry and sharp. It must have been just this sort of bitter Chicago night that had spawned the street expression, 'the hawk's bitin'.' We were in the nine-to-five section of the loop, where few restaurants served dinner, and no shops stayed open past six. The magnificent mile and the nocturnal circus that was Rush Street were just a five dollar cab ride away. But for all intents and purposes, on a weeknight like tonight when the symphony did not perform and the Schubert Theater was dark, we might as well have been on the far side of the moon.

Patty and the driver unfolded a rented wheelchair from the trunk. Under the baleful eye of the cadaverous night doorman, they extricated me as carefully as they could from the backseat of the Bentley. The revolving door presented another obstacle, and there was some fumbling in the deep pockets of his moth-eaten, velvet-collared topcoat while the doorman scrounged for the key to the other door. I realized that I was just four blocks from my office. It seemed like a lifetime since I'd last been there.

The lobby of the University Club was silent and dark, with mahogany paneling and deep oak floors, exactly the same as it had always been. It had not changed since I was a little girl and my father took me there every Christmas to have lunch with Santa.

I belonged to several clubs. I never went to most of

them. The University Club was the one I used. For one thing, despite the carved beams and doleful portraits of old men that hung from the paneled walls, it wasn't exclusive. Anyone who had graduated from college and who could afford the modest dues was eligible for membership. It had also been one of the first clubs in the city to unsneeringly accept women. And while it was primarily a business club with the usual emphasis on power lunches and old men drinking sherry and reading the paper in the club library, there were fourteen squash courts, and you could always find a free lane in the pool.

A bushy Christmas tree sat by the elevators, filling the city air with the scent of evergreen. A typed calendar of December events, including lunch with Santa and caroling, was tacked inside a glass-fronted case between the doors. There was also a notice that Mr. Cyrus Rocque was two months behind on his dues and that his name was being posted in accordance with the University Club bylaws. Merry Christmas, Mr. Rocque.

The University Club was the perfect choice for a secret summit meeting. It was deserted except during the lunch hour, and even though there were a handful of overnight guest rooms, no one who ever stayed there reported seeing anyone there after 5:00. Clients whom I had put up there had more than once accused me of booking them into the morgue for the night.

Anthony Azorini punched the UP button, and we waited in silence for the elevator to arrive. The bell rang, and Patty turned me around and backed me into the car. When the polished brass interior doors closed in front of me, I saw myself for the first time since I'd been attacked.

It was much worse than I'd imagined. The left side

of my face, the one with the twenty-nine stitches, was horribly swollen. I looked like a lopsided black-and-blue melon with hair. I just hoped the sight of me would have the desired effect on the board.

The elevator deposited us on the fourteenth floor. While Anthony Azorini held the door and Patty struggled to get my wheelchair over the metal lip of the elevator car, the bell on the car next to us rang; the other elevator arrived and disgorged a load of passengers. Patty pushed me out of the elevator and straight into Edgar Eichel.

I jumped as if I'd seen a ghost.

Eichel, in the abstract, had been the focus of so much hatred and energy since the day that he announced his offer for Azor. I was completely unprepared to deal with the little man in the flesh. The sight of him and the wet end of his cigar made my throat constrict and my palms sweat.

Eichel cocked his head to one side and considered me in my wheelchair. He rolled his cigar between his thumb and his forefinger. "What happened to you?" he demanded finally. "Did Stephen Azorini punch you, too?"

Before I could reply, he made a sound that might have been a chuckle, turned on his heel, and headed for the conference room at the far end of the hall. Anthony Azorini, having received instructions from the board, led the way to the conference room at the opposite end of the corridor. Richard Humanski and John Guttman stood in front of closed oak doors, waiting for us. Richard seemed to have shrunk since I saw him last, as if he had been afflicted by some sort of wasting sickness. He held one of the doors open for Anthony Azorini. I heard Stephen's voice, loud and angry, and then Rich-

ard pulled the door shut behind him, blocking my way
with his body.

"You have to wait out here, Kate," he said severely.

"What's going on?" I asked.

"That's what I wanted to ask you," Guttman
growled. "What on earth do you think you're going to
achieve, pulling a stunt like this without consulting
me?"

"I hope to get the board to delay forcing Stephen to
negotiate with Edgar Eichel," I replied evenly, as if the
question had not been purely rhetorical.

"Well, I just want you to know you are way out on
a very thin limb, young lady, and I am not going to be
standing around with a safety net."

I could see another group of Eichel's people coming
off the elevator. This was clearly going to be a plenary
session.

"I don't even think they're going to let you into the
room," Guttman continued smugly. "Stephen and
Brian Gould have been in there for half an hour. It
doesn't sound good."

I had neither the energy nor the inclination for small
talk, so we just waited. The dim lights and dark wood
of the corridor were depressing. Occasionally, the taut
silence was pierced by a raised voice, unintelligible
from behind the closed doors of the Azor conference
room. A few times we heard muted laughter from the
room at the other end of the hall where the Eichel team
awaited their victory.

Finally, Stephen emerged. He was in shirt-sleeves.
Half moons of sweat ringed his crisp white shirt. His
face was grave.

"They're not going to let you speak," he told me.
"They think we're trying to beat a dead horse for the
sake of my pride. They think you've come here for per-

sonal, not business reasons. They don't give a shit what's right or wrong, what happened or didn't happen. They just want to get this over with.'' He seemed disgusted and depressed.

But I was just plain mad. I hadn't dragged myself downtown only to be turned away at the door. I was willing to use whatever lever or bluff I could think of that might get me a hearing.

''Ask Tucker to come out here and talk to me for a minute,'' I said.

Tucker appeared a moment later. His face was tight, and his hands were jammed tensely into his pockets. This was a high-stakes game, and Tucker was much better at corporate schmoozing than corporate hardball. He looked like a man who was in over his head.

''Kate, please, don't drag me into this,'' he pleaded. ''When it's over it's over. This is just so . . . unseemly. You have let your feelings for Stephen cloud your judgment.''

''You tell your buddies on the board this from me,'' I said in a voice filled with venom. ''I have a story to tell. They can either be the first ones to hear it, or I can go down the street right now and tell it to the business editor at the *Tribune*, and they can read about it in the paper tomorrow morning. I don't give a shit one way or another. It's up to them.''

Three minutes later the oak doors swung open, and Stephen Azorini motioned me inside.

Angry faces ringed the polished conference table. On one side sat the shareholders. Most of them were scientists, early recruits of Stephen's who had, over the years, accumulated substantial positions in Azor Pharmaceuticals. Stephen had opened new horizons for them and made them wealthy in the process. Tonight, they sat together in a row like schoolboys in detention, squirming under the relentless gaze of their mentor. Stephen, consciously or not, was using every inch of his physical presence and every ounce of his personality to put the squeeze on these men whom he had once counted as his staunchest supporters. To describe the atmosphere in the room as strained would have been a gross understatement.

Anthony Azorini was there, of course, as was Jeff Bassman from the trusts and estates department at Callahan Ross, ostensibly to represent the estate of Gretchen Azorini. Joey Azorini was there, too. I found myself missing Vito.

On the opposite side of the table sat the board of directors. Stephen, the chairman of the board, sat closest to me on my right. Next to him was Dick Porter, then Carl Swensen, Peter Chou, a physicist named Adrian Cowling, a banker named Eugene Waldman, and finally, Tucker Sweet.

Brian Gould was standing at the head of the table next to me, talking about something, but I didn't listen. The directors had captured my attention. Funny, I thought to myself, they've seated themselves in the same order as they appeared in the photograph in the annual report.

The photograph in the annual report.

For a moment everything was suspended—my breathing, the sound of Brian Gould's voice, even the throbbing of my bruises. Suddenly I knew why a sixteen-year-old girl would keep a photograph of the board of directors of a pharmaceutical company. She hadn't wanted a picture of them all, just of one man. But it was someone whose picture she could not display alone. The rest of them were just camouflage.

And then the room returned to me. I was breathing again. Stephen was touching me on the shoulder, prompting me to begin my address to the special meeting of the board.

I didn't know what to say. I grabbed Stephen's hand. "No matter what, back me up," I whispered urgently. I stared at the faces that looked back at me from around the table, and the hair stood up on the back of my neck.

Anger is an excellent anesthetic. So is fear. It is the only explanation I can give for how I pulled myself forward in that wheelchair to address the men sitting in that room.

"I am sure that Stephen has told you why I have come from my hospital bed, against the strongest advice of my doctors, to speak to you tonight. I did not come to ask you not to sell out to Edgar Eichel. I did not come here to ask you to consider the finer points of corporate finance. I came here to plead with you for one thing—more time.

"Edgar Eichel has been buying confidential information about Azor Pharmaceuticals and using it illegally to help in this takeover attempt. I was getting too close to finding out who is supplying that information, and that someone tried to kill me."

"That's all very well, Ms. Millholland," said Dick Porter, self-consciously clearing his throat. "And I don't want you to misconstrue this as lack of sympathy for your injuries, but Mr. Sweet tells us that you were assaulted when you surprised a burglar. What proof do you have that your assailant was anyone other than a burglar—other than the strong desire to see your boyfriend remain as the president and CEO of Azor Pharmaceuticals?"

"Gretchen Azorini found who was sending Azor documents to Eichel. She was killed to prevent her from making that information public. When I announced that

I was close to uncovering the traitor, he tried to kill me, too.''

"I have heard of lawyers going to any length to assist their client, but these histrionics strain the imagination," Porter said with a mixture of pity and disgust. "We all appreciate your physical suffering and your loyalty to Dr. Azorini, but your story is, frankly, incredible. Mr. Chairman, I move that the board vote to institute an amicable merger with Edgar Eichel with negotiations to that end to begin immediately."

Stephen looked at me.

"Wait!" I implored. "I may not have enough evidence to convince Mr. Porter here, but I have a good enough story to drag this company through whatever mud the media can dredge up."

"I hardly think the board should allow threats of this kind," Tucker Sweet protested.

"All I ask is that you take a vote on whether or not to delay. If you vote to proceed without hesitation, we'll call Edgar Eichel in here right now to begin negotiations. But, please, at least vote."

Stephen rose and moved for a vote on the delay. He glared at Peter Chou until the chemist meekly rose to his feet and seconded the motion.

"There is no need for the shareholders to leave the room," I instructed. "We'll take the vote in writing. Richard, hand each of the directors a blank sheet of paper. Gentlemen, I ask that each of you write whether you support or reject Dr. Azorini's motion to delay negotiations with Edgar Eichel for forty-eight hours. Then sign your name, fold the paper in half, and pass it down to John Guttman. He and I, as outside counsel, will count the votes and report your decision."

Richard Humanski produced sheets of blank paper and passed them to the directors. Guttman glowered at me, clearly furious at having to take the backseat. For a moment, Anthony Azorini caught my eye, his chin resting in a giant gnarled hand, his sharp bird's eyes twinkling at me in amusement.

The directors hastily scribbled on their makeshift ballots and folded them in half. Tucker slid his down toward my end of the table, and the chain progressed until a stack of seven ballots rested in front of me. The room was brittle with suspense.

Guttman and I retreated into the nearest corner where we opened the ballots and counted them twice.

The vote was five to two against any delay. Even Tucker Sweet had voted against me. I clutched his ballot in my hand.

"Don't say a word," I hissed to Guttman. "Just go and get Eichel."

"I don't think—" he protested, but I cut him off.

"Just get him," I commanded.

No one looked at me as we sat in silence, waiting for Edgar Eichel to make his triumphant passage down the hall. Everyone cringed as he entered the room. They may have all wanted Stephen to meet his adversary face-to-face, but none of them had planned on being around to witness it. Eichel looked puffed up, as only short men do when they are very pleased with themselves. Stephen's revulsion was undisguised. Guttman motioned Eichel into an empty chair near the head of the table across from Stephen.

"The vote of the board of directors of Azor Pharmaceuticals was five to two in favor of immediate negotiations with Mr. Eichel's group," I announced while Eichel beamed. "But before we proceed, I'd like to beg your indulgence for just one minute."

Guttman shot daggers at me with his eyes. I ignored him.

"From the very beginning Edgar Eichel's bid for Azor Pharmaceuticals bothered me. There was just something about it that didn't seem right. For one thing, a large portion of the company's shares are held by people thought to feel deep personal loyalty to Stephen Azorini." I looked at the sheepish faces of the various shareholders and directors around the table and continued. "For another thing, Azor Pharmaceuticals is a very high-tech, skill-intensive, specialty company. And while Mr. Eichel argues that he can hire people with the same specialized knowledge as Dr. Azorini's, it always struck me as strange that someone with Mr. Eichel's particular background would choose, from all the publicly traded companies in the world, a company that was so beyond his experience and expertise."

Eichel looked uncomfortable but said nothing.

I looked at the directors. I finally had their undivided attention.

"Your high-rolling days are over, my friend," I said, turning to Eichel with undisguised contempt. "You'll be lucky if you get a chance to sell mufflers again. The only way your bid for Azor Pharmaceuticals makes sense is if you had the fix in from the start. It wasn't even your idea. Someone made you an offer you couldn't refuse."

"I don't have to sit here for this," Eichel sputtered.

"I'd like to show you all something," I continued, ignoring him. I motioned to Patty to bring me my briefcase. From it, I extracted the copy of Azor's 13-D, the document with the "Dear Edgar" note scribbled across the top.

"This is Azor's forthcoming Thirteen-D form, the one that has yet to be filed with the Securities and Exchange Commission. It is one of many corporate documents that have been transmitted to Mr. Eichel, beginning well before the launch of his takeover attempt. Look carefully at the handwriting and then compare it to this sample.''

I laid the 13-D on the table in front of the directors. Next to it, I laid the ballot that Tucker Sweet had just written in full view of everyone in the room. The handwriting was the same.

"Just because he wrote it doesn't mean he sent it!" Eichel exclaimed angrily. "You can't prove any wrongdoing on my part."

"I agree. Even once a handwriting expert confirms the match, there is no proof that the documents were ever sent. But I am confident that once the SEC starts looking, they'll find that the connection won't be that hard to prove. Financial transactions of the size involved here are notoriously difficult to conceal. My guess is that you didn't even bother to be that careful. You probably never expected anyone to come looking. Nobody in a million years would suspect that Tucker Sweet would sell out a company that he helped run.''

"Kate," Tucker implored, "you've been injured. You don't know what you're saying. Stop before you make an even bigger fool of yourself.''

"You can't stop me now, Tucker," I snarled. Fury rose up inside of me like a living thing. "You should have stopped me while you had the chance. You should have finished me off like you finished off Gretchen.

"It must have been hard for you to kill her," I continued. "After all, you really liked her. You've always liked little girls, haven't you, Tucker? About the only thing you like better is money. Lots of money. And you have such very expensive taste. It must cost a small fortune to cover just your club bills for the year.

"The problem is, it's Eunice's money, isn't it? How degrading to have to go to your horse-faced wife and ask her for your allowance, to have to justify every penny. That must make it difficult to cover up your extramarital adventures. That's why you had to use Joey's ratty little cottage in Mannetuoc, so drafty and inconvenient, because Eunice goes through all the bills with a fine-toothed comb!

"Selling out Azor was your bid for freedom. You must have cut quite a deal with Eichel to make it worth the risk. But Eichel would be willing to pay quite a premium to have a feather like Azor in his cap. They wouldn't be snickering at him behind his back as they politely asked if he lunched at the Yale Club or the Harvard Club, once he ran a pharmaceutical company, would they? Eichel might be willing to pay through the nose to end that kind of sniggering.

"But when Gretchen found out, it put the whole plan in jeopardy, didn't it? It put you in terrible danger, too. Exposure would ruin everything. Even if she didn't tell everyone that you were sleeping together, they wouldn't be so happy to have you at the Choraliers or the North Shore Club once your name had been dragged through the mud for leaking inside information to a sleazeball like Eichel. No, the best people look down on any sort of money grubbing, especially the illegal kinds.

"You had no choice. You had to stop her.

"So you told her that you were doing it all for her. You had to get free from Eunice, and you needed money to do that. I'm sure it wasn't that hard to convince her. You are a pretty persuasive guy; most men who seduce children are, I should think. The rest was easy.

"Gretchen's diabetes made her pathetically vulnerable. No need for mess or violence. No painful struggles on the beach with her. Every day her life hung in the delicate balance between insulin and food. All you had to do was interfere with the equation, and she would literally kill herself.

"But you had to be sure that she would come up to Wisconsin with you, and your relationship had gotten a lot shakier since she found out you had sold out to Eichel. Her conscience bothered her. Her loyalties were divided. Telling her you were going to marry her was good, very good.

"But there were some last minute obstacles. Bad weather at LaGuardia delayed the board meeting and forced you, at the last minute, to call Gretchen to tell her to drive up herself and meet you. You know, the phone records show that you called her from here. The transcripts of the meeting show that you were out of the room at the time the call was placed.

"Having two cars was also a problem. You left Gretchen's in the K mart lot. You went back the next morning and left the keys in the ignition. But it was really bad luck that no one stole it. Without the car registration, the sheriff's department would never have made the connection between a missing girl in Chicago and a body found on a back road in Wisconsin.

"And, of course, you didn't count on me. You must have had a heart attack when I marched into Stephen's office and announced that I had discovered that someone had been faxing material to Eichel. And I was so confident that I was about to discover his identity. You panicked. You had to do something.

"You knew that I was going to my parents' house for dinner that night. You overheard my call. You even went so far as to offer me a ride. That would have made things easy. You must have been desperate, sitting out there in the dark waiting for me. You probably couldn't believe your good luck when I appeared with the dog and headed down those dark stairs to the beach.

"The trouble is, you didn't finish the job, did you? Did you think I was dead, or did the dog scare you off?"

"You can't prove any of this!" Tucker protested in a constricted voice. "The police say it was a burglar. Guttman said you don't even remember what happened."

"My memory is coming back. But you're right. I don't have enough proof for a jury. Not yet. But what do you think will happen when they compare your DNA to the semen found in Gretchen Azorini's body, to the hair found in the bed in the cabin, and to the blood on the clothes I was wearing when you tried to kill me?"

"I don't have to hear this," Tucker hissed. He rose to his feet. Anthony Azorini nodded to Joey, who was behind Tucker Sweet in an instant. Joey grabbed him by the shoulders and drove him back down into his seat.

"Show me your hand, Tucker," I said.

"I don't have to show you anything," he answered defiantly. "You'll be hearing from my lawyers in the morning."

Joey grabbed Tucker by the hair and slammed his head down onto the table with a sickening thud. Blood spurted from his nose and made a sticky puddle on the polished wood. Stephen was at his brother's side. Joey twisted Tucker's arm painfully behind his head while Stephen extricated Tucker's other hand from his jacket pocket and slowly unwound the bandage.

Holding his wrist, Stephen displayed the back of Tucker's hand for everyone to see. A jagged flap of skin was pulled back from a puffy wound in the dark semi-circle of a bite mark. My bite mark.

Suddenly, Tucker bucked savagely, sending both brothers to the floor. He rushed through the door while Stephen and Joey scrambled to their feet to go after him. The rest of us just sat there like idiots, as if we were watching it all on TV.

Anthony Azorini rose to his feet. "Don't bother to chase him," he said quietly. "Where is he going to go?"

CHAPTER
20

I woke up in the hospital. Elliott was sitting with his feet up on the side of my bed, drinking coffee and reading the newspaper. I wondered if I was still paying him by the hour.

"What am I doing here?" I asked. I actually felt good compared to the last time I came to in a hospital bed.

"You must have popped a blood vessel at the Azor meeting. Claudia says they almost lost you on the way to the hospital. It was close, but they pumped you full of anticoagulants. You've lost another day, but they say you'll be fine."

"Have you been here the whole time?"

"I'm just the day shift. Stephen Azorini spent the night. He didn't want to leave this morning, but his office kept calling. I told him I'd keep an eye on you. He said he'd be back this afternoon. You saved his ass. He'd be looking for a job today if it weren't for you, and he knows it."

"That's okay. I owed him one."

"You had a couple of other visitors. Your sister came by. We had a long talk. I don't think she's as screwed

310

up as everybody thinks. She just needs to get away from your nutcake family.''

"Thank you, Dr. Freud.''

"You're welcome. Also Claudia was here twice. And Guttman keeps calling. You know, I don't know how you work with that Guttman guy,'' remarked Elliott, folding up the newspaper. "Every time he calls I say, 'I'm sorry, she can't come to the phone right now, she's unconscious.' And then he yells at me like it's my fault. What an asshole.'' '

"He's an asshole who makes five hundred dollars an hour,'' I said.

"You'd have to pay me a lot more to get me to act like that,'' Elliott said with one of his wonderful smiles. "How are you feeling?'' he asked.

"Not as bad as I thought. Do I still look awful?''

"Yeah. Maybe you could show me a picture, so I could see what you look like when you're not beaten up. Do you feel up to some news?''

"Good news or bad news?''

"It depends.''

"Tell me.''

Elliott handed me the newspaper folded to the front page of the metro section. There was a picture of a Mercedes sedan. The window on the driver's side was splintered around the starburst of a bullet hole. Inside, you could make out the shape of a man's head slumped onto the steering wheel. The headline read: MILLIONAIRE MURDERED. I didn't need to read the article.

"When did they get him?''

"About an hour after he left the University Club. According to the article, there were packed suitcases in the trunk, and he was on the Dan Ryan heading toward the airport. It was a clean hit. Professional job. All the Azorinis were probably miles away, in church.''

I thought of my godfather, the man who had sex with his teenage mistress right before he killed her, the man who left me to bleed to death on the beach where he'd taught me to fly a kite when I was seven.

"So how do you feel?" Elliott asked after a while.

I thought about it. "Hungry," I answered.

"What do you want to eat? I'll send out for it."

"Corned beef on rye with coleslaw and Thousand Island dressing."

"You've got to be kidding about the corned beef."

"I never joke about food," I answered. "Especially when I'm hungry."

ABOUT THE AUTHOR

Gini Hartzmark attended the law and business schools of the University of Chicago and has been a business and economics writer for textbooks. She has written articles on a variety of topics for the *Chicago Sun-Times*, the *Chicago Tribune*, and a number of national magazines. PRINCIPAL DEFENSE is her first novel. Ms. Hartzmark and her husband, an economist who often works as a consultant on controversial mergers and acquisitions, live in Ohio with their three children.